COME TO CASTLEMOOR

The ruins of Darkmead—first the ill-fated Donald came to study them, then his beautiful sister, Kathy.

Dried blood stained the stone altar. As Kathy stepped into the circle the stone circle seemed to expand, closing her in. The darkening sky pressed near. Footsteps grew louder, came nearer. She backed against the stones, wanting to scream, but no sound would come. Fear held her powerless. Powerless, she waited....

A terrifying thought struck her: Were those bloodstains from some ancient druid sacrifice—or had there been a more recent victim?

COME TO CASTLEMOOR

COME TO CASTLEMOOR

by
Jennifer Wilde

MAGNA PRINT BOOKS
Long Preston, North Yorkshire,
England.

British Library Cataloguing in Publication Data.

_____

Wilde, Jennifer
    Come to Castlemoor.

    A catalogue record for this book is
    available from the British Library

    ISBN 0 7505 0140 5
    ISBN 0 7505 0141 3 pbk

First Published in Great Britain by Severn House Publishers Ltd.,
1991

Copyright © 1970 by Tom E. Huff

Published in Large Print 1992 by arrangement with Severn House
Publishers Ltd., London.

Printed and bound in Great Britain by
T.J. Press (Padstow) Ltd., Cornwall, PL28 8RW.

CHAPTER ONE

The men in leather aprons lifted the huge mahogany chest. Their brows were beaded with sweat, and their muscles strained. They carried the chest out of the room and down the stairs. The empty room was a shell now, stripped of life, bleak and depressing. The rich maroon carpet had been rolled off the floor, revealing the ugly grey boards, and the heavy pearl satin draperies had been taken down, exposing the dirty windows that looked out over the dingy roofs and chimneys of the congested neighbourhood. The room held only memories, but I had no time to grieve.

I heard the cart clattering over the cobblestones and knew the men had finally gone, carrying with them all the things I had once cherished. I had saved only my brother's books and a few mementos. It was all over now, and in the morning Bella and I would be leaving London. A new life was beginning, but I was finding it painful to part with the old one.

Footsteps rang loudly on the stairs and came

pattering down the hall. Bella whirled into the room, her cheeks flushed pink, her blue eyes radiant. The moment I saw her saucy, captivating smile, I knew she had been up to some mischief. Bella herself was captivating with her tousled brown curls and pert face and hoydenish mannerisms. She was impudent and vain, bold, bossy, and frequently exasperating, but she was completely devoted to me, more close friend and confidante than maid.

'Stevie Green!' she cried. 'What brass! Just because I'm leavin' he thinks he can take liberties! I guess I showed *him!*'

She rubbed her backside and grinned, no doubt contemplating the liberty Stevie had taken.

'He begged me not to go,' she said, 'and I asked him why I'd want to stay and put up with the likes of him. A blacksmith's apprentice! Can you imagine me settlin' for *that?*'

'Stevie's a fine lad,' I told her. 'He'd make you a fine husband. You might be better off if you accepted his offer. I don't know what we'll find in Wessex....'

'Marry Stevie Green and let you go off to them moors alone? No thank you, Miss Kathy. You can forget that right now! Besides,' she said, wrapping a long brown curl around her finger and smiling pensively, 'there are *bound* to be lots of good-lookin' fellows in them parts, lusty lads that haven't seen *anything* like me!'

'If there are, you'll find them,' I said. 'Or they'll find you.'

'That's what I'm countin' on,' she replied confidently.

She put her hands on her hips and looked around at the bare walls. She frowned and seemed very firm and resolute. Although she was only nineteen, three years younger than I, I sometimes felt she was much older. Bella had been a scrawny little scullery maid in the old house, a minx of twelve who broke china and forgot to dust and quarrelled constantly with the other servants. When my father died, bankrupt, leaving Donald and me alone and penniless, the other servants had been discharged, but Bella had begged to stay with us. She was an orphan, without a friend in the world, and I had persuaded Donald to let her remain.

Donald went off to Oxford on a scholarship, and Bella and I had to go live with Aunt Clarice for the next four years. Aunt Clarice, a widow with three unwed daughters, lived in a large grey-brick mansion with blue shutters, a rose garden in front, in back a green lawn that rolled down to the bank of the Thames. Bella was given a room in the attic and put to work in my aunt's pantry. I was given a small, dim room on the second floor and put to work stitching embroidery and memorizing sermons.

Life was not pleasant in the large grey mansion. My three cousins saw me as an intruder and never let me forget that I was living on charity. My aunt saw me as a flighty, frivolous creature who needed to be taught severity and Christian virtue. My mother had died when I was an infant, and my father had reared Donald and me as a couple of young heathens. Neither of us had the least idea of what was right and proper, she claimed, and it was amazing to her that a young man as headstrong and blasphemous as Donald had won a scholarship to Oxford.

I lived for his letters during those four long years, and the whole bleak pattern of my life took on an incredible sparkle on those rare occasions when he was able to come for a short visit.

'I'll get you out of this, Kathy,' he had promised. 'Just you wait. We'll show the old hag what the Hunts are made of.'

I wanted to believe in this promise, but it was difficult. Donald was studying archaeology, leaving Oxford periodically to study the Celtic ruins that are so profuse in certain parts of the country, and while his professors considered him one of the most brilliant and imaginative students they had ever had, I did not see how such study could possibly bring him the fame and fortune he so intensely desired. He was planning a book about the ruins and filling notebooks with observations and research. He participated in an excavation in Cornwall that received national notice, and his articles on this discovery were published in several prominent journals. He was receiving a lot of attention but very little money. The money was to come from a completely unexpected source.

Donald and I were both aware that we had an uncle in America, but we had never met him and didn't even know his full name. My mother's brother, he had crossed the ocean at the age of seventeen and been swallowed up by that vast country. We knew that he had been connected with lumber in some way, and I had always imagined him in heavy wool jacket and boots, chopping down trees with a mighty axe. A month before Donald was to graduate, he received an amazing communication from America. Our uncle had died, and Donald was his only surviving male heir. Lawyers came to call, papers were signed, and my brother received a small but impressive sum of money. Most of it was tied up in investments that would provide an annual income, but there was enough immediately transferred to him to enable him to rent and furnish an apartment and finish writing his book without financial strain.

He kept the inheritance a secret. After graduating with honours, he found an apartment large enough for both of us, with a room for Bella. He hired workmen to come in and redo the whole apartment, and had a firm furnish it with style and taste.

I'll never forget the day he came charging into my aunt's home, young and virile and audacious. We were all in the parlour, stitching fine linen napkins and presenting a picture of typical Victorian womanhood. Donald stormed into the room, his brown eyes ablaze, his tawny gold hair dishevelled. He was wearing tall brown boots of shiny leather and an expensive brown suit that fit his large body with dandyish elegance. A white silk stock flowed at his neck, and he carried a brown leather riding crop. To my eyes he looked like Saint George, come to slay the dragons. My cousins tittered in alarm, while Aunt Clarice gasped and rose to her feet, haughty and imperious. Donald ignored them all. He seized me by the wrist and jerked me up. Startled, I dropped my stitching.

'You're leaving this place!' he cried out.
'But Donald—'

'Now! This minute!'

'My clothes—'

'Forget them!'

'Bella—'

'She's waiting in the carriage!'

He dragged me outside and thrust me into the carriage. My cousins came running outside to watch the spectacle. My aunt stood on the front steps, her face pale. Donald leaped up on the seat and seized the reins. Bella was clapping her hands in delight. When the wheels began to rattle on the cobblestones, Bella stuck her head out the window and made a face, sticking her tongue out at my aunt. One of my cousins fainted. Donald drove straight to the apartment and led me up the stairs, calm now, and gentle. His brown eyes were tender as he held my hand and opened the door and led me through my new home. He scolded me for my tears and told me I would never have to cry again.

He was wrong, but he had no way of knowing that.

The next day he escorted me to the shops to help me choose a whole new wardrobe. No more drab grey and brown, he informed me. No more coarse cotton and heavy wool. I would wear bright silks and soft cambrics, take down the severe braids and let my hair fall loose and lovely. I would look like the girl of nineteen I was instead of an old maid of thirty. When that day was over, I was completely exhausted, but glowing with a happiness never felt before.

The next two and a half years passed quickly. Donald wrote his book. It was a chaotic time, the apartment littered with books and journals and papers, pots of ink tipped over, important documents lost, lamps burning in the small hours, my brother wildly ecstatic or bleakly dejected, snarling, laughing. I helped him with the manuscript and was soon as absorbed in the subject as he. The book was published, and while such books seldom came to the attention of the general public, it was hailed by scholars and historians, all of whom hoped he would continue with his writings on this unusual subject.

Donald went to Wessex on a research expedition, prowling on the moors outside the town of Darkmead. He came back seething with excitement, telling me about the fantastic ruins and the book he was planning about Celtic religions. He said we would have to move to Castlemoor County so he could be near the source of his research. Leaving Bella and me in London, he went back to Wessex, promising to send for us soon. He bought a small house on the moors, near Castlemoor, a relic of ages past that stood in the middle of the desolate land and gave the county its name. His letters were full of scholarly information as well as references to the Rodds, the peculiar people who actually lived in the castle. He said he would send for us in a month, and when the month passed he wrote again and said it would take some time before arrangements could be made. Then his letters no longer made any mention of our joining him. He said his manuscript was growing, that the book would astound the world. It was all rather mysterious and puzzling. He asked me to do some minor research at the library and send him the results, along with some books he needed. Then a month passed without any letters.

During all this time I had become interested in the Celtic tribes, and while I could hardly have been called an authority, I was more than well versed in their customs and religious ceremonies. Their exotic pagan rites were fascinatingly bloody and bizarre, some so graphically erotic in nature that I couldn't obtain books on them. Such studies were clearly not suited for proper young ladies, the librarian informed me, shocked that I had even asked for such scandalous volumes. I seethed with frustration and did the best I could, all the time waiting for Donald to send for us.

15

He never did. Three weeks ago his body had been found on the moors. He had apparently tripped and fallen down a crevasse, his body battered on the rocks below. He died instantly. The body was shipped to London. My world collapsed; the funeral was almost unbearable. The minister spoke of golden youth and lost dreams and eternal rest, his voice solemn and monotonous. I could hardly stand by the graveside when they lowered the casket and began to shovel the dirt over it. Bella stood by me, holding my arm, a pillar of strength for me to lean on.

Aunt Clarice wanted me to come back with her. It wasn't at all proper for a young woman to be living alone, she claimed, not at all. I told her it was out of the question. Donald had left everything to me, of course, and I needed neither charity nor sympathy, particularly the kind I would find at the large grey mansion. I had money in the bank, an annual income, and owned a house in Wessex. Nothing could have induced me to accept her offer.

The apartment where I had known such joy became intolerable. It held too many memories, each one painful. I could see Donald striding through the rooms, his hair spilling over his forehead, his shirt opened at the throat, his eyes blazing with intelligence and curiosity. I could

16

see him with a pen in his hand, scribbling furiously at his desk, then pacing up and down expounding his theories, completely oblivious to the rest of the world. There was the fireplace where we had sat and talked, and there was the table where we had eaten bread and cheese and drunk the hearty ale he loved so well. It was too much to bear, and I realized I would have to leave.

Though I was bowed with grief, I knew I couldn't go on this way. Donald had liked to see me full of life and vitality, busy with some project, lively, gay, amusing. The woman with tearstained cheeks and shadowy eyes would not have pleased him at all. I had to find something to tear me out of my lethargy. I decided I would go to Wessex. My brother had left a half-completed manuscript. I might be able to finish it. At any rate, the house was mine, and I thought I would like to live there for a while until I could find some kind of purpose for my life.

Aunt Clarice protested violently, as expected. I needed a husband, she declared, and she reeled off a list of young men she knew who would be only too glad to take my hand in marriage. Though not really wealthy, I was nevertheless an heiress, and London was full of suitable men who would find such a match eminently desirable. I wanted nothing to do with them. The money was mine, and I didn't see why I should turn it over to some man who would spend it as he pleased and relegate me to kitchen and bedroom to obey his orders and satisfy his whims. I was stubborn and independent, and when I decided to marry I would choose my own man. Aunt Clarice took it as just another sign of my barbaric upbringing.

'If you carry on this way, no man will have you!' she exclaimed.

'I'll take that risk,' I replied calmly.

'Impudent! Always were! You go running off to those moors like this, and you'll regret it, mark my word! It isn't decent. Reading about those filthy pagans with their stone circles! I couldn't hold my head up in public when my own nephew published a *book* about them—'

'I see you read it,' I said.

'With horror!' she retorted. 'No God-fearing Christian would have such garbage in his home—'

I didn't argue with her. I managed to break the lease on the apartment and arranged to sell the furniture. Now Bella and I stood in the empty room. It was not yet noon. In a few minutes the carriage would be here to take us to the hotel. Our trunks had already been shipped to Wessex, where they would be waiting for us. We each had only a small valise for the journey the next day. I stared at the barren walls, remembering those days when they had surrounded happiness. Bella sensed my mood. She took my hand and squeezed it.

'You know Mr Donald wouldn't have liked to see you lookin' so sad and gloomy,' she said.

'I know, Bella.'

'He liked you best when you were laughin' and carryin' on. Remember those parties when he'd have his friends come up and you'd be the only girl and they'd all flirt with you, 'n' you'd let 'em tease you? Mr Donald was mighty pleased when he could show you off.'

'I remember,' I said quietly.

'They were a wild bunch—all them students. Some of 'em mighty handsome, too. Not as handsome as Mr Donald, though, not by a long chalk! They were all in love with you, Miss Kathy.'

'I never noticed,' I replied.

'Sure they was, every last one of 'em. They were afraid to be too brassy 'cause they knew Mr Donald didn't want 'em givin' you any ideas. They were brassy enough with me, I can tell you! I was black and blue for days after every one of those parties. Such cheek! No wonder he wouldn't let any of 'em take you out!'

19

'I never wanted to go out with any of them,' I told her.

' 'Course you didn't. You had too much sense. Mr Donald always said you were going to marry a real gentleman, someone fine and good and worthy of you. He wanted you to have the best. Maybe you'll meet someone in Wessex, Miss Kathy.'

'Maybe,' I said, humouring her. Bella was incurably romantic.

'Someone tall and dashin',' she elaborated. 'Rich, too! He'll sweep you off your feet, and he'll be madly in love with you. I'm not just sayin' this, Miss Kathy, and it's God's truth: you're the prettiest girl in London, and if you think I'm lyin', just look in the mirror.'

'Nonsense.'

'Those gorgeous cheekbones and deep blue eyes, that coppery gold hair! So elegant and refined—'

'Oh, hush!' I scolded.

'It's going to be grand,' she said, 'a real adventure! New places, new people! The past is over and done with, Miss Kathy. The future's the thing! I have a feelin' it's going to be lively for both of us.'

'Maybe so,' I said.

'I'm countin' on it!' Bella exclaimed.

20

CHAPTER TWO

The road was a long, twisting ribbon that stretched for miles and miles, and the mail coach rumbled along at an easy pace. I had never seen such emptiness, such space. The plains were vast, covered with short green grass, rolling in gentle slopes and hills to touch the horizon. Sometimes we would see a farmhouse in the distance, a barn, a round red silo, and cultivated fields, but mostly there were just the hills, green and brown, with a few enormous grey boulders occasionally breaking the monotony. We had left the regular coach hours ago, for it did not come to Castlemoor County, and we had had to wait for the mail coach to carry us to Darkmead, the village on the edge of the moors.

'I'm as sore as sore, and that's a fact!' Bella complained. 'Aren't we *ever* going to get to that place?'

'Patience, Bella,' I said. 'Just a few more miles—ten or so.'

'It's at the end of the earth!' she protested.

'I've never seen so much grass, so much *sky*. I'll bet we haven't passed five farms since we left the regular coach.'

'There are several farms this side of Darkmead,' I told her. 'It's a rich agricultural area. They even raise sheep.'

'Sheep!' she cried.

'And wheat and barley. Darkmead is famous for its pottery, too. They have huge kilns there, and clay pits, and glassblowers. Their dishes are shipped all over England.'

'Bully!' she said. 'Sounds like a lively spot.'

'Where's your sense of adventure, Bella?'

'I lost it about thirty miles ago,' she said contrarily. 'I haven't seen a single man since we left the main station.'

'There'll be plenty in Darkmead,' I replied.

'Lot of good that'll do *us*. We'll be passin' right through that place and headin' for the moors.'

'The house is only a few miles from the village,' I said. 'We'll be going there often for food and supplies. Cheer up, Bella.'

'I *am* eager to see that castle,' she informed me. 'Imagine people livin' in a castle in the middle of a moor. Must be mighty peculiar folks! And they're going to be our neighbours!'

I nodded, thinking about the letters my brother had written about the mysterious

22

Rodds. Dorothea Rodd was a widow, living in complete seclusion, and her son, Burton, owned the local pottery factory. He had been to Oxford and spent some time on the Continent, cutting quite a figure in society, but now, in his thirties, remained at Castlemoor, a strange and enigmatic figure. Donald had found him extremely unfriendly and wrote that Rodd was both feared and hated by the local people. There was also an Italian girl, seventeen or so, Dorothea's stepdaughter, and a distant cousin, Edward Clark, who had published an authoritative book on the Celts and was now collecting Celtic folk songs. Donald had sent me a copy of Clark's first book and said the man had been most interested in his own project.

I wondered about these people, wondered if I would meet them, if they would be as bizarre as they sounded. Why would people choose to live in isolation, completely cut off from the world?

The coach rolled on and on. Bella was silent, eating chocolates and peering out the window. The empty plains began to take on a more cultivated look, still stark, brown and green, but now we passed fields with rich, loamy earth ploughed into neat furrows, some of them already covered with the jade-green crops that would grow tall and turn gold. There were more farms along the way, some quite impressive, with large stone houses surrounded by oak trees. We saw men working behind ploughs and pitching hay from the lofts of barns. The land grew richer, greener, with trees and wildflowers and a river that flowed sluggishly along its banks. The sky stretched blue and white over everything, but the sun was already sinking, and soon it would be dark. I hoped we'd reach Darkmead soon. I wanted to get to the house before darkness shrouded the moors.

The coach had gone over the road for miles and miles without passing a single cart, but now there were more signs of life. We passed a farmer with a wagonload of fertilizer. Bella coughed and made a face, and I lifted a handkerchief to my nostrils. The farmer cracked his whip, waving his hand at us. Farther down the road a smart rig passed us, coming from the direction of Darkmead. The handsome dappled grey trotted briskly, pulling the neat black surrey with its fringe swaying and its wheels spinning. A woman in a pink dress sat beside a man in black broadcloth, and two flaxen-haired children peered around them. I guessed they were a family who lived in one of the prosperous farms. We passed two farmboys who were walking home from the fields with their rakes and hoes. Bella sat up, all attention now.

We passed a slope covered with sheep, a black-and-white dog barking as they chewed the grass, the sheepherder in leather jacket leaning against a stunted tree and whittling a stick. The sheep spilled down to the edge of the road, baaing and looking at us with placid faces. The coach moved at a faster pace now that we were getting nearer Darkmead. There were many small houses now, and, in the distance, great cavities in the earth that I assumed were the clay pits. The earth was reddish brown, and there were several wooden buildings with tall black chimneys surrounding the pits. I saw men pushing wheelbarrows, tiny from this distance and silhouetted black against the darkening sky.

As we drove into Darkmead, Bella rubbed the smudge of dust off her cheek and patted her long brown curls. I smoothed the folds of my skirt and took down our valises. The coach stopped, the driver opened the door for us, and we climbed out, eager to see the village, eager to stretch our legs. We were in front of the post office, a tiny building on a street lined with stores and shops. The street was unpaved, the sidewalks wooden; the stone fronts of all the buildings were brown and grey, gritty with soot. I could see the small square at one end of the street, oak trees growing around it, and at the other end, a bleak yellow-brick church lifted a tarnished bronze steeple up to touch the dark sky. A wagon of hay stood in front of the feed store, two farmers standing by the horse and talking in subdued voices.

'It isn't London,' I said, trying to sound cheerful.

'That's for sure,' Bella replied, tapping her foot.

'Look at the oak trees. I've never seen them so enormous.'

The whole village was surrounded by these gigantic trees, and we could see the mighty limbs projecting up behind roofs and chimneys. A river circled the village, small stone bridges spanning it, and I supposed the water caused the trees to grow so tall. The new leaves gave a greenish cast to the air, and the smell of mud and water and moss permeated the village. It was a pleasant smell, completely different from the oily odours that rose from the Thames.

'I think I'm going to like it,' I said.

'I'm not so sure *I* will,' Bella retorted.

The driver swung the sack of mail out of the coach and heaved it over his shoulder. I asked him where we could hire someone to drive us out to the moors.

'Best try the inn, miss,' he said. 'It's down the street a ways. Old Rufus can tell you 'bout

26

anything you want to know.'

'Thank you, driver,' I said.

He nodded his head. 'Luck to you, ma'am,' he replied.

Bella and I walked along the sidewalk. It was crowded with people, but none of them paid any attention to us. They studiedly ignored us, although I suspected they were taking in every detail of our dress and manner. I was wearing a lilac-coloured dress with a purple velvet bodice and a purple bonnet trimmed with pink and white ribbons. I felt highly conspicuous, but I held my chin firm and lifted my skirts to keep them from trailing in the dirt. Bella sauntered beside me, openly eyeing every man we passed. Most of them were tall and husky with sullen eyes and dark beards, wearing dirty clothes and smelling of the farmyard, but occasionally there was a blond giant with the native Saxon features of this part of the country. Bella was delighted, her feet fairly dancing.

'I may grow to *like* this place,' she said.

'I wouldn't be surprised,' I replied.

She nudged me with her elbow. 'Did you see that blue-eyed brute?' she whispered. 'The one with the brown boots and leather jerkin? I'll bet *he* could hold his own in a wrestling match! They grow 'em big here, Miss Kathy, and that's no lie!'

'You're shameless, Bella,' I scolded.

We passed a dry-goods store with bolts of shimmering silk and colourful cotton displayed behind the dingy grey glass windows, and a milliner's with surprisingly chic bonnets prominently exhibited. We smelled the delicious fragrance of newly baked bread as we passed the bakery, and kegs of nails and shelves of tools stood in front of the hardware store. The blacksmith's shop stood open, horses standing under the shed, flames roaring, sledgehammer pounding on anvil. A wagon rumbled down the street with three coops of chickens squawking in back, and a small boy hurried past us with a tiny brown pig in his arms. Darkmead was small and ugly, but it had its own flavour, and the fascination of the new and unexplored. I couldn't help but feel a certain excitement as we moved along this main street. London was far behind me, and the life I led there might never have existed.

A red-and-brown sign in the shape of a bull's head hung over the local inn the driver had mentioned. It was on a corner, overlooking the square, the lower floor a restaurant, rooms to rent above. We pushed the swinging wooden doors and stepped inside. It was dimly lighted, the walls a moss-green colour, black oak beams supporting a low ceiling. Sawdust littered the floor, and the air was filled with smoke and the odours of beer and ale. The place was almost empty, two men sitting at one of the crude wooden tables, another man standing at the bar, the rest of the vast, shadowy room deserted. Bella and I stood hesitantly in the doorway. Old Rufus, the proprietor, came out from a back room. He was a burly, middle-aged man in a soiled white shirt and brown trousers. His sleeves were rolled up, and a thin black leather apron was tied about his waist. His face was ruddy, his eyes glowing black, his head a gleaming bald globe. He came toward us.

'I'm starved,' Bella said. 'Let's get something to eat before we do anything else.'

'Very well. I'm hungry, too.'

Old Rufus nodded jerkily and looked at us with the glowing black eyes. He seemed to resent our presence, and I wondered why. 'Miss Hunt?' he said.

'Why—yes,' I replied. 'How did you know my name?'

He grunted and led us to one of the tables without answering my question. The other men in the room watched us silently. I wished I weren't dressed quite so elegantly. Old Rufus told us we could have roast beef and boiled potatoes or meat pie. We chose the beef. I asked him to bring us a pot of coffee while

29

we were waiting.

'I wonder how he knew your name, Miss Kathy?' Bella asked when he had gone.

'The trunks, I'd imagine,' I replied. 'They probably got here several days ago, and my name was plainly printed on them. They'll be at the house when we get there.'

More men came in, all of them wearing heavy jackets with the collars turned up. Although April was already here, it was still chilly outside, and I imagined Darkmead would turn cold as night fell. Old Rufus tossed a log in the enormous rough-stone fireplace and lighted the kindling. Soon a merry fire was roaring, orange-and-blue flames licking at the log and throwing flickering shadows on the wall. Even more men came in, a few of them with their women, dour, silent creatures in plain black or brown dresses. I was amazed at the subservient manner of these women. They did not speak unless spoken to, and they kept their eyes lowered, although I caught a few casting sly glances at our table. I felt even more conspicuous.

A barmaid in a vivid red dress served our food. She had tangled black hair and vivacious brown eyes, and the dress was cut far too low, flaunting the overripe body. Cheap golden bracelets dangled at her wrists. The men followed her with their eyes, and the women tried to pretend she wasn't there. I was almost pleased to see the lusty creature in this drab, solemn community. Hearing one of the men call her Mrs Rufus, I assumed she was married to the proprietor, although that didn't keep her from throwing coy glances at various men. She settled behind the bar and began talking to one of the men standing there.

'Take a look at that,' Bella said.

'What?'

'The lad she's talkin' to. Have you ever seen anything so glorious? I declare, Miss Kathy, he's the most appetizin' morsel of man I've seen in *months!*Can you believe it?'

The man she referred to was leaning against the bar, one heel hooked on the brass footrail. He must have been six-foot-four and had a body that would have done justice to a Rugby player—well-turned legs, slender hips and waist, powerful shoulders. His raven-black hair curled at the back of his neck and spilled in dishevelled waves over his forehead, and he had the bluest eyes I have ever seen, sapphire blue, snapping with life. His features were rather coarse but granite-strong, large nose, wide mouth, firm jaw. He wore mud-splattered black boots, tight black trousers, and a heavy brown suede jacket lined with sheepskin, the

31

collar turned back to reveal the fleecy yellow lining. He was teasing the barmaid, his manner bantering and jovial and extremely male. The proprietor's wife seemed to glow in the warmth of his attention.

'Look at that tart lappin' it up!' Bella whispered.

'Jealous, Bella?' I inquired, smiling.

'Humph! I guess not. I guess *I'd* know how to handle a man like that! He thinks he's pretty big stuff with the womenfolks. Maybe he is with these country girls, but he wouldn't last long in London. I'll tell you that free of charge! He has mud on his boots and probably smells of manure.'

'I thought you were admiring him a minute ago,' I teased.

'Big louts like that don't interest me a bit,' she lied. 'Finish your roast, Miss Kathy, not that it's fit to eat. When we get settled in that house, I'm going to cook some *decent* food!'

She lapsed into angry silence. The cause of her anger continued talking with the barmaid, exuding a robust charm that captivated the creature in red. Although the inn was almost crowded now, it wasn't rowdy. The men talked in low voices, and more than once I discovered groups of them staring at me in silence. I was glad when we finished the meal and were ready to settle the bill. Old Rufus came up to our table, beads of sweat on his naked brow, a napkin folded over his arm. 'That be all, ladies?' he inquired.

'I wonder if you could tell me where I can find someone to take me to Castlemoor?' I asked quietly.

He stared at me, the burning black eyes suddenly flat. He made no effort to answer my question. The room grew painfully silent, all ears attuned to our table. I looked around, puzzled. The men were staring at me as though I had asked someone to commit a murder.

'Not the castle itself,' I clarified. 'I—I own a little house on the moor, across the hill from the castle. That's where I want to go.'

'I know where it is, ma'am. Your brother stayed there. You ain't intendin' to live there, are you?'

'I certainly am,' I retorted in my haughtiest manner. I was on my feet now, Bella standing beside me. I was appalled at the rudeness of the proprietor and the blatant stares of the men. I could feel a blush burning on my cheeks.

'Will you tell me how I can get a ride there?' I asked icily.

'You'd best stay here till morning,' Old Rufus said.

'Why should we?'

'Night's fallin'.'

'So?'

'Ain't no one here goin' to go out to the moors when night's fallin',' he said. I heard some of the men grumbling in agreement.

'But—that's absurd,' I protested. 'I'll pay—'

'It ain't a question of money,' he replied, his voice gruff. 'In the morning there's dozens of men who'll drive you out for nothin', but no one will drive out there with night comin' on.'

'Why—I never heard of such a thing,' I cried.

I stared at the solemn, leathery faces of the men in the room. I saw hardened mouths and sullen eyes, and I saw fear, too. It was quite plain. These men were afraid of something. My brother had written that the superstition here was something to behold, but I never expected to find anything as strong as this. The moors were full of ruins, and legend had it that the ghosts of the Celtic dead rose from their rock-piled graves and worshipped the stone circles at night, but surely these men couldn't believe any such nonsense. Nevertheless, the fear was there, as well as open resentment of Bella and me, strangers, intruders.

'You mean to tell me there's no one here who'll take me to my house?' I said, my voice trembling.

'That's a fact, ma'am,' the proprietor retorted.

'You're all afraid? All you big, strong men are afraid—'

'No need to go insultin' us, Miss Hunt. There's things strangers ain't equipped to understand. I've got some nice rooms upstairs you and your maid can have for the night, and I won't charge you for 'em—'

'I'll take you, ma'am,' a slow, drawling voice said. 'Soon as I finish my beer.'

There was a general stir among the crowd. All eyes turned to where the man Bella had pointed out earlier stood with a mug of beer. He gave the men a slow grin and lifted his mug to them, a mocking toast. He sipped the beer and clanged the mug down on the bar. He hitched his thumbs in the corners of his trouser pockets and started toward us, the grin still on his lips. The men grumbled in low tones. The few women looked at each other with pale faces. The air seemed to crackle with tension.

'Alan Dunne!' one man hissed.

'Aye, and a fool he is!' another answered.

'He's up to no good!'

'Aye, nor has he ever been.'

The man ignored the muttered comments. He came up to us and gave me a jerky little

35

bow that would have been humorous under other circumstances. I saw that the blue, blue eyes were crackling with mischief, and the face, though rough-hewn and unquestionably coarse, had the amiable and endearing look of a naughty little boy's. He was in his early twenties, but despite this, despite his immense size, he reminded me of a boy who delighted in pranks.

'Alan Dunne, ma'am, at your service.'

Although he was speaking to me, his eyes were on Bella. I sensed his rather cocky, arrogant manner was for her benefit. She sniffed disdainfully and shot me a quick glance. He *did* smell of manure, but it was mixed with the odours of sweat and leather and hay and blended into a not unpleasant male scent.

'I've got my wagon out back, ma'am, if you and the little lady don't mind ridin' up front with me.'

'We'd be delighted,' I said, before Bella could make the cutting comment that was shaping itself on her lips.

'Fine, then,' he said. 'I'll just take them valises you've got there and go bring the wagon around front.' He eyed the room with jaunty disdain and made a face. 'I just wanted you to know *all* the men in Darkmead ain't a bunch of sissies!' he remarked loudly. He sauntered out of the inn as his fellow townsmen grumbled menacingly. I paid Old Rufus for our meal and left with my head held high. The swinging wooden doors made a swooshing sound as we stepped outside.

'I'd just as soon *walk!*' Bella said irritably. 'Did you get a whiff of his clothes? Enough to knock you flat! And that drawl! I bet the oaf can't even read and write!'

'I thought he was charming,' I told her.

'Ah, Miss Kathy, you're no judge of the menfolks, and that's a fact!'

She smoothed the folds of her vivid pink skirt and tugged at the tight pink bodice, pulling it a bit lower than modestly permitted, and toyed with her glossy brown curls, arranging them casually on her shoulders. The toe of her slipper tapped merrily on the sidewalk, and there was an undeniable sparkle in her eyes.

'Bella,' I said teasingly, 'I think you're getting ready to make your first conquest.'

'What? Why, Miss Kathy!' she cried, outraged. 'That was a downright *wicked* thing to say! Whatever gave you such a crazy notion?'

CHAPTER THREE

The sky was darkening and taking on a greenish cast, and long black shadows were falling heavily over Darkmead, as though wrapping it up for the night. The air was cold, and I wished I had brought a cape, but Bella didn't seem to notice the chill. Any kind of wrap would have spoiled the effect she hoped to create with the tight pink bodice. She stood with her hands resting on her hips, her chin tilted haughtily. As Alan Dunne drove the old farm wagon around front, she gave a snort of disapproval. Her manner clearly indicated that she wasn't accustomed to riding in such a disreputable conveyance, and she made certain he noticed it.

The wagon was old, its wooden sides warped, its wheels creaking. It was piled high in back with foul-smelling damp straw and gunnysacks. The horse that pulled it was an ancient chestnut with a swayed back and enormous hooves. Alan Dunne tossed the reins aside and leaped down to help us climb up on the wide wooden seat.

I climbed up first, but Bella scrambled over me so that she would be sitting in the middle. She arranged her skirts prettily and stared straight ahead, paying no heed to Alan when he sat beside her and snapped the reins. The old wagon creaked forward in a series of jerky motions, but the horse soon found his stride, and we rolled along the unpaved street smoothly enough.

'Don't you ever *clean* this wagon?' Bella snapped. 'It smells like a stable, and a filthy stable at that!'

'Aye, I clean it now and then,' he replied in his slow drawl, 'when I take a mind to. I wudn't expectin' to be haulin' any fine ladies around in it tonight, though. I had something else in mind.'

'I know well enough what you had in mind, Alan Dunne,' Bella retorted. 'I saw what you were up to with that hussy in red!'

'So you noticed me?' he said, grinning broadly.

'Don't you be gettin' any ideas!' she cried. 'A person couldn't help seein' you standin' there like you owned the place, not that I was at all impressed!'

'Aye, you noticed, all right,' he replied.

Bella saw fit to make no reply to this outrageous comment. She developed a suddenly

39

intense interest in the scenery and folded her hands primly in her lap.

We left the main street and passed down a street of small neat houses, brown and grey, mostly brick, with small green lawns and picket fences and blue morning glories. The oak trees soared, their limbs arching overhead to make tunnels through which the fading light dripped feebly. We passed over a wide stone bridge that arched across the river, and on the other side the last grove of oak trees stood, as if protecting the village from the moors. The trunks were thick and strong, greyish brown, the limbs mighty things that seemed to scratch the sky. I had never seen such tall trees. I knew that the druids had worshipped the oak, a symbol of strength and power to them, and now I could understand why. They seemed to dwarf everything around them. I felt small and insignificant as the wagon rolled under their boughs. Primitive man must have found them mysterious and forbidding.

Beyond the oak trees the ground was rough and uneven, sparse brownish grass growing in patches over the flaky grey soil. Here, on the edge of the moors, there was an abrupt change in mood. The rich farmland, the village, might never have existed. The land rolled on and on until it touched the green-cast sky, without a single shrub or tree to break the vista. Time and space seemed to merge into one, and we might have been driving over the land a thousand years ago or a thousand years into the future. The earth might really be flat, and we might be driving to the rim to pitch into the void. These sensations were acute, but I could tell they were merely my own personal reactions to the land. Alan and Bella seemed to feel none of this mystic quality as the wagon bumped and jogged over the rocky road.

'Do you know how to get to the house?' I asked. My voice sounded peculiar to my own ears, as though I had spoken aloud in church.

'Sure,' Alan replied. 'Many's the time I've been there. My Aunt Maud cleaned up for your brother, ma'am, and sometimes when I needed the wagon I'd drive her out in the morning and come fetch her 'fore night.'

'You knew my brother?'

'Aye, he was a fine fellow. I helped him get settled in the house when he first came to Wessex, put a new roof on the smokehouse for 'im, built some shelves for all his books, fixed the flue so the fireplace wouldn't smoke him out. Amiable chap, he was, real educated, and not a stuck-up bone in his body. Used to listen to 'im talk for hours when I didn't have nothin' else to do.'

Alan clicked the reins. 'I was real sorry, ma'am, about the tragedy. I liked your brother, and he liked me.'

There was a moment of awkward silence.

I wouldn't give way to the surge of grief that swept over me. I would learn to live with the memory of my brother and speak of him naturally with none of the maudlin sentimentality he would have despised.

'You must have been a great help to him,' I said calmly. 'Donald was brilliant with books and papers, but he couldn't get near a hammer without smashing his thumb. The flue in our apartment was always a great mystery to him. When it smoked, he just opened the windows and tried to ignore it until I got someone to fix it.' I paused, pleased with myself. 'Is—is the house in good shape? I know my brother didn't pay much for it. That makes me wonder—'

'It's a fine house,' Alan told me. 'Nice fittings, good furniture. It used to belong to the folks at the castle, you know, but they sold it years ago, when the father was still livin'. Lots of people've lived there over the years, but not many of 'em stayed. That's why your brother bought it so cheap—no one else'd have it.'

'What do you mean—not many of them stayed?'

'The moors drove 'em away. These moors—

42

they do things to you. They ain't friendly 'less you're receptive to 'em. Your brother, now, he was real receptive. He took to 'em right away and could spend all day out alone and come back smilin'. Not many people can do that—the moors get to 'em. They haunt you, they take over, little by little—'

'Is that why the men were afraid?' I asked.

'Ah, that's somethin' else. Bunch of children! They're afraid of the stones.'

'The stones?'

'Them ruins and graves and things farther on. We ain't passed any of 'em yet. Folks say the dead come back. Old Ted Roberts was lookin' for a stray lamb one night and came back and said he saw 'em dancin' around, all in white. Live, they were, and chantin', and they had knives and branches of mistletoe, and there was a girl tied up to one of them stones—' Alan shook his head, his mouth grim. 'Them stones—some of 'em are pretty indecent if you know what they're supposed to represent. Old Ted claimed the girl was tied up to one that looked like a—uh—'

'I'm familiar with the symbols,' I said primly. 'I know what you are referring to.'

Alan blushed ever so slightly, the lobes of his ears turning pink. He clicked the reins loudly and told the horse to move, Bessie, move.

'Did Old Ted drink?' I inquired.

'Considerably,' Alan replied. 'That's why folks didn't pay him no mind at first. Then they found Milly Brown on the rocks, all cut up. Caused quite a fury in Darkmead, I'll tell you that! 'Course what folks wouldn't see was that Milly wudn't no better than she should have been and was tryin' to make Jud Hawke marry her, and they'd had a big tiff two days before. Jud was always a mean 'un, and he suddenly found it convenient to leave for Liverpool to work for an uncle there, he said. No, folks'd rather believe them spirits mutilated poor Milly.'

'How horrible,' I said, shivering.

'Aye, it's that, all right.'

I folded my arms about me, staring at the vast empty land and thinking of what Alan had said. I was slightly alarmed, a hollow feeling at the base of my spine and a nervous pattering in my stomach. The alarm was foolish, of course, but it was still there.

I knew that the ancient druids had held ceremonies around the phallic rocks. They frequently wore long white robes, and the mistletoe played an important part in their rites. They made an aphrodisiac from its berries, and this beverage created a catatonic trance. Virgins, both male and female, were sacrificed upon the

44

altar of Priapus after duly worshipping the generative powers. I wondered vaguely how a drunken villager could possibly have known all these details, and then I smiled at my moment of alarm. Even today villagers all over England hung bunches of mistletoe over their doors at Christmastime, and any lad or lass who stood under it had to give a kiss to the host or else suffer a curse. Although I doubted that many of those who indulged in this quaint custom were aware of its origin, I could see how the people of Darkmead, so near its source, might know more about it. Old Ted Roberts had probably been raised on legends of the druids. Besides, I told myself, from what Alan said, poor Milly Brown could hardly have qualified for sacrifice.

'The men of Darkmead really believe such nonsense?' I asked.

'Aye, there's been talk for years, long before they found Milly. Lots of strange things happen on the moors, all right, and some of 'em are pretty mysterious, but I ain't buyin' a bunch of ghosts comin' up and slittin' a poor girl's throat.'

'I should hope not,' I said.

'Them old superstitions—they hang on, even though we've got a fine church that's packed solid ev'ry Sunday, and a fine choir, too. Folks tell you they're Christian, and most of 'em are, but they don't take no chances. They still have a powerful fear of them pagan ruins.'

'I suppose it's a carry-over from the old days,' I remarked.

'Per'aps it is, but I'm twenty-three years old, and a man to boot, and I for one ain't believin' none of it.'

I smiled at the vehemence of this statement. Alan Dunne was a true man of the soil, strong, forceful, realistic, with no place in his life for native superstition and legend. He was firmly rooted in today, and the past had no claims on him.

The old chestnut jogged along placidly. The wagon wheels creaked with shrill protest, and I was finding the wooden seat highly uncomfortable, but these things seemed small in the cathedral-like vastness of the land. The sky was dark green now, streaks of black merging in like drops of ink on a wet green paper, and the sun had already vanished, leaving behind a few lingering yellow rays that slanted across the horizon. We had come at least two miles into the moors now. A few scrubby bushes and stunted trees broke the monotony. Grey rocks littered the ground, and as we drove farther on I began to see huge boulders that seemed to hang suspended on the sides of the sloping hills.

Bella had been silent all this time, but she was unable to keep up her pretended uninterest any longer. After their first exchange of barbed conversation, Alan had ignored Bella as studiously as she ignored him. He had leaned around her to speak to me, paying not the least bit of attention to her glossy brown curls or low pink bodice. He and I might have been alone on the wagon for all the notice he took of my maid. She didn't like that at all and decided to change her tactics.

'What do you *do?*' she asked abruptly. 'When you're not wastin' time with some no-account like that tart at the inn, I mean.'

'I do lots of things, little lady. What would you like to hear about?'

'My name's Bella Green—*Miss* Green to you—and I couldn't care less, really. I was just makin' conversation.'

Alan grinned and shrugged his shoulders, a gesture calculated to drive Bella to distraction. She sulked, a pout on her lips, and Alan shifted his great body on the seat and leaned forward a little, taking a firmer grip on the reins. The raven-black hair curled on the back of his thick neck, and the wind tousled those locks that fell over his forehead. The bulky brown suede jacket emphasized his powerful torso. Bella leaned a little closer to him, her pink skirt touching his black pants leg. The pungent male odour did not seem to bother her now, though pride prevented her from speaking again. I secretly felt she had finally met her match.

'Do you work in the pottery factory, Alan?' I asked, hoping to break the strained silence.

'The factory's no place for a man who's a man,' he retorted. 'It sucks the life out of you, makes you pale and weak. The work ain't so bad, but the hours are long, and there ain't enough ventilation inside, and a man sees the sun only when it's comin' up or goin' down.'

'It seems Mr Rodd would do something to improve conditions,' I said. 'He took over the factory a few years ago, I understand.'

'Aye, and there was lots of groanin' and complainin' when he did. The men of Darkmead hate 'im, and that's a fact. First thing he did was pass a rule sayin' no child under thirteen could work there—and over a hundred families lost a source of income. Rodd don't believe in child labour, and I go along with 'im there, but folks'd rather see a few shillings comin' in every week than see their young 'uns growin' up tall and healthy. Rodd also shortened the hours the women were allowed to work and passed rules on the kind of work they could do—packin' and sortin' and labellin' consignments, and that sort of thing. They couldn't work in the kilns or pits anymore. A lot of folks depend on the factory for livelihood and think all these radical changes're going to spoil industry.'

'Don't they know Parliament is trying to pass laws against child labour and improve working conditions for women? It would seem Mr Rodd is on the right road—'

'Aye, Miss Hunt, but them things are happenin' in London, and Darkmead ain't much interested. Folks're thinkin' of those few shillings that don't come in no more since the kiddies ain't workin'.'

'Does Mr Rodd visit Darkmead often?'

'He inspects the factories twice a month—woe unto anyone who hasn't been doin' his job properly! He's got a vicious temper, he has. Marches in like a general and sticks 'is nose in everything. You'd better hope everything is smooth as silk. Ever so often, he'll bring Mrs Dorothea and the Italian girl to church, but most of the time the whole bunch of 'em stay at the castle.'

'If you don't work at the factory, where *do* you work?' Bella asked, breaking her self-imposed silence.

'Here and there,' he replied, not looking at her. 'I had a fine herd of sheep last year, but the blight took 'em, took every last one of 'em. I do a little farmin' when someone needs an

49

extra hand, but mostly I just do stray jobs, runnin' errands, deliverin' goods. A handyman of sorts, I guess you'd call me.'

'Oh,' Bella said, her tone of voice clearly indicating how totally unimpressed she was.

'My time's my own,' Alan added. 'I can spend it near'bout any way I've a mind to spend it.'

'Really? I suppose that delights a lot of girls in Darkmead.'

'Aye, there's a few of 'em who don't mind seein' me hangin' about.'

Bella made no comment. She had gained the information she wanted, and now she was contemplating just what she would make of it. I could visualize seeing quite a lot of Alan Dunne in the future as he found excuses to come to the house.

The wagon jolted as we pulled up a long slope. A dark brown bird flew in aimless circles against the greenish sky, his wings spread wide. We came up over the slope and moved over level ground again, and I saw the first ruin. It was far away, silhouetted sharply against the horizon. Tall brown rocks rose like rough, round columns, supporting long, flat rocks that balanced on top like a sloping, uneven roof. It was a weird sight, primitive and bizarre, standing so starkly on the barren soil.

50

Even from the distance I could feel the power it generated. It dominated all the land around, and it seemed to cast a spell. It seemed to draw one to it, and at the same time it warned one not to come too near. It was undeniably majestic, but there was something sinister as well.

Alan noticed my interest in the ruin. He slowed the horse down a bit so that I might have more time to study it. One of the lemon-coloured rays slanted across the ruin like a mystic finger pointing it out to me. I felt a sense of awe.

'It's—beautiful,' I whispered.

'If you like that sort of thing,' Alan said matter-of-factly.

'It's so big—'

'That 'un's small,' he said. 'The really big 'uns are farther on, beyond your house. I imagine you'll be spendin' a lot of time studyin' 'em, just like your brother did.'

'I imagine so,' I replied, as the wagon rolled down a gentle slope and the ruin vanished from sight.

'Funny thing about them stones,' Alan said. 'No one knows where they come from. Great hunks of rock they are, most of 'em, unlike any around here. Ain't no rock like that anywhere in the county, anywhere in the whole of Wessex for that matter. One of them fellows

51

that studies rocks—what do you call 'em—'

'Geologists?'

'Yeah, one of them geologists from a German university was out here a couple of years ago. Spent several months studyin' the rocks and the soil, and he said it was a bloomin' mystery—where them big stones come from.'

'There are several theories,' I told him, feeling very erudite. 'The most popular is that England and Europe were once joined by a strip of land where the English Channel is now and that the Celts got the rocks there and transported them here, thousands and thousands of years ago. It hasn't been proven, of course, but it does sound likely.'

Alan looked very impressed. I had been unable to resist showing off a little, though I realized it was quite unfeminine.

'You sound just like your brother,' he remarked. 'Talk like 'im—'

'Miss Kathy's *terribly* smart,' Bella said proudly. 'She helped Mr Donald write his first book, and she intends to finish the one he was workin' on. We're not *ordinary* people, I'm pleased to say.'

'Aye, and that's no lie,' Alan muttered.

Although it was not yet completely dark, the sky still more green than black, I could see the first stars flickering dimly like chips of diamond scattered recklessly in space. We passed through a grove of scrubby trees, over a marshy stretch, and then I got my first sight of Castlemoor. It was an enormous grey structure, perfectly square, with a round-turreted tower at each corner, stone battlements around the top. There was no moat, no drawbridge, but the front entrance door must have been twelve feet tall, seven across, ancient black oak embellished with brass studs. The windows were recessed at least a foot within the thick stone walls, the leaded glass as dark as steel. Oak trees grew around it, though they were by no means as immense as those we had seen earlier, the topmost branches barely reaching the battlements. The castle was like something out of Sir Walter Scott, and it looked all the more incredible sitting there in the middle of the empty, desolate land.

'Land o' Goshen!' Bella cried, unable to restrain herself.

'Aye, impressive, ain't it?'

'I'm not believin' my own eyes,' Bella retorted. 'People *live* there? Why, it could hold an army—'

'Aye, people live there. There's two hundred rooms—some of 'em big as a barn—and that's not countin' the dungeons.'

'Dungeons!'

He nodded, grinning. 'And some say a secret tunnel that leads out to the moors a mile away, though I ain't never seen it myself. There's a vast courtyard with trees and a vegetable garden, and stables, too, right there inside the castle. It's somethin' to see, though ain't many folks had that privilege.'

'You've been inside?' I asked.

'Aye, I've delivered supplies and packages.'

'How many servants?' Bella wanted to know.

'Ten or twelve. Most of the place is shut up, all dust and cobwebs, white shrouds over the furniture. Used to be fifty servants, they say.'

'It looks scary,' Bella said. 'I'm sure *I* wouldn't want to work in such a place. It'd give me the creeps.'

We rounded a bend, and the castle was partially concealed by a curving slope of land. The wagon headed down, and I saw the house. It was small and neat, two stories high, with a blue-slate roof and a crooked chimney of dusty-orange brick. The stone was the same dark grey as the castle, but it looked lighter, not so dark and ponderous. Neat blue shutters framed the leaded-glass windows, and an oak tree towered up in the front, spreading its limbs to touch the roof. There was a small garden to one side, protected by a low stone fence, and in back there was a smoke shed and an ice house. I thought it was beautiful, a mellow, comfortable oasis here in the middle of the moor. Alan stopped the wagon in front. I felt something wet on my cheek, and only then realized my lashes were brimming with tears.

Alan helped us down and took our valises out of the back of the wagon. I wiped my eyes and looked with love at my new home. Bella gave it a quick inspection and then turned to Alan, who was standing rather awkwardly beside the horse, stroking its chestnut coat.

'Aunt Maud came out this mornin' and straightened up,' he said. 'She put fresh linens on the beds and checked the pantry. There's hams and bacon in the smoke shed, cheese and eggs and butter in the ice house. You'll find lamps and candles on the hall table just inside the door.'

'Thank your aunt for me, Alan,' I said.

'We knew you'd be gettin' in. Aunt Maud, she was mighty fond of your brother, and she wanted to make you feel right at home.'

'Do tell her I'm looking forward to meeting her.'

'I'll do that, ma'am.' He dug his toe in the dirt and seemed reluctant to leave. 'I—uh—I reckon I'll be stoppin' by tomorrow to see if you need anything.'

'I reckon you will,' Bella said tartly. They

55

understood each other perfectly. 'You might just take a bath first!' she snapped. 'And when you come, I want you to bring a new broom and lemon oil and a pail of wax and—' She paused, giving him a saucy look. 'I might just be able to use a new ribbon for my hair.'

Alan gave her a long, slow look that was almost menacing. The sapphire eyes crackled and the wide mouth grimaced. Bella glared at him impudently, her hands on her hips. Alan started to say something, then thought better of it. He shrugged his shoulders and climbed back up on the wagon. He saluted us and drove away, whistling softly to himself. There would be no ribbon tomorrow, but there would be verbal fireworks, and Bella would be in her element. She smiled, watching the wagon disappear over the slope. She turned to me, radiant, full of merry expectations. I wiped a final tear from my cheek and took her hand. We went inside just as the final yellow ray died on the horizon and night fell black over the moors.

CHAPTER FOUR

Waves of sunlight washed in through the open window, spilling over the old green carpet and reflecting brilliantly on the green-and-white-striped wallpaper. I felt the warmth on my eyelids and opened my eyes, to see the leaves of the oak tree rustling, and beyond, the towers of Castlemoor sticking up over the hill. I stretched luxuriously, rustling the coarse linen sheets and disturbing the brilliantly hued patchwork quilt at the foot of the bed. The room was small, the furniture plain—golden oak with a gloss of varnish over the natural grain. A white porcelain pot with delicate green leaves sat on a low table, and the light-blue curtains billowed at the windows. It was a wonderful room, and I already felt at home.

Delicious smells drifted upstairs from the kitchen. I stretched again and got out of bed, slipping my feet into the yellow slippers and pulling a yellow robe over my white nightgown. I tied the sash and pushed dishevelled golden curls away from my face, then walked down the narrow hall and paused at the head of the staircase with its shabby green carpet and glossy oak banister. I tried to identify the smells. Coffee, for sure, and sausage, and freshly baked bread? Impossible. Not at this hour. Then I saw the white porcelain clock in the hall and realized it was after ten. I had slept incredibly late, but the bed had been heavenly and the house a haven after the rigours of travelling. I hurried down the stairs and passed through the parlour and on into the compact little kitchen at the back of the house.

Bella was just taking the bread out of the squat black stove. Her hair tumbled about her shoulders, and her cheeks were a bright pink from the heat of the oven. She took out two crusty golden loaves that would have pleased a master and set them carefully on the zinc drainboard. The drainboard was smeared with flour, and particles of flour were sprinkled over the dull red floor like white dust. Bella tossed the potholders aside and took out a long butcher knife and a piece of pumice stone. She started to sharpen the knife, making a noise not at all endearing to one who had just awakened.

'There!' she cried, testing the edge of the knife with her finger. 'I see you finally woke up! I was goin' to wake you, but I thought it'd be nice to have breakfast all ready. Then

I decided to make bread so you'd have a bit of toast with your coffee.'

'You spoil me, Bella,' I protested, though weakly.

'That's what I'm for,' she retorted.

'What time did you get up?' I asked.

'Hours ago! Couldn't sleep a wink for thinkin' about them awful tales that Alan Dunne was fillin' our heads with. There's heaps of work to do, Miss Kathy. Our trunks are piled in the front room, and books are spillin' all over the place in the study. The windows need cleanin', and the place needs a whole goin' over—'

'It can wait till after breakfast,' I said wearily.

'Oh, it'll take us a week at least!'

Bella was surprisingly enthusiastic about domestic affairs. She loved to cook, to clean, to sew, to stock the pantry. She had a genius for such things and loved doing them almost as much as she loved exchanging insults with strapping young men. I sat down at a table spread with a dark-yellow cloth and set with chipped blue dishes. Bella sliced the bread and toasted some of it while I admired the copper pots and pans hanging on one wall and the golden oak cabinets that dominated another.

'I want to go through Donald's things this morning,' I said.

'That study's a mess, and that's no lie! All those files and papers! Mr Donald never let me get anywhere *near* his workin' quarters, and I'm not goin' to start now. I'll unpack the trunks while you're in there. Alan Dunne can take the empty trunks down to the cellar when he gets here.'

Bella served a delicious breakfast of toast, coffee, and sausage, producing a jar of wild-strawberry jam she had found in the cabinets. We chatted as we ate, discussing a wide assortment of subjects. Bella was satisfied with her small room adjoining the kitchen, although she wanted new curtains for the windows and said all the mattresses needed airing. She intended to make a list of food and supplies for Alan to purchase in town, and she had a mind to bake a chocolate cake this afternoon if she could find the time. I had several cups of coffee, lingering at the table. Bella was able to get up in the morning and radiate vitality. It took me quite a long time to be really certain that I was actually awake.

'Come on, Miss Kathy! Let's get started!' Bella cried fifteen minutes after she had cleared the table. 'It's practically *noon.*'

'All right!' I retorted, none too pleasantly.

'For shame,' she said, frowning. Bella had always been bewildered by this post-rising stupor which was a Hunt-family trait. My brother had been even worse than I. No one dared speak to him for at least an hour after he got out of bed, and he had even been known to throw old shoes at birds who sang on the window ledges of our old apartment. I finally got up from the table, noting that Bella was clanking the dishes together with unnecessary noise. I yawned, stretched, and finally went up to my room.

I changed into a light-blue dress with tiny pink print roses and tied my hair back with a long blue ribbon. I went back downstairs with a feeling of reluctance. I didn't want to go through Donald's desk and files, but I knew it was something that had to be done.

Donald had turned the front sitting room into his study. The room had been light and airy, with pearl-grey walls, light-blue carpet, graceful white furniture, but he had managed to amass a masculine clutter that marred the intended atmosphere. The sky-blue-velvet sofa had been shoved into a corner to make room for a bulky brown desk on which sat a huge lamp with red-glass shade, a black-onyx desk set, an elephant of carved ivory, several paper-weights, and at least twenty books. Boxes of magazines and journals sat beside the desk, and on the other side of the room an immense filing cabinet stood between two delicate blue-and-white chairs. One wall was covered with the shelves Alan had built for my brother's books, crammed full, and pipe racks and tobacco boxes and ashtrays rested sturdily on tables meant for fragile ornaments and flowers.

Going through all the desk drawers, I found several sketches of the ruins he had made with charcoal and ink, and I discovered a mushroom-shaped rock with a hole in the top, through which a leather thong had been inserted. I examined it with curiosity and blushed when I realized that it was a Celtic amulet of the sort described in several forbidden books. I wondered where Donald had found it. In the ruins, perhaps? Although it repelled me, I knew it was valuable, a museum piece, something he could certainly never have afforded to buy. I found various magazines, letters from myself and his professors, and several meaningless papers, but the manuscript I had been looking for was not there.

I put everything back in the desk, puzzled. Something bothered me, and at first I didn't realize what it was. I fingered the ivory elephant, trying to remember something. Then it struck me. Although the rest of the desk drawers had been hold-alls and invariably messy, Donald had always kept four of them scrupulously neat. One held blank paper, neatly stacked, and the next held pens, blotters, and ink, while the third was reserved for pages of manuscript in rough draft. The fourth drawer, usually locked, was for the final draft. Though everything else might have been heaped in messy piles, these four drawers had always been tidy. There had been no such system in the desk today. All the drawers were full of clutter, which wasn't at all like my brother.

I frowned. Oh, well, I thought, maybe he gave up his regular working habits while he was out here all alone. They were eccentric, some of them. It doesn't mean anything....

I attacked the filing cabinet next. Before I started working with him, Donald's files had been hopelessly jumbled. Whenever he had wanted to locate something, he had had to go through piles and piles of material before he could find it, and it had been a source of maddening frustration to him. I had devised a simple and effective filing system, purchasing hundreds of manila folders and labelling each one. Thereafter the files were admirably neat and completely serviceable. They weren't now. They were incredibly messy, papers and articles stuffed in the wrong folders, stacks piled loose in the back of each drawer, clippings scattered. I gasped. No, no, Donald wouldn't have done this...something is wrong.

I spent two hours putting the files in order. I sat down on the floor and separated all the materials and put them in their proper folders, putting each folder in order, placing everything back in the filing cabinet. I found manuscripts of articles Donald had written, rough drafts of articles he had planned but never completed, the original manuscript of the book published a year ago—but there was no sign of the manuscript he had been working on when he died.

I went through the boxes of magazines and journals. The manuscript was not among them.

I stood in the middle of the room, alarmed and yet afraid to give way to the alarm. There was bound to be a logical explanation for everything. The manuscript was not here. It was somewhere else, then, perhaps in one of the drawers in the bedroom, perhaps in a box on the floor of one of the closets, perhaps...perhaps he had lent it to someone. It would turn up. There was no reason to be alarmed, no reason. The desk, the filing cabinet, the mess and confusion—there were explanations for that, too. There must be. I couldn't give way to alarm, not on my first day. It was utterly foolish to feel this way....

Bella came into the room, her blue-and-white-striped dress dusty and soiled with perspiration. There was a smudge of dirt on her forehead, and she smelled of camphor and mothballs.

'What a job!' she exclaimed. 'I got all the trunks unpacked, though. All the clothes are put away, and everything else sorted out. There's those books you wanted, a couple of dozen of 'em, and the little painting of Mr Donald that wild artist friend of his painted. They're the only things I didn't know what to do with.'

'We'll find room for the books on the shelves,' I replied, 'and I'll put the painting here on the desk.'

We toted the books into the study and managed to squeeze them onto the shelves with the others. Although most of the books pertained to the work my brother had been doing, there were also many novels, volumes of poetry, history, biography. Some were so old that their bindings were worn, some new with flashy jackets, some bound in fine leather, and a few from France that had stiff yellow-paper covers. They gave the room a certain character and flavour strongly reminiscent of the man who had owned them.

Bella handed me the painting, and I started to put it on the desk. Donald's friend Damon

65

Stuart had painted it two years ago, a small canvas not quite eight by ten, framed in polished brown wood. I had packed it away, not wanting to look at it, but now I studied that face, so lifelike, so vital. The dark-brown eyes blazed with intelligence, the wide pink mouth curled with humour, the tawny gold hair tumbled boyishly over the high forehead. The strong, ruggedly handsome features had been perfectly duplicated on canvas, and I caught my lower lip between my teeth and looked down at the portrait with misty eyes. I wanted to tell Bella to put it away, hide it. I couldn't look at that face every day, not now, not yet. I started to hand the painting back to Bella, but the blazing brown eyes stared up at me from the canvas and seemed to admonish me. I stepped over to the desk and placed the picture beside the ivory elephant. No tears. No maudlin sentiment. A living memory. That's what he would have wanted, and that's what I intended to preserve.

'He'd be proud of you, Miss Kathy,' Bella said quietly.

'I—I certainly hope so.'

'He's here. Don't you feel it? It's strange.'

'I know. It seems he just stepped into the next room—'

'I like that feeling,' Bella said. 'It's—comforting.'

66

'Not sad,' I said. 'Not like the apartment.'

'Come, Miss Kathy. I want to show you the pantry.'

It was after two o'clock when we heard the wagon pulling up in front. Bella's hands flew to her hair, and she darted to the nearest mirror. I went to the front door to see an outrageously dressed old woman climbing down from the wagon Alan had brought us here in yesterday. She wore a shapeless blue dress that hung like a sack on her plump, stocky body, and a mothy old grey sweater with bulging pockets. Her feet were shod in a pair of boots, and a sad black felt hat drooped about her face. She gave the horse a smart pat on the rump and plodded up the flagstone path toward me.

'Mornin'!' she cried. 'Or is it? Ain't never been able to keep track of time! Busy from mornin' to night, an' not a minute to spare. Thought I'd pop by for a minute and welcome you to Castlemoor, Miss Hunt. Yes, and I'd know you were your brother's sister in the middle of the desert. Same eyes and same nose, though your hair's a bit brighter, not so tarnished-lookin'! I'm Maud—you probably guessed that—and I worked for Mr D. Smashin' gent 'e was! Bleedin' shame—'

Her face was marvellous to behold, fleshy

and lumpy, as though patted in shape by a generous though amateur sculptor, as plump as the rest of her. The blue eyes were lively and shrewd, and the mouth was mobile. It was a face that registered emotion: first delight, then sadness, then distress as she referred to my brother's death. I could see she was afraid she had upset me by the reference. I smiled, warming to her immediately.

'My brother wrote me about you,' I said. 'I'm so glad he had someone like you to take care of him—'

'A rascal 'e was, always playin' tricks an' teasin'. I'll tell you this, an' I'm not jokin': if 'e'd a been twenty years older or I'd a suddenly lost thirty years, that young man wouldn't a stood a chance. I'd a nabbed 'im for sure. A charmer, 'e was, a regular charmer—'

'Won't you come in, Maud?'

'Cain't stay long. Gotta go see Fanny Potter, who's got 'erself pregnant again, an 'er a woman of forty! Mornin' sickness you wouldn't believe! I'm takin' 'er some herbs—'

'Why don't we go into the kitchen,' I suggested. 'Bella's just made some tea, and there's bread and jam—'

'Ta-ta to your tea, luv! I brought me own nourishment.' She dug into one of the lumpy pockets and dug out a flask. 'Old cuss like me

68

needs somethin' a mite stronger than tea to keep the blood a-boilin'. No offence, you understand.'

'None taken,' I replied, smiling. I led her into the kitchen.

During the short time that Maud and I had been talking, Bella had miraculously changed into a jade-green dress with puffed sleeves and a swirling skirt, bits of ruffled white petticoat showing beneath the hem. Glossy brown curls had been hastily piled on top of her head, tied with a ribbon. The change had been accomplished with phenomenal speed, and she had doused herself with cologne water, smelling of mint. When she saw Maud, her face underwent a drastic change. The blue eyes filled with disappointment, and the saucy mouth drooped at the corners.

'Ah-ha, luv!' Maud cried. 'Guess I know who *you* was expectin'! Consider yourself lucky it was me instead of *'im!* 'E's bad news from the word go, an' that's a fact. Should see the way 'e treats 'is poor old aunt. Last night 'e was as surly as a bear, near 'bout snapped me head off when all I did was ask 'im if 'e was feelin' all right. I knew then an' there 'e'd met a new filly.'

'Oh?' Bella said. 'Well, I don't know what you're talking about, I'm sure. If you won't

69

be needing me, Miss Kathy, I'm going to see about those curtains in my room.'

'Don't grieve, luv,' Maud said with a lusty cackle. ' 'E'll be comin' 'isself later on this afternoon. Wild 'orses couldn't stop 'im.'

'In that case, I wish you'd give him this list,' Bella said, picking up a slip of paper off the drainboard. 'It's things we need, and I'd appreciate it if he'd bring them. Miss Kathy will reimburse him when he delivers the items.'

She was a parody of primness and decorum. She left the room with her chin at a haughty angle. Maud cackled again, thoroughly amused. 'She's a ripe 'un!' she exclaimed. 'Don't know who's gonna get 'urt worse—'er or 'im, but I'll be willin' to bet she'll hold 'er own with my nephew. Time 'e met someone who can put 'im down good and proper like.'

'Bella didn't mean to be rude,' I apologized.

' 'Course not! 'E's a dazzlin' fellow, 'e is, a regular devil with the women. That little filly's already been marked for disaster.'

'I'd be more inclined to say Alan has.'

'It'd be tit for tat,' Maud agreed.

I poured a cup of tea for myself and handed Maud a glass for her whiskey. She tipped the flask over the glass and filled it full, then jammed the empty flask back in her pocket and drank the whiskey as though she had gone for three days without water in the middle of the desert. She sighed, plopped the empty glass on the table, and looked at me with crackling blue eyes. Her cheeks were flushed ruddy. I sipped my tea while Maud told me all about her herb garden, the medicine she made, her farm, her nursing, the four husbands who had preceded her to the grave, and the blacksmith who hoped to be her fifth. She related some salty gossip about the people of Darkmead and then began on the Rodds.

I learned that Dorothea Rodd had been the beauty of the county before she married and shut herself up in Castlemoor, that she and her husband had lived in Rome for two years while their son, Burton, was at Oxford, and had adopted a little girl whose mother, their cook, had died of tuberculosis. Nicola was seventeen now, and a bloomin' beauty from all reports, although being shut up in a castle was no life for a girl, and that was a fact. Dorothea's husband had died years ago, and her son had taken over the family affairs. Maud said that Burton Rodd had saved Darkmead from industrial disaster when he took over the pottery factory, and was roundly despised because of it. No pretty girl was safe when he was town, she said, and many a maid had slipped into the castle under the cloak of darkness and come out with a bagful of coins but a maid no more. Maud talked with a lusty relish for each anecdote, but I imagined much of her talk needed to be liberally sprinkled with grains of salt.

'Wait till 'e sees *you*,' she said, nodding briskly. 'That's goin' to be somethin'. 'E'll go out of his mind.'

'I see no reason why I should meet Burton Rodd,' I told her. 'We may be neighbours, but it's not likely—'

'You'll meet 'im, all right!' Maud cried. 'When 'e 'ears about that golden hair and them eyes—you'll meet 'im. Then look out!'

'I'm sure I—'

'He's a fascinatin' devil. Cold, 'eartless— irresistible. The girls in Darkmead are all a-pantin' for 'im, and them that're proper—the gentry lasses—they all want to reform 'im and save 'im from 'imself. You'll see what I mean.'

'Not likely,' I said, my voice cool.

Maud grinned. Her eyes sparkled. 'Aye, it's a situation that promises fireworks,' she said. 'I can see that right now. A lad like 'im, a lass like you—'

'I want to thank you for straightening up before we arrived,' I said, changing the subject abruptly. 'It meant a great deal—'

Maud saw that she had carried the other as far as she could without offence. She sighed and leaned her elbows on the table. 'No offence, luv,' she said.

'Of course not,' I replied. 'I am grateful for what you did here. We would have been up half the night if—'

'Don't mention it, luv. Glad to do it. Wudn't no trouble at all. I wanted things to be nice when you got 'ere. Good thing I came, too. That study was a shambles.'

'Oh?' I said carefully.

'Place looked like a gale swept through it—which is probably exactly what 'appened. A window was open, you see, and we had a big storm a couple of days ago—wind like you never seen! That big cabinetlike thing where Mr D kept all 'is papers had been tumped over, and the papers were all over the floor. Desk drawers were open, too, but I imagine they'd been left open before—took me quite a while to pick everything up and put it back.'

'A—a window was open, and the *wind* blew the cabinet over?'

'Sure, luv. You ain't seen nothin' till you've seen the wind cuttin' across the moors. It's a wonder the whole 'ouse wudn't blown away.'

I felt a wave of relief, but at the same time I couldn't quite accept this explanation for the disorder in the study. There was doubt in the back of my mind, but I wanted so much to accept Maud's explanation that I shoved the doubt even farther back and managed to forget it for the moment.

'Did you ever see the manuscript my brother was working on?' I asked.

'Not close up, I'll tell you that! He'd a 'ad my 'ide if I so much as touched that precious pile of yellow paper. He kept it in a neat pile in one of the drawers and threatened to blister my rump if 'e ever saw me near that drawer. It was the only thing 'e was fanatical about, them papers.' She grinned. 'He could be pretty rough at times, 'e could, snarlin' and snappin' when 'e'd been up all night workin', but most of the time 'e was a lamb, a regular lamb. I usta bake 'im a cake now an' then—'

Her eyes were moist, and her lumpy face looked as though it might crumple up. She sniffed once and folded her arms about her and smiled, fond memory overcoming grief.

'Those first months, 'e was full of ginger, all eager an' enthusiastic, talkin' all the time, and in love with the place. He mentioned you a lot of times, said 'e was gonna bring you an' the girl out here to live, said you'd love the moors just like 'e did. Then—I don't know—'e changed. Still a lamb, mind you, but moody—'

'Moody?'

'Nervous-like. Lost a lotta weight, an' 'is face

got kinda pale-lookin', with shadows under 'is eyes. He wouldn't eat proper, no matter how much I got after 'im, and 'e looked kinda— well, kinda haunted-like, like 'e'd seen some of them ghosts them fools're always talkin' about.' Maud shook her head. 'He was workin' too 'ard, that's all. Many's the time I come in to find 'im slumped over 'is desk, sound asleep, the candles burned out and the oil lamps still splutterin' in the middle of the mornin'—'

'How did the—the accident happen?' I asked.

She hesitated, clearly reluctant to tell me. 'I want to know,' I said. 'Everything—' 'I understand, luv, but—' 'Please,' I said firmly.

'These moors are bad—bogs, quicksand, sudden crevasses in the earth. He stumbled over a rock, seems like, and tumbled into a crevasse, great hole twenty feet deep with sharp rocks at the bottom. He was missin' about three days, and finally Buck Crabbe found 'im.'

'Buck Crabbe?'

'One of the servants at Castlemoor, ugly fellow, vicious, real rough an' rowdy. He was strollin' with a village girl, little Jennie Payne—she ain't so little anymore—an' they found 'im at the bottom of the crevasse. Real —real banged up, 'e was, but—'e musta died instantly. It was one of them horrible freak accidents—'

I listened to all this calmly and found that I was able to maintain my calm even as she told me further details of the accident and how the body was placed in a closed coffin and shipped to London. Maud's wonderful face registered her grief, the blue eyes welling up, the mouth quivering. She frowned and forced back the tears and looked at the empty glass as though she would have gone to the stake for another drop. She stood up, scraping the chair across the tile and tugging at the folds of her old grey sweater. I walked out to the wagon with her.

'It's been pleasant, Maud,' I said. 'You must come back.'

'I keep mighty busy,' she retorted. 'Don't 'ave much time to visit. You're a luv, luv. You take care of yourself, hear?'

'I will.'

'And—don't mind my ribbin' you about Rodd. I talk too much, always 'ave. Old coot like me cain't do much *but* talk—'

'Nonsense,' I said.

'One last word, and then I gotta rush—Fanny Potter's expectin' me, and she might be ready to burst out all over—if you do 'appen to meet Rodd, be careful, you hear? You're a luv, an' I wudn't want nothin' to 'urt you.'

'I haven't been hurt yet,' I said. 'Not in the way you mean.'

Maud looked at me with shrewd eyes, and she started to say something. She shook her head instead and climbed up on the wagon. I wondered what it was she had been about to say, something about love? I knew that Maud was undoubtedly an expert on that subject that I knew nothing about. Her eyes had conveyed a message far more effectively than words could have. What had that shrewd look meant? I shrugged my shoulders, dismissing it. I had too much to do to worry about something as trivial as love.

Maud drove away, and I walked back toward the house. I noticed a horseshoe nailed over the door, and I stopped, startled. I felt a chill, and my pulses leaped. It was another evidence of Celtic superstition, a token to the pagan goddess of fertility. I wanted to jerk it down, destroy it, and then I realized how foolish I was acting. Centuries ago the womb-shaped object had been nailed over doorways in hopes that the goddess of fertility would bless the house and keep it from evil, but the original meaning had long since been forgotten by all but a few scholars. Now people nailed them up for 'good luck,' and they had no pagan symbolism at all. Foolish of me to have been so startled, absurd to have been frightened. My nerves were on edge, and I was reading evil into the most innocent of things. Nevertheless, I intended to take the horseshoe down. It certainly hadn't brought Donald good luck. Just the opposite. I didn't want it over my door, no matter how innocent it might be.

CHAPTER FIVE

Blue had drained from the sky, leaving it a watery grey expanse over which ponderous clouds, darker grey, rolled menacingly. A brisk breeze scurried low on the ground, ruffling through the stiff brown grass on the moors with a whispering sound. It was after four o'clock, and I was walking aimlessly, hoping the exercise would relieve some of the tension I had felt ever since Maud left. The wind caught the hems of my skirt and petticoats and caused them to billow, and my hair whipped like long golden ribbons about my head. I sensed a certain animosity about the land, as though it were savagely aware of my presence and resented it. Climbing a slope behind the house, I turned to look back. The house seemed frighteningly unprotected in the middle of all these barren acres, while beyond, over the hill, Castlemoor seemed a huge, bulky monster eager to snarl mightily and sweep down to devour the timid little dwelling.

I went down the other side of the slope, and both places disappeared. I walked carefully over the hard greyish-brown earth with its chalky patches. Small rocks and bits of shell crunched beneath my shoes. I wondered about the shell but assumed there was a geological explanation for it. Once, ages ago, this whole land had probably been the surface of the ocean. Even now it retained some of the bizarre features—cracks, crevasses, huge boulders with waterworn smoothness and deep holes through which dark sea creatures might once have sailed. At the bottom of the slope the land stretched flat and empty, undulating at the edges and twisting up distant slopes, curving around great boulders. The grey-and-brown and chalky-white drabness was relieved only by the occasional moss-green growth on a boulder or the stark black stretches of tarlike peat.

I walked carefully, overly aware of quicksand and bogs. I knew cattle had vanished before the very eyes of their herders, sinking from

79

sight in a matter of seconds, and I had heard gruesome tales of wagonloads of people who had come to the moors on outings, never to return. Many of the most treacherous stretches had been marked with poles and roped off for safety, but I carefully avoided any ground that didn't look firm. The wild terrain was desolate, full of menace, but it had a kind of barbaric splendour, something prehistoric, older than time. The land seemed to defy man and challenge his civilization. I seemed to feel some primeval power watching me, tolerating my presence here but warning me not to look too closely. It was an eerie feeling, almost tangible in the air around me.

I walked for perhaps half an hour, letting the wind tear my hair and sting my cheeks, enjoying the sensation of movement and the feel of muscle used. Overhead the clouds rolled heavily and massed together, grey lined with black, weak white rays of sunlight spilling over their edges. I could smell the sea, miles away, a faint salty tang in the air, and the stronger, earthier smell of the peat. I came to a great cluster of rocks protected by a grassy brown slope that rose behind them. A gnarled oak tree grew in front of the rocks, a dwarf oak with crusted bark and bare, tormented limbs. The back of my knees ached, and I was breathing heavily.

I decided to rest for a few minutes before starting back to the house.

I sat down on a low, flat rock, leaning my back against another. I had enjoyed the walk, and it had been good for me. All the doubts and worries that had plagued me earlier were gone. The manuscript would turn up. There was nothing to be alarmed about. It would be foolish to work myself into a state over nothing. So it wasn't in the study? Well, I would find it. My brother had had rigid work habits, but they weren't entirely inflexible. He may have —he may have put the manuscript in a suitcase, or in a cupboard. It didn't necessarily have to be in a certain desk drawer. Maud's explanation of the confusion in the study was a perfectly logical one. Donald left a window open when he went out for—for the last time, and a storm caused the damage, knocking the cabinet over, scattering the papers. There was no reason to make a mystery of it all.

I was thinking about this when I heard the first growl. I thought it was thunder and paid no attention. Then it came again, followed by a fierce bark. I jumped to my feet, terrified. A huge greyhound stood at the top of the slope, his strong, sleek body rigid, his hair bristling. He growled again, and another greyhound, as strong, as fierce, came up behind him. I was petrified. My pulses leaped, and my throat went dry. The dogs snarled and snapped at the air, their vicious eyes burning at me with savage fury. I could see the tensed muscles under the silver-grey coats and the gleaming white teeth like monster fangs. The air was charged with hot animal rage. I was too terrified to scream. I watched with horrified fascination as the first dog pawed at the ground, leaped up on its hind legs, threw its body into a rigid stance, and flew down the slope, a live silver arrow streaking through the air toward me.

I closed my eyes. I saw death.

I felt the thud of the heavy body against my legs and heard the shrill ripping noise as my skirt was torn. In an explosion of horror I saw flashes of red, felt black wings flapping inside my head, heard the sharp command shouted, staggered, opened my eyes, saw the dog crouching beside me, body quivering. My skirt was torn, but I was unharmed. The dog whimpered and looked up at me as though in apology, abject now. A girl came rushing down the slope toward me, the other dog leaping beside her.

'I'm sorry!' she cried. 'They didn't know—'

I was still too stunned to speak. My knees felt weak, and my wrists were limp. I took a deep breath, pressing my hand against my heart. The black wings grew still, receded. The orange flashes vanished, and I began to focus again. My heart stopped pounding so rapidly. I made a jerky little gesture with my hand and had to curb an impulse to break into hysterical laughter.

'They—they don't like strangers,' the girl said. The incident seemed to have affected her even more strongly than it had affected me. Her cheekbones looked chalky, and the corners of her mouth quivered. Her enormous black eyes were cloudy with anguish, and I could tell she was on the verge of tears. I managed a weak smile of reassurance.

'I'm all right,' I said. 'At least—I think so.'

'Your dress!' the girl exclaimed, as though my torn skirt represented a tragedy of epic proportions.

'It's not a bad tear. It can easily be mended.'

'Duke! You *bad* dog!'

The animal at my side crouched down and whined, his large eyes filled with humiliation. He looked perfectly harmless now, even beautiful, with the sleek silver coat and distinct lines. I reached down and stroked his head, the bravest thing I have ever done in my life, and Duke responded by slurping his long pink tongue over my fingers. I felt as though I had been given a medal for bravery above and beyond the call of duty. The other dog came over to me, sniffed my feet, and whined, demanding similar attention. When I stroked its head it gurgled in ecstasy. The girl watched, her eyes still dark with tragedy, but she seemed to be recovering.

'They *like* you,' she said, amazed. 'They never do that, particularly Duchess. She's afraid of strangers and doesn't let *any*one touch her. I don't understand it—'

'Neither do I,' I retorted, 'but I'm relieved.'

'They must have frightened you to death,' the girl said.

'Not really,' I replied glibly, 'though I wouldn't be surprised if my hair has turned white. It hasn't, by any chance?'

The girl shook her head, still solemn. I shrugged my shoulders. She seemed to relax a little and watched with great interest as I examined the tear in my skirt.

'You're Katherine Hunt,' she said.

'As a matter of fact, I am.'

'I knew that. You couldn't very well be anyone else.'

'Not in this life. Perhaps in the next.'

'You're—you're teasing me,' she said.

'Just mildly, Nicola.'

'You know my name?'

'You couldn't very well be anyone else,

now, could you?'

The girl smiled. All traces of the tragic heroine vanished, and she became an incredibly beautiful young girl. Her skin was dark, her jet-black curls fell in a rich cascade to her shoulders, and her features were exquisitely moulded. The pink mouth looked vulnerable, the nose was classic, and the enormous black eyes were surrounded by soot-black lashes that swept her cheek. She reminded me of a gypsy, and I sensed a gypsylike abandon in her nature that had been carefully repressed by years of enforced decorum. She was probably not even aware of this streak in her makeup, yet it was clearly there. I thought of a wild colt captured and trained, forced to go through thoroughbred paces while longing instinctively to leap the fence and return to the wildlands.

The beauty was natural, yet the girl did not seem to be aware of it. She had none of the vanity, none of the little affectations that so often mar such beauty. She wore a white dress with clusters of vivid yellow daisies printed on the full, billowing skirt. It fit tightly at the waist and bosom, emphasizing a figure both beautiful and startlingly mature. She was like some earthy, Mediterranean flower mistakenly transplanted on English soil. Her childlike charm, her girlish gestures, and her obvious innocence only made this other quality all the more disturbing. In her native Italy, Nicola would have already been married, with a home, children, and a fund of worldly wisdom. Instead she had the charming naïveté of a proper young English girl carefully schooled and sheltered from all but the most inane aspects of life.

'I so wanted to meet you,' Nicola said enthusiastically. 'I knew you had come.'

'Did you?'

'Yes. Your trunks arrived a few days ago, and everyone was surprised at that. They thought you'd probably sell the house. Then Buck saw you in town yesterday, and he told us about it.'

'Buck?'

She nodded. 'He works for Burton. He was walking down the street, and you and your maid passed him.' She smiled. 'I made him describe you, but he couldn't remember what you were wearing. I wanted to know everything—' She sighed, looking at her feet. 'Not too much happens around here. When someone new comes, it's an event.'

I sat down on the low rock. Duke came and put his head in my lap, but Duchess cavorted around her mistress, leaping up and down, wanting to play.

Nicola stroked the dog's head. Her eyes were

sad. 'I hoped maybe I'd have a friend,' she said with disarming simplicity. 'I—I haven't had many.'

'I could use a friend myself,' I said lightly. 'I don't know anyone here.'

Nicola came and perched on a rock slightly higher than the one I sat on. She spread her skirts out and folded her hands primly in her lap. The rocks protected us from the wind, but there was still enough to ruffle her curls and blow wisps of hair about her temples.

'I haven't been very lucky with friends,' she said. 'There was your brother—'

'You knew him?'

'Oh, yes! He came to Castlemoor once to talk with Edward. I listened to them, and when your brother noticed me, he asked me to join them. Edward didn't like that much, but I sat on the sofa, and your brother talked to me and treated me like—like a person, not a child.'

'Donald liked people,' I said. 'He knew how to make them feel important.'

'*I* wasn't important,' Nicola continued, 'but he always had time for me. I used to slip out of the castle and visit him at the ruins. He told me all about the history of the rocks, and—and when I told him about my nightmares, he didn't laugh.'

'Nightmares?'

She seemed to stiffen, grow wary. 'I—I imagine things. At night I hear noises, and once I saw—' She hesitated, her brow creased. 'I saw a ghost—I *thought* I saw a ghost, all in white, slipping down the hall.' She looked up at me, studying my reaction. 'I don't believe in ghosts,' she added quickly. 'I don't want you to think that! I—just imagine things sometimes. Dorothea says I read too many novels, and Burton is very stern and says I have to get hold of myself.' She paused, frowning. 'I don't tell them about my nightmares anymore.'

'You still have them?'

'Sometimes,' the girl said, bowing her head as though ashamed. 'But I try not to.' She was uneasy, glancing around as though someone might be eavesdropping on us. 'They're so *real*,' she whispered.

She jumped off the rock and darted over to the oak tree. Both the dogs followed her. Nicola seemed to forget I was present. She snapped her fingers at the dogs. They leaped in the air about her. She clapped her hands at them, and they ran merrily. She laughed, a lovely, tinkling laugh like wind blowing through the crystal prisms of a Japanese wind chime. There was something desperate about this childish conduct, as though it were her defence against something darker, something that threatened her.

She finally came to rest beside me, out of breath, her cheeks flushed a vivid pink. What a strange girl, I thought. She was like an instrument upon which emotions played—sadness, gaiety, affection, fear. One never knew which chord would be plucked next. She caught her breath and smiled and looked at me with lustrous black eyes that seemed to beg me to like her. I was strangely moved, and bewildered, too.

'I—I don't like to talk about sad things,' she said simply, 'but I was desolate when they told me about your brother's accident. It was just after they'd sent Jamie away, and I had no one. I stayed in my room alone and cried and cried.'

'Who was Jamie?' I asked, hoping to change the subject. I didn't want to discuss my brother's death.

'He was a boy,' Nicola said. 'He worked in the stables. He taught me to ride when I was a little girl, and when I grew up he—he would talk to me. The doctor said I needed lots of exercise, so Dorothea let me go out riding. Jamie would go with me, my escort. I loved those days. We'd ride over the moors and laugh, and it was like Castlemoor didn't exist. He was my only friend at the castle.' Her eyes grew cloudy, and she seemed to be remembering something very lovely. 'He was tall and strong, with blond hair like dark honey, and the kindest brown eyes I've ever seen. Dorothea thought I was spending too much time with him—I'd slip out to the stables to talk to him. She didn't like that. Burton sent him away.' She looked up at me, suddenly intense. 'He'd worked at the castle for seven years, and they sent him away! Jamie hadn't done anything. He was just a friend—just a friend! They couldn't understand that—'

I thought she was going to cry, but she mastered her emotion. She clasped her hands in her lap and stared down at them. When she continued to speak, her voice was level, carefully controlled. 'I don't know what happened to him. There was no way I could contact him. I—I wanted him to know how sorry I was. But—he just vanished. He stayed in Darkmead for three or four days, then—just left. No one knows where he went. I think about Jamie a lot.'

There was a rumble of thunder in the distance. The clouds were moving slowly across the sky, and dark shadows moved across the moors at the same pace. Duchess whined, burrowing her head in Nicola's lap. Duke stood before us with his silver-grey body stiff, his eyes alert. Nicola seemed to be lost in thought. She crooned softly to Duchess, stroking the dog's head and rubbing its ears.

'Tell me about yourself,' she said abruptly.

'What would you like to hear?'

'About you—your life.'

I gave her a brief résumé of my life. I told her about the years with Aunt Clarice, about the apartment Donald had found for us, about the work I had helped him with. I talked about the excitement of London—the streets, the theatres, the parties. She listened with her elbow on her knee, her chin propped in her palm, her eyes filled with longing.

'How I'd like that,' she said quietly. 'Being free, being able to do just what I liked.'

'I always thought it would be rather nice to live in a castle,' I said airily. 'Do you sleep in a tower?'

'My room's downstairs,' she said. 'Near the stairs that lead down to the dungeons.'

'That sounds exciting,' I replied. 'Imagine having real dungeons! I would love to explore them.'

Nicola looked grim, unresponsive to my humouring. 'They're horrible,' she said. 'Dark and damp and—I don't go down there. I did, and I heard something—' She drew herself up, fighting back the tremulous emotion in her voice. 'It was another nightmare. Buck found me. He told me I hadn't heard anything. Dorothea gave me a sedative and sent for the doctor. They put me to bed and thought I was asleep —and they talked about me. I'm not sick—'

'Everyone has nightmares—' I began.

'I'm not sick,' she continued, 'but I let them think so. It's easier that way.'

'What—what do you mean?'

'Exactly what I said.'

She looked at me with eyes that were perfectly lucid. There was a hard set to her mouth, and I felt for the first time that she was actually communicating with me. The skittish, nervous girl had gone. The Nicola who stared at me now was intelligent, alert, almost formidable. I felt a cold chill pass over me, and I was afraid. What had she seen? What could possibly have happened to give a seventeen-year-old girl that hard, defensive look? I started to reach for her hand, but she drew away from me, standing up and brushing her yellow-white skirt. I felt she had been on the verge of telling me something of paramount importance, but the moment had passed, and she was lost to me again. I stood up too, frowning.

'I'd better go,' the girl said quietly.

'I—I hope you'll come to visit me at the house, Nicola.'

She shook her head. 'I won't be able to do

that,' she said, her eyes averted. 'They don't like for me to—to talk to people. I've talked too much. I shouldn't have talked—' She looked at me, and there was a pleading quality in her voice. 'Don't pay any attention to me. I—I just wanted to meet you. I didn't mean—'

'Nicola—'

'I have to go back now. Buck'll be furious when he finds I've run off again.'

'You ran off?'

'You might say so. I merely eluded my keeper. That's what Buck is, my keeper. If I go for a walk, he goes with me. For my protection. There are so many—accidents, you see. I—I just had to get away for a little while today. I told Dorothea I was going to my room to rest, but I slipped down the back stairs and got the dogs and left. Buck'll be livid.'

'Nicola, tell me—'

The dogs barked. Nicola froze. A man came down the slope toward us. He was tall and slender, with thin hips, a large chest, and huge, bony shoulders. He wore tall brown boots, tight beige doeskin trousers, and a leather jerkin over a coarse-cloth white shirt with long, gathered sleeves. He had bronze-blond hair that clung to his skull in small tight curls, and a broad, bony face. His nose was long, his mouth was wide, and his blue-grey eyes were flat, expressionless. He came toward us slowly, swinging his long arms.

'Buck,' she told me in a low voice. 'He's come for me.'

'What will he do?' I whispered.

'Nothing,' the girl said firmly.

He stopped a few feet from us. He stared at Nicola, not even glancing at me.

'You followed me,' she said.

'Soon as I seen you was missin'.'

'Do—do they know?'

'Not yet.'

'Are you going to tell them?'

'I might. I might just do that. The master'll be plenty mad—'

'He'll be mad at you, too, Buck.'

'I think not,' the man said.

'He'll be mad at you for letting me run away.'

Buck Crabbe glared at the girl. He loomed there in front of us like a giant. He must have been at least six-foot-five, but the sharp, bony physique made him seem even taller. The ugly, belligerent face had a kind of harsh, male attractiveness, a coarse strength that made the ugliness seem almost like an asset. The man was crude, with crude emotions and crude instincts. I shuddered at the thought of the authority he evidently had over the girl.

He frowned, curling his large hands into fists. Nicola smiled a wry, triumphant little smile.

'I'll tell Burton myself,' she said crisply. 'We'll see what he has to say to you.'

'You shut up,' he said, his voice flat.

'What are you going to do, Buck?' she taunted.

'You'll find out.'

'Aren't you smart enough to watch after me?'

'Come along!' he said sharply.

'Why don't you tell?' Nicola said sweetly. 'And I'll tell about last Wednesday—'

'What're you talkin' about?'

'What was her name? Sally? I wasn't supposed to see you slipping out to meet her, was I? Come to think of it, you were supposed to be with me while I practised my piano—'

'You little devil!'

Nicola's laughter rose in the air in silver peals, and it did, indeed, have a demonic quality. It ceased as abruptly as it had begun, and Nicola stared at Buck with flashing eyes. I knew then that she was more than a match for this gigantic, ignorant peasant.

'Come now,' he said. 'They'll miss us.'

'But you were with me, Buck, weren't you?'

He turned and started walking back up the slope. Nicola looked at me, her brow creased.

She made a futile little gesture and then hurried up the slope after Buck Crabbe. The dogs danced along beside her. At the top of the slope she turned around and looked down at me. For a moment she was silhouetted against the grey sky, her hair tossing in the wind, her yellow-white skirt billowing, and then she was gone.

I sat quietly for several minutes. The moors seemed to close in on me. The wind died down, and everything was still, silent. I thought about the girl. Here, on the moors, with their strange, mystic spell, it would be easy to convince myself she had been merely an apparition, not real at all. She was clearly disturbed—she had mentioned a 'doctor' and called Buck her 'keeper'—but somehow I couldn't pass it all off that easily. She had seemed to be silently pleading for some kind of help, and there had been that moment when she was as clear, as intelligent as anyone could be at that age. I was deeply puzzled by Nicola and upset by the veiled hints she seemed to make about Castlemoor.

The air stirred around me. It was damp. The clouds looked swollen and ready to burst. I started back toward the house. Almost all the light had gone, but there was a faint greenish glow, as though the air were stained with the eerie colour. I moved hurriedly, avoiding the tar-black patches of peat. The first drops of rain pelted down as I came up over the slope behind the house. Alan's wagon was in front of the house, and he and Bella were outside, looking frantic. When she saw me, Bella gave a cry of relief. The rain began to fall in earnest as I ran toward them.

CHAPTER SIX

Alan put the last packages in the back of his wagon, heaving a sigh of relief. He looked thoroughly exhausted after trailing around after us all afternoon as we shopped. He had been awkward and embarrassed in the dry-goods store while Bella selected material for her new curtains and then devilishly examined corsets and asked his opinion of them. He had blushed furiously when she held one up in front of her and asked him what he thought about the blue-ribbon trim. Like a loyal and devoted puppy, he had followed us, obeying Bella's orders without hesitation, but now he was slightly sullen, ready to rebel. He stood beside the wagon with his hands in his pockets, a scowl on his face. The wagon was sparkling clean and still smelled of the new coat of paint he had applied, and Alan himself wore tight black pants and a loosely fitting blue shirt that bagged at the waist, the sleeves full, gathered at the wrist. His tall black boots were gleaming, and he smelled of strong soap. His hair was as unruly as ever, thick locks tumbling over his forehead.

'I guess that's everything,' Bella said. 'I keep thinking about those birds—'

'Why don't you go back for them?' I suggested. 'They were lovely, and they'll make the front room so cheerful.'

'I guess I *could*,' she replied. 'You wouldn't mind, Miss Kathy?'

'Not at all,' I said. 'Why don't you and Alan go buy them, and I'll start walking.'

'But—'

'I want to explore a bit,' I insisted. 'I'll meet you at the bridge. You needn't hurry.'

Bella looked delighted. I could see that she wanted to be alone with Alan for a little while. During the past three days he had come out to the house every afternoon, lingering long after the sun went down, and once he and Bella had gone for a stroll that lasted a good two hours. Her skirt had been streaked with grass stains when they returned, and both of them had looked sheepish. Bella had never seemed so radiant and vivacious. I wondered if this new conquest was going to be more permanent in nature than a dozen similar ones in London.

'We *might* stop at the inn for a few minutes,' she told me.

'Fine,' I replied. 'We have plenty of time.'

Bella climbed up on the wagon, arranging her green-and-yellow-striped skirts. Her long brown curls were held back with a yellow ribbon, and she had stained her lids with faint jade-green eye shadow. Alan climbed up beside her and took up the reins. His chest swelled with pride, and he held his head at a cocky angle, plainly pleased to be seen with such a fetching girl beside him. The other village lads would be filled with envy, and he would sneer at them and fling his arm about Bella's shoulder in a quick and manly gesture to proclaim his possession.

'See you at the bridge, Miss Kathy!' Bella called as they drove away. 'We won't be too long.'

I walked slowly down the street toward the square. It was after five, and the sky was pearl grey, cloudless. The street was not crowded. Some of the shops were already closing, and I could hear a deep whistle blowing at the factory outside the village, signalling a change of shifts. Crossing the square, I lingered a moment to look at the tarnished bronze cannon that stood in the middle, a heap of black cannon-balls beside it. Blue and grey pigeons waddled around the cannon, scratching the dirt. The square was surrounded by oak trees whose heavy limbs made a dark-green-and-brown canopy above, leaves rustling, sunlight seeping through to stain the walk with dabs of yellow. The pigeons cooed, the leaves trembled, my skirts rustled silkily as I walked, and the whistle blew again. I turned down the street of small brown and grey brick houses we had passed in the wagon that first day in Darkmead.

I noticed that a horseshoe was nailed over the door of every house. No children played in the neat front yards. No windows were open to let in the sunlight and fresh spring air. No one passed me as I sauntered along the sidewalk. I wondered what went on behind those closed windows and doors. Life in Darkmead was curious, private. London was bustling, alive, every street marked with its own personality. There life spilled out on the pavements, lusty and vibrant, but here everything was shut in. I had the strange feeling that Darkmead would seem like a ghost town at night, the streets empty and silent, lights hidden by tightly closed window curtains. I remembered the grim men at the inn that first night and their dour, subservient women. These were strange people, sullen, taciturn, weighed down with outdated standards and ancient superstitions. It was almost as if the moors reached out and cast their spell over the town, smothering that robust vitality so common in most English villages.

Leaving the houses behind, I followed the road through a grove of tall oak trees, sunlight and shadow flickering at my feet. The stone bridge we had passed over stretched across the river, enormous brown and rust-coloured stones cemented together. I strolled to the centre and leaned over to look down at the water. It was greyish green, clear, rushing rapidly over smooth brown and gold rocks. The banks rose up steeply on either side, dark-green grass growing thickly, and the oak trees grew all around, spreading shadows over the surface of the river and allowing only a few rays of sunlight to sparkle and reflect in the water. The water made a soothing sound rushing over the rocks, and insects buzzed loudly as they skimmed the surface. The sound had a hypnotic effect on me, making me forget the present and carrying me back over the past three days.

They had been busy days. Bella and I had gone over the house thoroughly, washing all the windows until they had a diamond sparkle, cleaning the woodwork, waxing the furniture, nailing down the carpet on the stairs, and scrubbing the floors. Mops, soapsuds, brooms, wax, polish, satisfaction, and fatigue had filled each day. We had gone through every drawer, every closet, every cupboard, every box in the cellar, but we had found no trace of the manuscript. It was not in the house. Of that I was certain. Donald had done something with it— but what? I had asked myself that question at least a dozen times, and each time I could find no logical answer. I kept thinking about the confusion in the study that first day, and Maud's explanation seemed less and less likely. Had someone stolen the manuscript? That question magnified itself in my mind. But why should anyone want to steal an unfinished manuscript?

At night, my bones aching, the house smelling of wax and polish, I tossed and turned in my bed, trying to sleep, staying awake to think. The desired oblivion would not come, no matter how hard I tried to summon it. In a state of semiconsciousness, the night air cool, a bird singing in the tree outside my open window, I saw a puzzle, jagged pieces that wouldn't quite fit together, although I rearranged them over and over in my mind. The pieces taunted me—my brother's accident, the fear I had sensed at the inn when I was trying to get someone to take me out to the moors, the missing manuscript, an enigmatic girl who lived at the castle, a stable boy who had vanished. When the night was heavy over the moors and the bird was silent, I finally slept, to dream of gigantic ruins and figures in white in a circle, chanting.

In the morning, calm, logical, I told myself it was all nonsense. I tried to be very cool and intelligent about it all. I was trying to find a mystery where no mystery was. Nothing was wrong. Donald had either lent the manuscript to someone or disposed of it in some other way. Nicola was a disturbed young woman, and there was no reason to let my encounter with her bewilder me. The people of Darkmead were superstitious. There was nothing to be alarmed about—and yet that alarm lingered in the back of my mind. I was busy all day long with the house, cleaning, rearranging, making lists, but at night the alarm came with night shadows like a living presence in my room, hovering over my bed, making sleep impossible.

Bella noticed my apprehension. She asked me if the moors were getting to me. I laughed at her. She frowned and said she was glad *she* didn't believe in ghosts. She had taken a stroll the night before, just after the sun vanished over the horizon, and she saw a figure in white running across the moors. One minute it was there. The next it was gone. She wasn't at all nervous or imaginative, and she knew there really hadn't been a figure in white, but just the same she wasn't going to take any more strolls alone, thank you, and she'd be just as happy if we weren't quite so isolated out here. She changed the subject and went on polishing the silver, and I wondered if the moors really did have some curious power, if a realistic and level-headed girl like Bella began imagining ghostly figures.

The sound of footsteps brought me out of my reverie. I looked up. A man was coming toward me. He was moving slowly, almost stealthily, walking on the grass at the side of the road, huddling against the tree trunks and glancing over his shoulder every now and then as if to see if something were following him. He was perhaps twenty-five, tall and lanky, with coal-black hair and a pale, thin face. There were dark smudges under his blue eyes and deep hollows under his cheekbones. I felt a wave of apprehension as he came toward me. He looked like a drug addict or one of the ravaged denizens of a crime-infested London slum.

I was all alone. If I screamed, no one could hear me. The man looked as though he carried a knife concealed in his boot. The peaceful scene was shattered by his presence. I could feel evil in the air, an evil as real as the smell of moss, as real as the sound of water rushing over the rocks below. In my mind flashed all the accounts of assaults I had read in the tabloids. Those things happened to other people, at night, in dark alleys or along the wharves. The man looked over his shoulder again. Then he came closer.

He stopped at the edge of the bridge and stood very still, his shoulders stooped. Those haunted blue eyes stared at me, taking in every detail of my dress and person. Then he raised his hands, hooked his thumbs together, crossed his palms, and spread his fingers out, closed them, spread them out again. It was a curious gesture, almost like some kind of greeting, or a signal. He seemed to be expecting some response from me. I backed against the stone railing of the bridge. He made the gesture again, his eyes never leaving my face. Was he a deaf mute? Was this some kind of sign language? I was trembling. He dropped his hands at his sides and seemed to relax.

'You don't understand?' he said. His voice was hoarse.

I shook my head, unable to speak.

He made the gesture again. 'This means nothing to you?'

I shook my head again. Fear held me captive, paralysing me. The sunshine, the fresh air, the rushing water, the green leaves—all vanished in the face of my fear. There was nothing but the fear and this man who I was convinced must be insane or at least a dangerous criminal. He took another step toward me, then sighed deeply, with relief. The ravaged face did not look dangerous now. It looked pathetic. Grief, deprivation, and fear had stamped those harsh lines, hollowed those cheeks, stained those shadows under his eyes.

He looked down at his hands as though they had been contaminated by the gesture he had used. He clasped them together and rubbed them, as if to wipe away the contamination.

'I had to make sure you weren't one of *them*,' he said. He uttered the last word as though it were some kind of disease.

'I—I don't understand,' I said, my voice barely audible.

He nodded briskly. 'Aye, an' that's good. Neither did your brother. He didn't understand either, till—'

'Who are you?' I cried, my heart pounding.

'Bertie Rawlins. Jamie was my brother.'

'Jamie?'

'He was a fine lad, bright an' golden-haired an' fine. None of us wanted him to work at the castle, but Pa, he said the pay was good, an' Ma didn't want Jamie to work at the kilns. He was her golden-haired laddie, he was, and she didn't want him to grow stooped an' pale like me. That's what workin' at the kilns will do—'

'What do you want of me?'

Bertie Rawlins looked over his shoulder, nervous. He came closer. I could see the fear in his eyes. The corner of his mouth twitched, and his whole body seemed poised, ready for flight.

'I was sick this afternoon. I didn't go to the factory. I saw you in town. I knew who you was, of course, an' I knew I had to speak to you. I didn't want no one seein' me—none of them. If they saw me—' His mouth quivered. His eyes seemed to be staring into an open grave.

He shuddered and stepped closer, and when he spoke, his voice was even more hoarse than before. 'You never know,' he said. 'It might be the man livin' next door. It might be your best friend. No one knows how many of 'em —everyone's quiet about it, 'fraid to speak. Someone's gotta help—'

I stared at him, incredulous.

'They got Jamie,' he rasped.

'What do you mean?'

'They got 'im. They were afraid he knew. Jamie came home after Mr Rodd fired 'im. Ma and Pa, they're dead now, been in their graves a long, long time, and when Jamie came back, I was glad, glad they couldn't see 'im the way he was. He was upset an' edgy an' he wouldn't say a word. He was scared. I knew that. Then he told me about 'em. He showed me the sign. I knew he *knew*—'

His large blue eyes stared at me, but they seemed to be focused on visions of horror. His lips were slightly parted, his shoulders hunched. He reminded me of someone, and I cast about in my mind, trying to remember who it was. Suddenly I remembered. Bertie Rawlins reminded me of the Countess of Court Street, a character I had frequently seen in London.

The Countess sold rags and junk on the street corner. She was old, her face withered, her hair frizzled. She regaled passers-by with tales of her imagined life. She had been rich and beautiful and powerful, but her rivals had stolen everything and reduced her to this, and still they weren't content. They were looking at her. They wanted to kill her. She had to sell rags in order to pay her lawyers. These lawyers were going to get back her estates and imprison her rivals. Every day, good weather or bad, she stood on the corner beside her cart, pathetic, demented, her frail body covered with rags. Bertie Rawlins' manner was identical to hers. His voice had the same beseeching whine. His eyes had the same haunted, tormented look.

I suppose every village had a Bertie Rawlins, a harmless creature who was pursued by imaginary demons, the only one aware of plots and intrigues that threatened disaster.

'They got Jamie,' he repeated.

'Who are "they," Bertie?' I asked softly. I spoke to him as one might speak to a child.

'You gotta leave,' he said, ignoring my question. 'You gotta get away. That's what I had to tell you. That's why I followed you here. You gotta leave and bring back help. You gotta help. Your brother—' He paused. He seemed on the verge of tears.

'What about my brother?' I asked.

'He wanted to help, but—'

We heard horse hooves pounding on the road. They were distant, on the other side of the grove of oak trees before the road curved around toward the bridge. Bertie looked stunned. His face went white. He bit down on his lower lip, and for a moment he could not move. 'The secret of the stones—' he whispered frantically. Then he darted off the bridge and disappeared into the oak trees.

The horse hooves drew nearer. Sunlight speckled the brown dirt road with flecks of gold. The green leaves rattled scratchily overhead. The water splashed beneath the bridge. Bertie had disappeared completely. I took a deep breath and pressed my hand against my forehead. The man must surely have been a lunatic, and yet...

Absurd, absurd, the whole thing. In a town riddled with superstition, Bertie, feeble-minded to begin with, took the superstitions even more seriously than the others. He had embroidered them with a sinister conspiracy, the mysterious 'them' with secret members and private signals that only the members could understand. It was like something out of *The Mysteries of Udolpho*, utterly ludicrous here with the sun shining warm, the birds twittering pleasantly in the oak boughs. Bertie probably stopped people on the street to pass on his dire warnings. Being a stranger in town, I was no doubt a prime target. I permitted myself a smile, far too sensible to be taken in by such nonsense.

The horse came around the bend, kicking up small clouds of dust. It was a gorgeous creature, powerfully built, with a milky-white coat, tail and mane pearl grey, flowing like silk. Its rider pulled the reins, stopping the animal at the edge of the bridge. The man sat on the horse, looking at me across the length of the bridge. He wore gleaming brown boots and a tan tweed riding suit, the pants tight and corded, the jacket skirt flaring open. Beneath the jacket he wore a beige silk shirt and a forest-green cravat that flowed loosely in Byronic fashion. He sat easily in the saddle, his feet resting in the stirrups, his hands holding the reins in his lap.

He smiled. He was the handsomest man I had ever seen.

'We meet at last,' he said, his voice rich and melodious. 'I planned to call on you soon and pay my respects. This pleasant accident makes that unnecessary. The setting is so much more appropriate—formality's a bore, parlours stifle me.'

The smile broadened on his lips, warm, radiant. 'Delighted to meet you, Miss Hunt,' he said, his voice making a slight mockery of the conventional greeting. 'I've heard so much about you. Donald spoke of you often. He said you were a breathtaking beauty. I'm afraid he was guilty of gross understatement.'

The compliment was casual, the voice sincere.

'Who are you?' I inquired.

'Edward Clark,' he said, 'your humble servant.'

CHAPTER SEVEN

Edward Clark dismounted, swinging his leg over the saddle and slipping off in one quick movement. He patted the horse's neck and pulled off his dark-brown leather riding gloves, jamming them in the pocket of his jacket. He strolled toward me, moving with a lithe grace unusual in a man so large. He was over six feet tall, big-boned, heavy-set, solid, and muscular. I found it difficult to believe that this man was a noted historian, author of the scholarly volume Donald had sent me, that a man so robust and virile could now be collecting Celtic folk songs. One might imagine such a man working in a coal mine or as a stevedore, but one would hardly associate him with a profession as academic as his own. Men as large as Edward Clark frequently seem hulking and awkward, but he had the carriage of a splendind animal whose great size and ruddy vitality only emphasize an innate dignity and pride. The elegant, casually worn clothes augmented this impression.

His hair must have been light brown at one time, but the sun had scorched it a burnished gold colour, streaked with bronze. His complexion was deeply tanned, making a startling contrast with the eyes, which were a very clear blue, the blue of a cornflower. His eyelids were heavy, his thick black brows arched. His nose was large, straight, his square jaw strong. His mouth was too wide, the lips thick, a dry, sun-parched pink. I realized upon closer inspection that he was not nearly as good-looking as many men I had known, but there was something vital about him that made those other men pale in memory. The natives Caesar had discovered on the shores of ancient Brittany must have had this same clean, rugged aura about them.

I dropped my eyes modestly, turning away from him a little. I wanted to study that face as I would study a sculpture in a museum, but convention forbade such inspection. A man might openly admire a woman all he wanted, examining her features with relish, but decent women must at least pretend to be oblivious to masculine charm. I looked at the water rushing over the smooth stones. I could feel his presence like something exuberant in the air, charging it with a crisp, intangible atmosphere. I thought of the sleek, golden lion I had seen at the London zoo. The beast had dominated the area with this same urgency, so that you were aware of him even when your back was turned to the cage.

I was glad I was wearing my leaf-green dress. The waist and bodice fit tightly, the puffed sleeves dropped slightly off the shoulder, and the full, swirling skirt was scattered with embroidered white and brown flowers, sewn on at random. The cut and colour of the dress showed me off to the best advantage, and it was only by pure chance I had worn it today. My hair was caught up in back with a single green bow, falling in rippling golden waves to my shoulders. I always wanted to look nice, but there was a special importance about it today. I desperately wanted this man to approve of me. It mattered, and I didn't exactly know why. The sensation was a new one for me. I was not equipped to understand it properly.

'I really had intended to call on you,' Edward Clark said, standing behind me. 'You've been here what—three days? Four?'

'Today's the fifth day since I arrived.'

'I wanted to give you time to get settled in. However, I'd have been on your doorstep the first morning had I known what I know now.'

'What's that, Mr Clark?'

'That you're unbelievably lovely. Donald

always said you resemble a portrait of Barbara Castlemaine that hangs in the National Gallery. You do. Now I can see why Castlemaine enchanted Charles—and half the men in England.'

'The comparison isn't flattering,' I said somewhat stiffly. 'She was hardly an admirable person.'

'Wasn't she?'

'Surely you've read your history books. Why, Pepys said—'

Edward Clark chuckled. It was a soft, rumbling sound, interrupting me. I turned around to face him, slightly flustered. His amusement irritated me, putting me on the defensive. He was standing so close that I could see the coarse, tweedy texture of his jacket. I could smell the shaving lotion he used, blended with the smells of leather and silk and the male body. I backed away a step or two, the back of my legs pressing against the railing of the bridge. He seemed to surround me, blotting everything else out, yet there was nothing brash or forward about his nearness. My own awareness of him just made it seem so.

He was aware of my discomfort. He stopped chuckling, even though his eyes seemed to continue the sound silently. He nodded his head, a lock of thick blond-bronze hair tumbling

115

across his tanned forehead. He spread his hands out apologetically.

'Forgive my gallantry,' he said. 'It's a habit I picked up in college when I was striving to win the favours of all the barmaids. My classmates'd grab and paw, with only a tongue-lashing for their efforts. I found a slow, searching look and a smooth compliment got marvellous results. I had a whole drawerful of garters at my digs, tokens from Dot and Sally and Bess—'

He grinned, no doubt remembering those easy conquests. I stared at him, coolly, not knowing exactly how to react. I knew it wasn't proper for him to be telling me such things, yet I didn't want him to think me a typical Victorian prude. Living with Donald and associating with his rowdy friends had long since made me immune to shock at masculine dallying, yet I could feel my cheeks turning pink, despite my efforts to curb the blush.

'I'm hardly a barmaid!' I snapped, more in irritation with myself than in affront.

'Hardly,' he said quietly. 'Forgive me—it seems I'm apologizing all over the place. No, you're not a barmaid, and I assure you my gallantry was most sincere.'

'I don't even *wear* garters!' I added.

The blush burned rosily now. Edward Clark threw back his head, laughing uproariously. I

116

couldn't help myself. I laughed too. I was acting outrageously. A sense of humour was all that could save the situation. When he laughed, the muscles in his thick neck worked strongly, pumping out the deep, lusty sound. My own laughter joined his, and it helped me to relax. I felt the nervous tension snap, flow, vanish.

'Tell me,' he said when our laughter had subsided, 'what are you doing here? Were you on your way back to the house? Surely you don't intend to walk all that distance?'

'No, I came to town with my maid and the boy who's been helping us. He brought us in his wagon. Bella, my maid, wanted to buy a cage of birds she saw earlier this afternoon. I told her I'd meet them here. I wanted to walk a bit, explore the town.'

'A shame,' he said. 'That they're coming for you, I mean. I had visions of sweeping you up and taking you back on my horse. A pretty girl, a white horse, a sunset....'

'You're being gallant again,' I told him.

'Perhaps "romantic" is a better word. When I was a boy I read about the cavaliers with their plumed hats and flamboyant mannerisms. I'm afraid it made a deep impression on me. Fortunately, I discovered the Celtic myths a little later on. They made an even deeper impression. I turned them into an academic pursuit

117

that's a way of life now.'

'I've read your book on Celtic folklore, Mr Clark.'

'Have you indeed? I would think the Brontë novels and the poetry of Byron would be more your sort of thing.'

'You *would* think that,' I replied.

'Remarkable,' Edward Clark said, shaking his head. 'Donald told me you'd helped him with his book, done research for him, kept his files. It's hard to imagine a woman doing those things—particularly a woman who looks like you.'

'I suppose you think doing embroidery and painting watercolours should be enough to fulfil a woman's ambitions,' I said, ready to launch a tirade about man's narrow viewpoint and woman's natural ability. He could see my sensitivity on the subject.'

'Not at all, not at all,' he protested, lifting his hands out again. His blue eyes danced with amusement, and he fought to keep the grin off his mobile lips. 'I *admire* bluestockings.'

'I'm not a bluestocking,' I retorted. 'I hate that term. It implies that any intelligent woman has to be some kind of freak. Women are just as intelligent as men. Society holds them down, and convention—'

'You were born too early,' Edward Clark

said, grinning openly now. 'I have a feeling women are going to come into their own one day. When they do, they'll rule the world, just as they did here until some smart man learned to count to nine.'

I stared at him icily, wondering if he were trying to shock me. I knew that the prehistoric ruins indicated that woman had ruled society thousands of years ago. She had the ability to create life, and this mystic power endowed her with a natural superiority that made man subservient, her slave. The earliest ruins were womb-shaped, celebrating woman's dominance. Later on, after man's role in the creation of life was discovered, the ruins took on an entirely different nature, and woman became the subservient sex. Edward Clark seemed to be amused by this, something that had happened before history began, and he knew I was aware of what he had referred to.

'Those were the days,' he said, grinning.

'You're insufferable,' I told him.

'That's just a first impression. After you get to know me, you'll find me quite charming, full of all kinds of endearing qualities.'

'I have no intentions of getting to know you,' I said stiffly.

'You'll change your mind.'

'I wouldn't count on that.'

119

'Attractive, intelligent—and stubborn. Quite a combination! Quite irresistible.'

'Your horse is waiting for you, Mr Clark.'

Edward Clark looked at me, looked at the horse, shrugged his massive shoulders. He backed away from me, jamming his hands in his pockets and staring at me with his head cocked to one side, his brows arched. Then he smiled. It was a radiant smile, and I was unable to resist its power. I smiled too. Edward Clark walked over to his horse stroked its mane, strolled to the railing of the bridge opposite where I stood, and looked down at the water, his back to me. I noticed the way the sun touched the burned-blond hair that curled untidily on the back of his neck, the way the tweed jacket fit so tightly across his shoulders, as though it taxed the material to cover so broad an expanse. He turned around abruptly, faced me with a boyish grin.

'This is ridiculous, isn't it?' he said from across the bridge.

'Of course it is. I don't know what came over me.'

'Friends?' he asked.

'Friends,' I said.

He leaned back against the railing, his elbows on the ledge, crossing his legs casually. The jacket fell open. The green cravat ruffled in the slight breeze. The width of the bridge was between us, but somehow it seemed he was closer than before. The gorgeous white horse tapped its hooves on the stones at the edge of the bridge, patiently waiting for its master to take command again.

'Donald wrote about you,' I said. I had to raise my voice a little, and curiously enough, this made the communication between us seem more intimate and direct.

'Did he?'

'He said he'd discussed his new book with you.'

'Yes, he did.'

'You weren't enthusiastic.'

He shook his head. 'He was way off course.'

'I find that hard to believe. My brother—'

Edward Clark came across the bridge and stood beside me. He spoke in a deep, serious voice, all frivolity and boyish charm subdued. 'Your brother was a brilliant man. I admired him. I even envied his scholarship. He was capable of astounding work, but this time he was all wrong.'

'He was working on the Celtic religions. I did research for him. There hasn't been a really definitive book on the subject. Donald intended to do one. He wanted to explore the subject thoroughly—'

'That's where he went off the track,' he replied. 'As you have probably already discovered, Darkmead is an astoundingly superstitious village. The past isn't dead for them. It's alive. It's here and now. Donald was infected with this superstition. It grew and grew, until he actually began to believe the tales and rumours that were circulating. He set out to prove as scholarly fact what is, in reality, mere fantasy.'

'I wish you would be more specific, Mr Clark.'

'Very well. He believed that the Celts still inhabit the moors, hold ancient ceremonies among the ruins. He believed there was a secret cult of druids in and around Darkmead. Is that specific enough?'

'Specific,' I said, 'and—astonishing.'

'The villagers talk about ghosts,' he continued. 'They say the druids rise from their graves at night, dance around the stones. People claim to have seen them, just as some people claim to have seen ancient ancestors roam the halls of old houses. It's a curious phenomenon. The mind is capable of imagining something so vividly, with such intensity, that frequently the imagined image is so strong that it actually seems to present itself before its creator, a separate entity, projected

122

by the mind and about as substantial as a dream. Ghosts exist, but they exist only in the minds of gullible people.'

'My brother was a scholar. His mind was like a diamond.'

'Quite true. That made the visions all the more sharp.'

'I don't think Donald was capable of believing in ghosts.'

'Ordinarily, no, but overwork and mental fatigue can do strange things to people. When your brother first came here, he was full of enthusiasm. His energy knew no bounds. He didn't eat properly. He didn't get enough sleep. He worked himself into a state of nervous exhaustion. Donald wasn't a well man toward the end. I'm sorry to have to tell you that.'

I thought of what Maud had told me about Donald's condition during the last month he lived. It fit perfectly with what Edward Clark had just said. I forced back the tears that threatened to spill over my lashes. Donald had needed me, and I was not there. I had been in London. If I had been here, I might have saved his life. He had been weak, tired, his ordinarily alert mind numbed by exhaustion. He hadn't seen the crevasse. His mind had been on other things, and he tripped...I turn-ed away from Edward Clark and stared down

123

at the water. I wasn't sure if I saw it or I was seeing my own tears.

Edward Clark stood beside me, silent. His presence was somehow comforting.

'I'm sorry,' he said after a while.

'Did you read the manuscript?' I asked, still watching the water flow over the rocks.

'I read it,' he said. 'It was rough draft, of course, many chapters unconnected, merely outlined. The early part, the factual reconstruction of the religious rites, was brilliant. The rest was—nebulous. You must have realized that when you read it.'

'I haven't read it,' I said.

'Oh?'

'I—I haven't found it. It's missing.'

'Then he *did* destroy it. He said he was going to. He intended to take a short vacation—the seashore, I believe he said—and then come back and start all over again. I talked to him two days before the accident. He was going to go to London, fetch you, and head for the sea. He realized he was in dire need of a break...' His voice trailed off. His blue eyes turned cloudly. The lines of his face were solemn.

'Life is like that sometimes,' he said. 'Sad, unfair—'

'But we go on,' I replied, calm now.

'It's been hard on you.'

'Yes,' I said, 'but the worst is over now. A new life has begun for me. I can't afford to grieve over the old one.'

'Why did you come here?' he asked. 'Castlemoor is no place for someone like you. In London there's merriment, music, diversion....'

'I'm not looking for diversion. I came to Castlemoor to finish my brother's book. I—I guess that's out of the question now.'

He nodded grimly. 'What are you going to do now?'

I didn't answer for a moment. I stood there looking at the sunlight filtering through the leaves, and I thought about Donald, about the book he had intended to write. It had been very important to him. It was important to me now. I knew, all at once, that I had to do that book myself. There was no manuscript to finish, no notes to guide me, but I would start from scratch. I told Edward about it.

'I have a file full of research material, all the books I need, and the ruins are right in my own backyard, so to speak,' I concluded.

'That sounds like quite a task for—' He paused.

'For a woman,' I finished the sentence for him. 'Do you doubt I have the ability to do it?'

'Not anymore,' he said, an amused lilt in his voice.

125

'You think I should go back to London,' I said in a flat voice.

'Perhaps I do. Nevertheless, I'm delighted with your decision to stay here. For purely selfish reasons.'

'Gallantry,' I said.

'Sincere gallantry. You can expect a lot of it in days to come.'

'Can I indeed?'

He nodded, his heavy lids drooping at the corners, his mouth stretched in a flat smile. He stood there beside me, so large, so confident. I tried to resist the powerful charm he exercised so casually. I turned away from him. He laid his hand on my shoulder and turned me back around. His hand on my chin, he tilted my face up so that I had to look into his eyes. They were full of amusement, and tender. 'Any objections?' he inquired softly.

'I—I'm not sure.'

'I've been waiting for you,' he said, 'waiting a long time. I believe you've been waiting, too.'

'That must have come straight out of a novel,' I said nervously, 'and a very bad novel, at that. People don't talk that way—particularly when they've just met someone not thirty minutes before.'

'I told you earlier, my life was shaped by the books I read.'

'Perhaps you read the wrong ones.'

'Surely you don't expect a proper Victorian courtship? Stuffy parlours, chaperons, polite, empty words, horsehair sofas, and Sunday concerts and magic-lantern slides and moss roses wrapped with fern—that's not the sort of courtship you want. We're both too adult, too intelligent for that.'

'What makes you think I want any sort of courtship at all, Mr Clark?'

'It's "Edward," ' he said, 'and you made me think that, the moment I rode up and you looked at me.'

'You're mistaken,' I told him.

He shook his head. 'I think not, Kathy.'

He looked into my eyes for a long moment. Then he stepped back, lifting his shoulders and dropping them in a slight shrug. He jammed his hands into his pockets and tilted his head to one side. A small grin flickered at the corners of his mouth. He was like an overgrown boy delighted with some marvellous toy. I stood at the railing, completely at a loss. I heard wagon wheels on the road.

'They're coming for me,' I said, my voice trembling.

'I'll see you tomorrow,' he informed me.

'Will you?'

'Count on it,' he said.

He stepped over to the horse and swung easily into the saddle, putting his feet in the stirrups and taking up the reins. He walked the horse across the bridge, turned, nodded his head, raised his hand in salute, and rode away, disappearing in the grove of giant oaks that stood on the edge of the moors. The scene that I had found so peaceful and lovely before, now seemed suddenly empty, as though in leaving he had robbed it of all its warmth and beauty. It seemed deserted now, whereas before it had seemed a restful haven. I waited eagerly for the wagon, anxious to be gone. It rumbled into sight. Bella held the bird cage in her lap, and she and Alan were talking in low, amused voices. Bella gave me a curious look as Alan stopped the wagon and leaped down to help me up.

'Anything wrong?' she asked. 'You look kinda—shaken.'

'I'm just tired,' I said.

'We didn't intend to stay so long.'

'That's all right, Bella.'

We drove across the bridge and under the boughs of the gigantic oaks. Bella showed me her birds. They were beautiful, one yellow, one gold, one brown, in a brass-wire cage shaped like a little house. The birds chirped merrily, as though aware of the attention they were getting.

Bella dropped a handful of seed in the bottom of the cage and set it down in back of the wagon. We started across the moors toward the house. I was silent, my arms folded across my waist, a pensive expression on my face. Alan and Bella seemed to be silently sharing some pleasant experience. I wondered what *had* kept them so long in town.

I suddenly remembered Bertie Rawlins. I asked Alan if he knew him.

'Aye, Bertie,' he said. 'Everyone knows him, more or less. He don't have no particular friends. He works at the factory turnin' a pottery wheel all day long and goes home to an empty cottage that's fulla dirty dishes and old rags. His parents died, you see, and his brother worked at the castle and never came around, and bein' all alone like that sorta unhinged Bertie. He's a harmless lad, but there's those who say stayin' to himself all the time's bad for him. None of the girls'll have anything to do with him, and some of the children laugh at him and throw rocks at his cottage, call 'im a loony. He's a poor sight, Bertie is. Why do you ask, Miss Kathy?'

'I—just wondered. What happened to his brother? You said he worked at the castle. Doesn't he work there anymore?'

'He was a stable boy. They say Rodd discharged him because he showed too much interest in the Italian girl. Wouldn't surprise me none if it was true. Jamie was a fine lad, quiet, polite, but he seemed to smoulder, sorta. You know what I mean? He seemed to be fulla somethin' that threatened to burst out, wudn't content to work in the stables, wanted to do somethin' better. Maybe he thought the girl could help 'im. I don't know. Anyway, he lost his job and came back to Darkmead, Jamie did, and stayed with Bertie a few days. The arrangement didn't suit 'im, though, and he left for other parts, thinkin' he could find better employment somewhere else, I guess, as Rodd wasn't about to let him work at the factory.'

'He left?'

'Just up and left one night without a fare-thee-well to anyone. He was like that. Independent as all get-out.'

'I see,' I replied.

I dismissed the subject from my mind. Everything was explained now. I was able to fit the pieces together. My brother had worked himself into a state of mental fatigue, and he had allowed the superstitions of the local people to take root in his mind. His work suffered from this, and he destroyed the manuscript. That's why I hadn't been able to find it. It didn't exist any longer. Jamie had been a robust stable boy who had undoubtedly tried to take advantage of a disturbed young girl, and after his dismissal he had stayed in Darkmead just long enough to see that it didn't have much to offer a lad with his ambitions. His brother shrouded the whole incident with his delusions, weaving it into a fantastic tale. Everything was perfectly clear.

I looked at the moors we were passing over, marvelling again at their terrible power. They seemed to have the ability to seep into the minds of people, distorting, building fantasy. The inhabitants of Darkmead, Nicola, Bertie Rawlins, my own brother—they had all been affected by this curious terrain. Even Bella had imagined a ghostly figure in white. I closed my eyes, upset, exhausted, wanting to shut everything out.

I couldn't shut out the image of Edward Clark. I found myself looking forward to seeing him again, and at the same time I hoped he wouldn't come. My calm, orderly life had just recently been thrown into an emotional confusion by my brother's death and all that followed, and I was just now taking hold again, restoring order. I wasn't sure I was ready to welcome the kind of joy and anguish I knew, already, Edward Clark was capable of bringing into my life.

CHAPTER EIGHT

Edward Clark came to call the next day, and the next. When he came through the door, the narrow entrance hall seemed to diminish in size, and the sitting room, clean and comfortable with its beige wallpaper and white-painted furniture, seemed to take on the proportions of a doll house. He sat on the lime-green sofa, and I feared it would collapse under his great weight. He walked about the room, examining the black-and-white etchings on the walls, touching the white milk-glass vases, and the room seemed like an elegantly appointed cage designed to confuse and confine a panther. On the first day he brought me an autographed copy of his book on Celtic folklore, on the second he brought a bunch of long-stemmed yellow roses which I promptly put in one of the milk-glass vases.

He was charming and completely at ease, yet I sensed a certain restlessness about him, as though his energy was so great he had to repress it, keep it under careful control when he was engaged in something as sedentary as talking with a young woman. His large hands with their broad palms and strong sinuous fingers seemed to have a life of their own. They gripped the edge of the sofa, stroked the worn nap of the cloth, rubbed the hard, polished surface of his leather boots. They didn't merely touch, they made contact. They were capable of crushing, capable of caressing with silken gentility. Even in repose, resting at his sides, they seemed eager to leap into action. I thought again how incongruous it was that such a man should have chosen the academic life full of books and quiet and thoughts when he would seem to be more suited for digging canals or building stone houses or fighting the enemy as a professional soldier.

Edward discussed his work. He brought manuscript copies of several of the folk songs he had collected here, each carefully annotated with a history of its origin. They were very similar to Elizabethan ballads, with an earthier, more direct quality than those smooth-flowing, prosaic pieces. He told fascinating stories about how he had collected them. He had heard a group of children singing one as they played around the blacksmith's shop, had bought candy for them, and had them recite all the verses while he hastily transcribed them into his notebook. A drunken factory worker bellowed one of the songs at the inn, hurling the Anglo-Saxon phrases about the room in a blustering, whisky-sodden voice. For the price of a few drinks he sang the song over and over again until Edward had every word captured on paper. The songs reflected the interests and attitudes of the people who had lived here hundreds and hundreds of years ago, and when the collection was finished and published, Edward's book would be a valuable contribution. He was doing something worthwhile and, apparently, having a great deal of fun with it.

'The folk songs, the ballads, the nursery rhymes, are the history of the country in capsule form,' he told me. 'A love song written by a young peasant for the daughter of landed gentry can tell us more about social attitudes than volumes of factual reconstruction of a period.' He gave a soft chuckle. 'Someday,' he continued, 'the raucous songs they sing in the music halls today will provide a far greater insight into the true Victorian character than any number of documented historical studies.'

'That's an interesting theory,' I said, 'though I have my reservations about it.'

'Nevertheless, it's a grand way to make a living. People have an insatiable curiosity about the past, perhaps because the present's so drab.

134

My books feed that curiosity—and they're fun to read.'

'When will you be finished with this one?' I inquired.

'I have a few more weeks of work here, a few more leads I must follow up, and then I'll go back to London and spend several months haunting the book rooms and libraries to authenticate what I've gathered. My publishers will have the completed manuscript in about six months.'

He spread his palms over his knees, leaned forward a little. Locks of burned-blond hair tumbled in a heap on his forehead. 'I hope to gather quite a lot of material at the festival in Darkmead next week,' he said.

'Festival?'

'Perhaps that's too grand a word. It's market day, and after the goods have been sold, the barters made, the profits turned, a bonfire is lighted and folk dances are performed in front of the blaze. It's all rather primitive. You might enjoy it.'

'It sounds intriguing.'

'You'll come with me?'

'I'd love to,' I replied.

Edward talked about his rooms at the castle. He had a study in one of the towers, a round room with high, slitted windows, filled with

135

books and hung with ancient tapestries. A flight of circular stairs led to his bedroom, directly above the study, damp, slightly mouldy, crowded with ancient furniture. Conversation turned naturally to the people at Castlemoor, and I learned that his second cousin, Dorothea, had become a recluse because of the smallpox that had marred her once-perfect face. As a very young woman she had travelled to Egypt and Arabia in high-buttoned boots and veiled hats, and even now, as a recluse, found life far more exciting and stimulating than most people Edward knew. He spoke of her diamond-hard mind, her sharp tongue, her devilish sense of irony. She sounded like a fascinating, enigmatic woman.

He had very little in common with her son, Burton Rodd, and I sensed that the two men did not get along at all well. Edward described Rodd as a hard, cold, realistic man whose life evolved around the factory, whose only other interests were the complicated business and financial transactions he carried on with London firms via the mail. He was a man without poetry, a man whose occasional fleshly indulgences were as sterile and devoid of emotion as his business deals. Edward hinted that Rodd resented his presence at the castle and that the two of them had had words. I wondered if any man could be as black as Burton Rodd had been presented by everyone who spoke of him to me. Surely there were shadings. Surely no man could be all that bad. I found myself wondering about him more and more.

I asked Edward about Nicola, without letting on that I had already met her. His face looked grim, weary, his mouth a straight line, his eyes dark. She was very disturbed, he said, had always been. The 'school' she attended in London for several years had, in reality, been a kind of private hospital, the 'teachers' especially trained nuns who were adept in dealing with the overly sensitive, the deluded, the young who carried a private anguish inside themselves. Nicola had 'graduated' and been sent back to Castlemoor, only to grow worse. She had developed a girlish crush on a young stable boy who had tried to take advantage of her. The boy had been dismissed, and she saw the whole thing as a conspiracy against her. Edward shook his head, a crease between his brows. I could see that he was genuinely fond of Nicola, genuinely concerned with her welfare.

'She needs to get away from here,' he said. 'She needs to be taken somewhere where there's bright sunshine and colour, music and laughter. She was born with those things as her natural heritage, then brought to a grim place the very opposite of what her nature demanded. I worry about Nicola. Sometimes I wonder if it's too late for her....' His voice trailed off, and he was lost in thought. I found his expression touching.

Bella came into the room after he left that second day. She tried to conceal her curiosity, but she couldn't repress the lively sparkle in her eyes. Bella thrived on romance. Now that she sensed one in the offing for me, she could hardly control herself. I felt she wanted to dance around the room and clap her hands in glee, and I was amused at the way she restrained herself. She stepped over to the bouquet of yellow roses, touched the sleek petals, then wandered over to the brass cage and watched the birds swing on their swing and peck at their seed. She stuck her finger between the wires. The brown bird perched on it, the gold one pecked at it gently, and the yellow bird ignored it completely. Bella seemed to be absorbed in her study of the lovely creatures.

'What do you think of Mr Clark?' I asked after a moment.

She whirled around, birds abruptly dismissed from her thoughts.

'Oh, Miss Kathy, I think he's simply *grand*. Fancy him bringing roses! It's ever so romantic.'

'It was just a gesture—politeness.'

She shook her head vigorously. 'No, no, he's *smit*ten. It's as plain as the nose on your face! The way he looks at you, the way he says one thing and means somethin' else. I can *tell*.'

'I think you're exaggerating.'

'Didn't he ask you to go to the festival with him?'

'How did you know about that?'

'Well—uh—'

'Bella!' I cried in mock horror. 'You've been eavesdropping!'

'Not really. I was dustin' the hall table, you see, the one right near the door to this room, and the door was open, and—'

'How long did it take you to dust the table?' I asked casually.

'About thirty minutes,' she admitted, grinning pertly. 'It was *very* dusty,' she added.

I smiled, wishing I could look stern and reproving. I couldn't, not with Bella.

'You may as well forget all that nonsense,' I told her. 'Mr Clark thinks of me as a friend—we've interests in common—and even if he *did* have another kind of relationship in mind, I wouldn't be interested. I have the book to write—I intend to start on it immediately—and I'm not interested in anything else right now, not at all.'

Bella smiled and looked very wise. She shook her head slowly from side to side, as though despairing of my total naïveté. 'You always *were* able to fool yourself, Miss Kathy,' she said.

'Don't be impudent, Bella,' I said sharply. 'What are we having for dinner?'

'Baked ham and biscuits,' she replied, 'and I *wasn't* bein' impudent. I was merely statin' facts.'

That night I thought about what Bella had said and wondered if there could be any truth in it. No, no, of course not. Bella was a dear girl, but quite silly and frivolous, addicted to penny-dreadful romances and tabloids, without the least conception of the really important things. The important thing now, for me, was to do the book Donald had wanted to do, do it in memory of him, do it as well as possible. I had no time for romance, despite Edward Clark's magnetic charms.... I really couldn't be bothered, I told myself, and I went to sleep resolved to put all foolish notions out of my mind.

When I woke up early the next morning, I could hear Bella busy clattering in the kitchen. The sun had just come up, and everything was hazy, the mist lifting layer by layer, the air cold

140

and invigorating. I washed and brushed my hair and put on an old dress of dull-gold linen, brown daisies scattered over the skirt. Feeling none of the lethargy that ordinarily afflicted me in the morning, I hurried down the stairs and burst into the kitchen. Bella looked startled, then concerned, sure something was wrong with me. I gave her a radiant smile, had a cup of coffee, and then went into the study for notebook, sketch pad, and pencils. I had been here a week now and hadn't yet visited the ruins. I intended to do so today. I asked Bella to pack a sack lunch for me. She was displeased when I explained my project to her.

'I just don't think you *should*, Miss Kathy, not by yourself.'

'Why ever not? It's absurd—'

'All sorts of things happen at those ruins—Alan's told me tales! You have no business goin' to that terrible place alone.'

'Nonsense. I want to start the book as soon as possible, and I need to study the ruins before I start reading about them. There's not any reason on earth why I shouldn't.'

'There's plenty!' she protested. 'I just have a *feelin'*—'

I shook my head, smiling. 'I think this place is getting to you, Bella,' I teased. 'First you see a figure in white, and now you have premonitions. A strong, sensible girl like you! You really must take hold.'

'I knew I shouldn't a told you about that figure in white,' she said, pouting sulkily. 'I was tired, and kinda uneasy after all that talk about ghosts, and I *told* you I knew it wasn't *real*. This is different.'

'Would you like to come with me?' I asked merrily.

'No, thank you,' she retorted. 'I don't want anything to do with those stones! I can't understand why you're so *cheer*ful at this hour of the morning. It makes me nervous.'

'I'm just eager to get started. Have you packed the lunch yet?'

'I'm gettin' to it,' she said grumpily. 'If you don't mind my sayin' so, Miss Kathy, I just don't under*stand* you. You're as pretty as a picture, and that's a fact—'

'Why, thank you, Bella!'

'—and the world's full of books,' she continued. 'I can't see why you want to shut yourself up for months and months and work and lose sleep and grow all tired and pale just to write *another* one.'

'Bella, you disappoint me! I thought you were proud of my intellect. I heard you bragging about it to Alan.'

'Intellect's fine and dandy when you're sittin'

142

by yourself. There's a *man* in the picture now, and such a marvellous man, too. That makes everything different.'

'Heresy,' I said, enjoying the banter. 'You think I should toss everything aside just because a man is—rather, might be—interested in me? Why, if it were left up to you, women would always remain just where they are now, servants, playthings.'

Bella raised her eyes to the ceiling, as though imploring heaven to give her strength. I couldn't help laughing. She looked properly offended by the sound. She was a treasure, and her impudence was a great part of her charm. She wrapped sandwiches and dropped them in a paper sack with a hunk of cheese and an apple. I told her goodbye and set off across the moors in an unusually good mood, feeling very young, full of energy.

I walked rapidly, eager to see the ruins. The sun was high now, a hot yellow ball that evaporated the lingering veils of mist and dried the grey-brown earth. The mystic spell of the moors was present, but my mind was occupied with other things, and I managed to ignore it. Perhaps that was the secret of the moors: the spell was there, the danger was there, but only if you allowed yourself to succumb to it. I was thinking of other things, and the moors had temporarily lost their power over me.

Now that I had definitely decided to write the book, I was filled with enthusiasm for the project. It would take months and months, but I had already done preliminary research in London, and I had everything at hand. I visualized the completed volume, impressively bound in brown leather, Donald's name on the dedication page. The thought of that book caused my spirits to soar, spurred me on. It seemed to have given me a whole new lease on life.

I had a definite purpose, and I knew it was an admirable one. The sense of direction that had been missing all this time since Donald's death was present now. I had come to Castlemoor full of apprehension, only to be mystified by a series of curious, puzzling events that made the apprehension even greater. The pieces of the puzzle were all neatly in place now, no mystery at all, and everything was sharp and clear. I saw exactly what I had to do, and it was going to be a satisfying task. It would be a tribute to Donald, and, too, it would be an affirmation of the intellectual abilities of women in general. Women had published novels, of course—the Brontë sisters, the scandalous George Sand in France—but had a woman ever written a book such as the one I contemplated? It would be a step forward for my sex, and a contribution, however minor, to a cause I firmly believed in—sexual equality.

I climbed up a long slope. The ground was harder, chalkier, than it had been, with crusty layers of broken shell and rock. Far off, I could see what looked like a small black lake. It was an expanse of peat, one of the largest on the moors. Alan had described it when he had told me how to reach the ruins. The slope rose, growing steeper, and when I got to the top, I saw the ruins. I stopped, stunned. I don't know how long I stood there, transfixed. I had expected to be impressed, even overwhelmed, but nothing had prepared me for this.

The ruins stood on an immense stretch of flat land that was completely surrounded by great slopes that rose up, protecting it, making it invisible from any other vantage point. They were like a great fallen city, some of the ruins still standing, others collapsed into great heaps of stone. I was reminded of the ancient Aztec cities hidden in the South American mountains, or those primitive cities just recently discovered in Africa. These ruins must be even older. Some were small, mere clusters of stone, while others towered up to touch the hard blue sky. There were other ruins scattered over the moors, like the one I had seen when Alan had first drove us to the house, but these were the major ones, a metropolis incredibly hidden away in a secret valley in the middle of the moors.

I walked down the slope, and the present vanished. When I reached the surface of the valley and started toward the ruins, even the moors seemed to disappear. There was nothing but this primitive civilization, amazingly alive in my imagination. The slopes rose all around like the rim of a cup, and the flat blue sky stretched directly overhead. The ground was a hard crust, grey and white, and the ruins were dark brown streaked with a dull-gold grain. Some were stained with green, moss that had become a part of the stones themselves. There were three or four acres of flat ground before I reached the ruins, and as I came closer they began to take on a shape and character I had been unable to discern from the distance.

I didn't blush. Not quite.

I had read dozens of books about these ruins, or similar ones, and I had seen hundreds of plates and engravings which depicted them with explicit detail. I considered myself a scholar, immune to the jolts and shocks of the fastidious do-gooders, those who put skirts around the bottom of pianos in fear that the sight of naked piano legs would incite evil thoughts in the minds of young people who used the parlour. Such hypocrisy was part of our society, and I despised it, and yet my reactions now were those of the traditional Victorian maiden. Book print and illustrations were one thing. Stark reality was altogether different. I scolded myself, yet it took a few minutes for the initial reaction to wear off. I was glad I was alone. I couldn't have faced these ruins with anyone else, not even Donald.

I rationalized. Evil was in the eye of the beholder. If certain Victorian matrons saw evil in wooden piano legs, that was only an indication of their own warped minds. They were, in actuality, far less healthy than those ancient druids who saw life and the creation of life as a joyous miracle and celebrated it in their architecture. I took a deep breath and tried to shake off the last vestiges of prudery. I examined the ruins with an objective eye, and soon I was able to see only their wonder and ignore their pagan symbolism.

I stepped toward the nearest ruin, a small brown stone temple, four stone columns with a huge flat rock balanced on top to form the roof. Something rolled under the sole of my shoe, and I almost fell, my whole body pitching forward as though shoved from behind. I threw my arms around one of the columns and broke the fall. I caught my breath, pushed a lock of

hair away from my cheek. If I were superstitious, I could almost have believed that I had
actually been shoved by some vengeful spirit
who warned me not to desecrate this sacred
ground. Nonsense, of course. Such things happened only in fantastic tales.... I had stepped
on a loose rock. I bent down and picked it up.

It wasn't a rock.

I felt as though my palm were burning. I
wanted to fling the loathsome object away, but
I couldn't. I stared at it in horrified fascination. It was an amulet, almost identical in shape
and size to the one I had found in Donald's
desk drawer. It, too, was suspended from a
leather thong. What was it doing here? Such
objects must once have been fairly common
around here, like the Indian arrowheads that
farmers were always turning up with their
ploughs in America, but these ruins had been
explored by experts, examined by hundreds
of scholars as well as the merely curious, and
any such valuable curios as this must have
been carried away years ago. There was no
logical reason for the amulet to have been here.
It must be worth hundreds of pounds.... Then
I noticed that the leather was new. It should
be withered with age, stiff, dried. It was still
soft and pliable. I frowned. I dropped the
amulet into my skirt pocket and rubbed my

hand briskly to remove the sensation of contamination.

Someone had been here, wearing the amulet. The strand of leather broke, and the amulet dropped off.... But who would wear such a thing? I creased my brow. A student, perhaps, come to study the ruins just as I had come today. It was curious that Donald should have had one in his drawer, that I should have stumbled over one as I visited the ruins for the first time. Such objects were rare, very rare. I decided to put it out of my mind, at least for the present.

Staring at the ruins that rose ahead of me, all shapes and sizes, I hesitated to step into that maze of ancient stone structures. I sensed an evil, a lurking presence that seemed to inhabit the place, and it seemed to be crouching, invisible, waiting for me to come within reach. I shuddered, the sensation was so real, and then forced myself to laugh silently. That spell again, even strong here, but I was determined not to let it overcome me. Uneducated villagers might believe in ghosts, might vehemently insist that phantom figures inhabited this ruined city, but I was above that sort of nonsense.

I walked into the midst of the ruins, stopping to examine each one. I jotted down notes on size and structure and made quick sketches of certain features they all had in common. I marvelled. The world of today was lost to me. Thousands of years evaporated, and the air around me was the air the druids had breathed, the sun was the sun that warmed them, the hard blue sky was the sky that stretched over them centuries ago. In my mind I could see the priestesses who climbed those broken brown steps, standing near the thick columns, chanting as the chosen one was led into the circle of stone. I stepped into the circle myself, bent down to study the flat altar stone that was stained brown with something that must have once run red. I could hear the voices, louder and louder, the monotonous chant rising until it threatened to shake the very earth. I felt the excitement, the fear. My pulses leaped. My throat went dry. I dropped my sketchbook and pressed my hand to my forehead.

The chanting died away, slipped back through the centuries. The stone columns became ruins, streaked green with moss. Reality returned, but the fear remained. I stood very still in the centre of the stone circle. I had let my imagination run away with me. I realized that, but why was my heart still pounding? Why did the air seem to be laden with some threat? I could feel the threat surrounding me, and I held my breath, every sense alert.

Something was here, something besides an overpowering illusion of the past. It was real. It wasn't just my imagination. Not now.

I heard a noise. It was like loose stones scattering. The sound echoed faintly. It was repeated. I heard heavy footsteps, several of them. The sound came closer. The stone circle seemed to expand, drawing away from me, and the sky seemed to waver overhead. I stood by the ancient altar, dizzy with fear. The footsteps grew louder, came nearer. I backed against the altar stone, wanting to scream, but no sound would come. Fear held me powerless. Powerless, I waited.

CHAPTER NINE

The horse stepped into the stone circle, small rocks clattering under its hooves. It was a beautifully proportioned creature with a coat as black as wet sable. A grey leather saddle with silver horn was fastened on its back, and the reins hung loose, dragging on the ground. The animal did not seem to notice me. It walked about the columns, its head close to the ground.

No doubt it was looking for grass where no grass grew. My heart stopped pounding and I heaved a sigh of relief. My whole body felt limp, and I had to brace myself against the altar stone to keep from falling. The animal continued to ignore me. Its hooves made a loud noise on the hard ground, and the sound echoed, magnified.

I set my sack lunch and notebooks on the altar stone and tried to summon enough strength to walk. I felt as though all energy, all courage, had been drained out of me by that sudden rush of fear. My knees were weak, and my hands felt numb. I chafed my wrists and took several deep breaths, turning my face up to let the warm rays of sun stroke it. After a few minutes I felt normal enough to scold myself for that absurd moment of fear. How Bella would laugh if I told her a horse had frightened me to the point of desperation. How she would smile if I told her I had visualized a swarm of ghostly figures closing in on me.

The horse walked across the open space toward me. It stopped two feet away and stretched its sleek neck, tapping one hoof gently on the ground, as though expecting a lump of sugar. I stroked its smooth jaw and ran my fingers through the silky black mane.

'You gave me quite a start, you know,' I said

quietly. 'What are you doing here? That's a lovely saddle. Whose horse are you? I don't have any sugar, but if I did I'd give it to you.' I smiled at the absurdity of my own words, but the horse stretched its neck and looked at me with enormous brown eyes and seemed to be delighted with the sound of my voice.

'You didn't come here all by yourself,' I said sensibly. 'I'd better see if I can find your master.'

I stepped away from the horse and walked toward the stone columns. Leaving the circle of stones, I looked around at the ruins outside it. I saw no one. I moved around a fallen temple and walked beneath a series of gigantic arches. The man was standing among a cluster of tall, thick obelisks that were graphic in their symbolism. His hands were thrust in his pockets, and his head was held down. He seemed to be searching for something on the ground. He bent down, picked up a handful of rocks, let them slip between his fingers. He frowned, shook his head, moved on, still examining the ground.

I knew immediately who he was, and I knew what he was looking for. He looked up and saw me. He showed no surprise but stared at me with mildly curious brown eyes, shoulders still hunched, hands still thrust in his pockets.

Neither of us said anything. We were perhaps ten yards apart, and neither of us made a move to come closer.

Burton Rodd was tall, and his slender, angular body made him seem even taller. The rawboned, lanky build gave an impression of strength, hard, wiry, formidable, and the face was seamed and craggy, a face ravaged by excesses. The lips were wide and thin, curling down at the corners, and the nose was large, twisted slightly as though it had at one time been broken. The cheekbones were sharp, and the eyes dark brown, with heavy, hooded lids that gave him a lazy, sleepy look. His dark brows arched sharply and flared out at the corners like black wingtips. It was a hard face, cold, and I felt those hooded eyes could witness great tenderness or great cruelty with an equal indifference. Thick locks of grizzled black hair tumbled untidily over his head, and his sideburns were frosted with silver.

He wore a rumpled black suit with tight pipestem trousers and a loose jacket that fell open to reveal a ruffled white shirtfront and a black cord tie awkwardly knotted. The clothes were elegant, the product of exquisite taste and expert tailoring, yet shockingly wrinkled and smudged with dust. I had the impression he had pulled them on because they were the first he laid his hands on in the closet. He wore them as he might wear a pair of pyjamas, with total nonchalance.

I stared at him openly, not even trying to hide my interest. The man was undeniably fascinating, and I could easily believe all the tales I had heard about him. That hard, angular body like whipcord could lash with fury and take with force, and those thin lips could curl with exquisite cruelty while the hooded eyes glittered with disdain. I could see that his prowess with women had not been exaggerated. Weak women would be unable to resist his dark fascination, would want to reform him, while the more sophisticated women would long to meet the challenge of his strong will, destroy it, and dominate.

Fortunately, I was neither weak nor overly sophisticated. I stared at him coldly, unmoved. He stood in front of the obelisks. I suddenly remembered them, and I blushed in spite of myself. Burton Rodd turned around and looked up at the obelisks behind him, then looked back at my flushed cheeks and grinned. He strolled toward me, hands still in pockets. Although I tried to control the blush, it burned rosily. I was infuriated with myself.

'So you're the little lady I've been hearing so much about,' he said. His voice was surprisingly soft, low-pitched, with a husky rasp that made it unique. It was as though it hurt him to speak.

'I'm Katherine Hunt,' I replied.

'Not at all what I expected,' he rasped.

'What did you expect, Mr Rodd?'

'You want to know? I expected a thin, pinched spinster with a soured expression and a drab dress buttoned all the way up to the chin.'

'Did you indeed?'

He jerked his head sharply, a nod, and grinned. The hooded eyes were examining me carefully, and I wished I *were* wearing a high-buttoned dress. The lips curled, the eyes glittered, and his expression clearly indicated what he thought of me. I wanted to slap his face.

'I'm disappointed,' he said.

'Oh?'

He executed the jerky nod again. 'If you were the prune I'd pictured, I could dismiss you from my thoughts. As it is'—he shook his head slowly from side—'it isn't going to be easy.'

'I'm afraid I don't understand what you're talking about,' I snapped. His eyes were still examining me.

'We're going to fight, you see,' he said.

'Are we?'

'You're going to leave Castlemoor. I'm going

to make you. Knowing your background, I expected resistance. I still do, of course, but I had no idea it would come from such a—splendid source.'

'You're talking in riddles, Mr Rodd. I'm going to leave Castlemoor?'

'Yes, ma'am.'

'You're going to make me?'

He nodded again.

'That's absurd,' I said.

He shook his head. 'You'll leave. I always get my way.'

'Not this time, Mr Rodd.'

'Always,' he repeated.

'You've got a fight on your hands,' I retorted.

'Delighted,' he replied.

'I—this is fantastic,' I said. 'Why should you want me to leave, and how do you think you'll make me?'

'I want you to leave because'—he paused, frowning—'because I don't like strangers on the moors. I tried to prevent your brother from buying the house. I lost that round. The agent who sold it to him no longer lives in Darkmead —he's bankrupt, as a matter of fact. Petty revenge, but all I could do under the circumstances. Your brother was a nuisance, and it seems you shall be, too.'

'You've only answered one of my questions,' I told him.

'How will I make you leave? Let's say I have means.'

'Are you *really* insane, Mr Rodd?'

'No, but it's insane to oppose me.'

'I don't believe a word of this,' I said. 'This is—why, it's *Alice in Wonderland*. I expect to see a turtle waddle up and tell me the story of his life. You can't be for real, Mr Rodd. Surely you're—you're pulling my leg.'

He arched a brow. My blush started burning again. I cursed silently at my unfortunate choice of words.

'I assure you I'm quite real,' he said.

'I don't believe it,' I said stubbornly.

'What would you have me do to convince you?' he asked in a tone that again made me want to slap his face.

I stared up at that seamed, ravaged face, so ugly and yet so fascinating. There were weary lines about his eyes and mouth and deep creases in his cheeks. The grin mocked me, his whole manner was mocking, but there was a hard, cold look in his eyes that told me he was quite serious. I felt a sudden chill, and I stepped back, appalled.

'I—I refuse to continue with this insane conversation,' I retorted. 'It's—preposterous.'

158

I turned away from him and started walking toward the arches. I heard him behind me, and then he was beside me, striding along casually, as though we were taking a Sunday stroll. I stopped dead still. He stopped too. I gave him an icy, disdainful look. He nodded his head and smiled. I continued on under the arches. Burton Rodd whistled softly, kicking rocks with the toe of his shoe as he moved beside me.

I stopped in front of the circle of stones. 'This has gone far enough,' I said. 'I—I have things to do. I have no intention of matching wills with you at the moment. You are without question the most loathsome man I've ever encountered.'

'Without question,' he agreed.

'And—and furthermore, your idiotic pose of villainy belongs to the Spanish Inquisition. This—this is the age of Enlightenment. Victoria is on the throne, and we're—quite modern. Just because you live in a castle and have a stranglehold on one little village doesn't mean—'

'Enough,' he said amiably. 'We don't have to fight just yet. You're on edge.'

'I am *not* on edge!'

I hurled the words violently. Burton Rodd jumped back, threw his hand out, and pretended to be on the verge of flight. Laughter welled up inside of him, and he had difficulty restraining it. I closed my eyes and took a deep breath, drawing on reserves of sanity which were fast deserting me.

I managed to speak in a calm, level voice. 'I am not a hysterical woman, Mr Rodd,' I said, enunciating each word carefully. 'I am, at the moment, extremely irritated, and I wish you had the common decency to leave me in peace.'

'Truce,' he said.

I turned to go into the circle of stones.

'What are you going to do?' he asked.

'I am going to eat my lunch,' I said nastily.

The horse was still inside the circle, reins dragging loose, wet-sable coat gleaming in the sunlight. I walked over to the altar stone, sat down on it, and started taking my lunch out of the sack. I studiedly ignored Burton Rodd, who stroked the horse's neck and then came over to pick up my sketchbook and examine the sketches I had done earlier.

'These are quite good,' he remarked.

I made no reply. I started unwrapping a sandwich.

'Of course, you know what they symbolize,' he said.

'I assure you, I know, and I assure you I'm not at all shocked. I intend to write a book about the ruins and the ancient rites, and I

160

have none of the maidenly sensibilities that might hinder some other woman.'

'You blush prettily.'

'I'm not blushing.'

'You really intend to write a book?'

'I most certainly do.'

'You think it's possible?'

'Mr Rodd—'

'So you *are* one of those?'

'I beg your pardon?'

'One of those "liberated females" so popular with the press.'

'You don't think women should be liberated?'

'On the contrary, I think they should be kept in chains. Women were created for one thing, and one thing only.'

'And what is that, dare I ask?'

'To serve men,' he said simply.

'Fiddlesticks!'

'Such language!' he mocked.

'I know a few stronger expressions, and believe me I'm tempted to use some of them now!'

I finished unwrapping the sandwich. Burton Rodd took it out of my hand and began to eat it, leaning on the altar stone, casual, unperturbed, infuriating. I pulled out the other sandwich, started to unwrap it, and found I had lost all appetite. I cast back in my mind, trying to remember another time when I had been as infuriated as I was right now, but I could think of none. Rodd finished the sandwich, said it was delicious, and asked what else I had in the sack. I took out the apple and handed it to him, livid. He examined it as though it were some curious object, then bit into it. I sat very still, trying to control my rage.

He ate the apple, ignoring me completely. He might have been alone in the ruined city. He seemed to be lost in thought. Occasionally he would glance up at the hard blue sky, a thoughtful look in his eyes, but he never once glanced at me. This bothered me even more than his brash impudence. I wondered why. Seething with rage, wishing he would vanish from the face of the earth, I slowly realized that these reactions were only a part of my response to him. The anger was real, but so was the thrill, the stimulation his very presence caused me to feel.

I tried to deny it. He was a horrible man, loathsome, yet there was something hypnotic about him, something that any woman would respond to. I blanched as I realized I was responding too, despite myself. This made my anger all the more potent.

'So you're interested in ancient history?' he

said. 'This is where it all started. Do you know what would have happened to a girl like you in a place like this several centuries ago? The stone you're sitting on was—'

I slid off the stone as though it had started burning. Rodd laughed. I stood rather shakily, knees weak. I started gathering up my notebooks. He took another bite of the apple, chewed, tossed the core to the horse. Now that he had finished eating my lunch, he gave his full attention to me. He leaned back against the stone, and his eyes examined me as they had the first time he saw me.

'You know, it's rather a shame we have to fight,' he said. 'Under other circumstances there could have been something—mmm—quite pleasant between us.'

'There could never be anything between us, Mr Rodd,' I said stiffly. 'Let me assure you of that.'

'You're mistaken,' he replied. 'No woman has ever resisted me, or even tried to, for that matter.'

'I'm sure the kind of women *you* consort with—'

'There've been all kinds. A duchess once tried to commit suicide when I refused to elope with her, and the wife of an ambassador—'

'I'm not at all interested in your—your dallyings, fictional or otherwise, and your—your preposterous conceit knows no bounds.'

'You're fascinated,' he said. 'You'd like to hear all about them, and in detail.' He smiled, and his eyelids drooped sleepily over those hypnotic brown eyes. 'If I were of a mind to have it that way,' he continued, 'you'd be in my arms by sundown, willingly. I'd place money on it.'

'You'd lose your wager,' I snapped.

I wasn't so sure of it, and I was horrified with myself when I realized it. I dropped the notebook, retrieved it, felt completely at a loss. I might have been an awkward schoolgirl, all thumbs, instead of an intelligent, self-possessed young woman. Burton Rodd sensed my confusion, and it delighted him. He was fully aware of his power, and he exercised it with malice. Even as he taunted me, there was something cold and disinterested about him, as though this were a slightly boring game that would pass the time until something more challenging came along.

'You really are as vile as they say you are,' I said, my voice barely audible.

'You're right,' he answered.

'And—and you're proud of it.'

'The world is full of placid sheep and pinchmouthed hypocrites,' Burton Rodd said. 'Fools

164

and knaves without the guts to be true to their instincts. I'm honest. I don't pretend to be a gentleman. I don't set out to charm and deceive. An honest man is a rarity in this age.'

'You needn't try to justify yourself for my sake,' I retorted.

He frowned. 'I wasn't trying to justify anything. I'm merely saying I'd rather be honest —and be called a cad—than to play the hypocrite and court the world while secretly despising it, like my cousin Edward, for example. I understand he's become quite attentive to you.'

'That's no concern of yours,' I said icily.

'He's very good at that. The ladies love him —young and old alike. My mother adores him, even while he sponges off her, eats her food, uses her home as a hotel, borrows money from her to finance his so-called "research," and secretly mocks her for her indulgences. But Edward's charming, very, so witty and warm and amiable. He's quite gallant, and gallantry always wins the ladies, all of whom are notoriously gullible.'

'You're incapable of understanding a man like Edward Clark,' I said.

'I understand him all too well. His beautiful manners amuse me.'

'He could give you a few lessons,' I replied.

He looked at me and shook his head slowly

from side to side, as though I were a mere child incapable of forming any real judgements of my own. 'We won't argue the point,' he said lightly, his voice expressing total boredom. 'It's been pleasant, Miss Hunt. We'll meet again, soon.' His dark eyes studied my face for a moment, interested, amused, and then they went flat. I seemed suddenly no longer to exist so far as he was concerned. He turned away, hands thrust in pockets again, and started strolling toward the entrance column. His head held down, he was studying the ground just as he had been doing when I first saw him.

His nonchalance, his obliviousness to me, was much harder to take than his antagonism had been. I frowned, furious. I called to him, in spite of myself. 'Mr Rodd!'

He turned, bored.

'Yes?' The word was a weary sigh.

'When I first saw you, you were—looking for something, weren't you?'

'As a matter of fact, I was.'

'Would you mind telling me what you hoped to find?'

'I don't think that need concern you,' he replied, slightly irritated now, as though a child dismissed for the evening had returned to plague an impatient parent.

'Could it be this?' I asked.

I pulled the amulet out of my pocket, holding it in the palm of my hand without looking down at it.

Burton Rodd lifted his bony shoulders, dropped them wearily, came back toward me, his brow creased, his lips curving down at the corners with impatience. He glanced at the object in my palm, and when he saw what it was, his whole manner changed. He stiffened. His face turned ashen. It looked even more ravaged, more deeply lined. He didn't say anything for at least a full minute. The expression on his face frightened me.

'Where did you get that?' he asked. He stressed each word, as though each had been slashed off with a sharp blade.

'I—I found it.'

'Give it to me.'

I didn't dare disobey. He stood in front of me, tall, thin, as hard as steel, as cold as ice. At that moment he looked truly menacing, capable of seizing my throat with those long, bony hands if I refused. He took the amulet and dropped it into his pocket without even glancing at it, his eyes piercing mine. I couldn't look away.

'You found it?'

I nodded, unable to speak.

'Where?'

I lifted my hand in an ineffectual gesture. My throat felt dry.

'Answer me!'

'I—as I came up to the ruins—I stepped on it. I—I almost fell. It was there—on the ground....'

His eyes never left mine. 'You know what it is?'

'Of course I do!'

'What does it mean to you?'

'Nothing.'

'Tell me!'

'Nothing!'

'What do you know?'

'I know the leather's new! It should be withered.'

'Are you—'

'I don't know anything else!'

Almost hysterical, I turned away from him. I leaned against the altar stone, staring down at my notebooks and the empty sack. My back was to him, but I could feel him behind me. The sky wavered, very blue. The sun was warm, a yellow pool on the brown-stained stone. The horse walked over the crusty ground, its hooves tapping pleasantly. These details registered sharply, yet seemed unreal. Burton Rodd laid his hand on my shoulder and turned me around to face him.

'You're telling the truth?' he asked. His voice was soft now, rasping, almost gentle.

'Why should I lie?'

'Why indeed?' he mused.

He studied my face, but without the ferocity of before. He seemed to be committing each feature to memory. His fingers still gripped my shoulder. He released me and stepped back. The wind ruffled his grizzled locks. He looked older, strangely vulnerable. At that instant a curious affinity seemed to join us together, and I felt closer to him than I had ever been to anyone in my life. It lasted only a moment, yet when it passed I realized there was much more to Burton Rodd than he revealed on the surface. He was enigmatic, a man of many levels, and I wondered if anyone really knew him completely.

'You'll have to leave Castlemoor,' he said in a thoughtful voice. 'I will see to it that the departure is profitable to you—quite profitable.' His eyes looked sad.

'I told you before, Mr Rodd: I have no intentions of leaving.'

'You'll leave,' he said.

He turned away from me abruptly. He took the horse by the reins and led it out of the circle of stones without once looking back at me. I heard the horse's hooves clattering on the ground for a while, then echoes, then no sound at all but the wind whistling softly as it blew gently through the great ruined city. For a long time I stood there amidst the ruins, stunned and shaken by the encounter with Burton Rodd. I frowned. Was he the demon people said he was, cold, cruel, amoral? At moments he had seemed so, and at moments he had seemed a man weighed down with some tragic burden, tormented and torn asunder by life. The ravaged face, the weary lines, the sad eyes—all gave weight to that impression.

I had run through a whole gamut of emotions in his presence, and now I felt depleted, unable to judge him. Perhaps that was part of his power. Perhaps he used it to weaken his victims before closing in for the kill. I wondered about that moment of curious affinity. Had it been real, or had I merely imagined it? I couldn't be sure. The only thing I was sure of was that Burton Rodd intended to try to drive me away from Castlemoor, for reasons unknown, and that I had no intentions of leaving, no matter what tactics he might employ in order to achieve his goals.

CHAPTER TEN

Dorothea Rodd's invitation came late that afternoon, after I returned from the ruins. I was in the study, compiling notes, when I heard voices. Glancing out of the window, I saw Bella, cheeks flushed, expression irate, arguing with Buck Crabbe. In boots, tight tan trousers, and leather jerkin, Crabbe looked the stupid peasant, his face sullen, his lower lip thrust out. He seized Bella's wrist, jerked her toward him. She looked small and helpless against his great frame, her brown curls tumbling about her shoulders, her pink skirts fluttering like butterfly wings against his legs. Buck Crabbe leaned down to whisper something in her ear. Bella pulled away from him and slammed her open palm against his face.

He looked stunned, an uncomprehending brute. Bella stood with hands on hips, cheeks blazing, daring him to do anything. Crabbe loomed up before her, incredibly large, incredibly ugly, and for a moment I thought he was going to strike her. His lips moved sullenly, but I couldn't hear the words. Bella threw her head back and laughed, the sound tinkling merrily on the air. Crabbe creased his brow, thrust his lower lip out, and seemed to stagger a little, as though he would topple over. Then he turned around and left, lumbering away like some enormous animal. Bella was still laughing. As she came toward the house, I noticed the slip of paper in his hand.

'What was *that* all about?' I inquired as she came into the study.

'He brought an invitation from the castle,' she said, handing me the slip of paper. 'And he had a personal invitation for me. Imagine the cheek! Stood there like a lummox and flexed his muscles and lowered his lids kinda sleepy-like and expected me to meet him behind the castle at ten! Just like that, as though he was doin' me a great big favour. I told 'im when I decided to dally I'd do my own choosin', and he said I didn't know what I was missin', and I said I'd as soon touch a boa constrictor!'

'And what did he say to that?'

'Somethin' perfectly *awful*, Miss Kathy! I wouldn't dare repeat it!'

Her eyes sparkled, and there was a saucy smile on her lips. I knew she had been thoroughly elated by the encounter. She fluttered about the study, her voluminous pink skirt rustling crisply over her starched petticoats. I could imagine how she would embroider the incident for Alan tonight when he came to take her for a moonlight stroll. She settled at the window to watch the last orange banners fade against the horizon, and I read the note from Dorothea Rodd.

It was more like a summons than an invitation. Dorothea Rodd would expect me for dinner at eight the next night, formal, and one of her servants would come to fetch me and escort me across the moors to the castle. I was irritated by the tone of the note, and I started to crumple it up and toss it aside, but my curiosity was too great. Few people had an opportunity to see the insides of the castle. I knew I would go even if the note had been openly insulting. I wondered if Burton Rodd had instigated the invitation. It seemed likely.

'You've got to make a marvellous impression,' Bella exclaimed after I had shown her the invitation. 'What will you wear? Something magnificent! Show them how *real* gentry dress.'

'I don't have anything magnificent,' I told her.

Bella narrowed her eyes, her head cocked to one side. She was mentally examining my wardrobe. 'The yellow silk? Not this time of year? The white linen—lovely, but it makes you look like a schoolgirl? The black-and-white-striped taffeta? Too severe. I have it, Miss Kathy! The garnet velvet! It'll be perfect!'

'Really, Bella, the dress is much too—'

'It'll be grand. You'll look like a duchess!'

My brother had bought the garnet velvet dress for me the day after his publishers accepted his book. He had paid an outrageous price for it, and I had scolded him for spending so much money on a dress when we needed new curtains in the parlour and were already two months behind in the rent. Donald had brushed all these arguments aside and insisted I wear the garnet gown to the opera. I wore it once and felt extremely uncomfortable as we sat in the box. I was certain that all eyes were upon me, and after wearing it that one time, I folded the dress away in tissue paper and mothballs and referred to it thereafter as 'Donald's folly.'

'I couldn't wear it,' I protested.

Bella was adamant. 'You shall!' she cried. 'And we'll have to do something spectacular to your hair!'

At seven-thirty the next evening I sat at the mirror, extremely nervous as Bella applied the finishing touches to my coiffure. It was already dark outside, and only one lamp burned in the room. In the shadowy glow, I studied the reflection in the glass. This wasn't Katherine Hunt. This was Katherine Hunt masquerading as something she wasn't. I knew that any man would be beguiled by what he saw, and most women would be envious, but I remained unmoved by the softly lighted reflection. Still, it would be pleasant to see the expression in Edward's eyes when he saw me tonight, and it would be interesting to note Burton Rodd's reactions to this woman who was so completely unlike the book-bearing, scholarly creature he had seen yesterday at the ruins.

The gown had long, tight sleeves that extended to the edge of my palms, and form-fitting bodice and waist, with a skirt that cascaded to the floor in richly gathered folds. It was extremely modest in front, completely covering my shoulders, yet it dipped down alarmingly in back, exposing an improbable amount of naked flesh. Bella said I had a lovely back, perfect shoulderblades, but I would have been happier had the cut not been so extreme. The soft, crushed velvet was a deep garnet hue, a silvery mist over the nap. Castlemaine herself might have worn the dress with flair, but Miss Katherine Hunt felt ill at ease.

Bella had pulled my hair back sharply from my face, moulding it tightly against my head like a golden skullcap, with three long ringlets dangling down. She arranged the ringlets over my left shoulder, stood back, sighed, clasped her hands together, and said I looked like a painting. I leaned forward to study my face, so painstakingly made up—violet-brown shadow applied lightly over lids, a hint of rouge brushed over sculptured cheekbones, bare suggestion of coral smoothed over lips. I looked like a sophisticated woman of thirty, and I felt like an awkward girl of thirteen.

I stood up. Bella handed me my wrap, a stole of gossamer black lace, exquisitely made like black cobwebs with frail jet flowers sewn on. It had been another gift from Donald, and I wrapped it about my shoulders now. He would have been pleased with me tonight, I thought. He would have loved to take me out, show me off, as though he had been solely responsible for all this sophistication and elegance.

'I see a torch moving down the slope,' Bella said. 'It must be the servant comin' to fetch you.'

'It must be,' I replied vaguely. 'You and Alan behave yourselves while I'm gone. He is coming?'

'He brought a tub of pecans this afternoon,' she said. 'We're goin' to sit in the kitchen and shell 'em. Have a good time, Miss Kathy.'

'I'll try,' I said.

I was waiting in front of the door when Buck Crabbe came up with the flaming torch. He was tall, impassive, dressed in a dark-brown livery that looked incongruous on his hulking body. He held the torch aloft. The flames cast flickering shadows over his broad bony face and caused the tips of his bronze-blond hair to glisten with orange. He turned, silent, and led the way up the slope toward the castle.

The night air was cold, stirring restlessly over the moor. I wished my wrap were more substantial. The gossamer net did little to protect my naked back. I could feel chills on the bare skin. Crabbe walked slowly, solemnly, like a zombie, I thought, but even so it was hard to keep up with him in my high-heeled black shoes. I stumbled once and had to catch hold of his arm to keep from falling. He stood still, waiting for me to right myself, his face expressionless, his mouth drawn tight. I felt like telling him he was a real bundle of personality, but I didn't quite dare. I felt sure the sarcasm would have gone unappreciated.

The sky was full of ponderous black clouds. Moonlight spilled over the dark rims, to drip a misty silver light over the moors. Everything was black and grey, slopes of grey rolling to a distant black horizon. The silence was heavy, broken only by the rasp of insects and the sound of footsteps crunching over the hard ground. The torch wavered, yellow and orange, throwing off an odour of tar and smoke. The castle was ahead, looking even more sinister shrouded in shadows, the thick grey walls stained with misty silver. Lights burned behind a few of the windows, and the great oak door stood open. We walked beneath the oak trees. Just as we reached the door, Buck stopped, turned to me. His blue-grey eyes studied me for a moment. His wide mouth curled down at the corners.

'Leave the girl alone,' he said.

'I beg your pardon?'

'The girl. Nicola. Leave her be.'

'What—what do you mean?'

'Don't meddle, miss,' he said in a flat voice. 'That's what I mean.'

Before I could form a reply, he turned and led the way through the huge door. It was very dark inside, the torchlight flickering over thick damp walls and an extremely low ceiling. I realized we were passing through a sort of tunnel that would eventually open onto the courtyard. My heels made a tapping noise on the cobblestone floor. I had a feeling of claustrophobia and was glad when we finally reached the courtyard. It was enormous, with several tall trees growing around a huge, cracked white pond full of dirty brown water, dead leaves floating on the surface, a broken statue standing dejectedly in the middle, holding a fish aloft. There were several buildings—a stable, a deserted blacksmith's shop, a granary. A white flagstone path wound among shabby flowerbeds, weed-infested, thorny. Torches were stuck in the ground, burning smokily, illuminating everything with a dim yellow glow.

I had an eerie feeling as we crossed the courtyard. The place was immense, the size overwhelming, and there was an atmosphere of decay—grey walls streaked with soot and glittering with moisture, loose stones fallen on the ground, everything suffering from neglect.

The castle had once been the home of dozens and dozens of people, and now only a handful lived here. I tried to picture them milling around in this vast, aged place. I saw long deserted halls, great empty rooms, cobwebs, dust, emptiness. I shuddered in spite of myself.

Buck led me up the curving grey marble steps that led to the portico in front of the main building. Round white pots held rubbery green plants, torches burned in niches, tossing wavering yellow shadows over the steps. We passed under the arch supported by smooth black columns and walked under the colonnade. A great oak door stood open, and we walked down a long hall tiled in black and white marble squares, ancient tapestries flapping on the walls. We turned, moved down a smaller, darker hall, illuminated only by Buck's torch, turned again, moved up a short flight of stairs, and passed through a great deserted room with tattered red damask on the walls, sheets over the furniture, cobwebs draped over the four chandeliers. I was completely lost now, could never have found my way back to the courtyard. One would need a map to get around in this place, I thought as Buck led the way down a long hall with padlocked doors on either side. We went around a corner and passed down another hall, well lighted now, the torches illuminating enormous dark portraits hanging in ornate gold frames.

Doors stood open at the end of the hall. Buck led me through them and stood back, his mission accomplished. I heard voices, but I couldn't tell where they were coming from at first.

The room was enormous, large enough to swallow up my whole house. The ceiling was two stories high, painted a dark blue and gilded with gold-leaf designs. The gold leaf was tarnished, the paint flaking. The walls were a yellowed ivory, adorned with gold leaf, and the floor was exquisite parquet, gold, brown, red woods all smooth from decades of wax, buckling a little at the seams. There were clusters of furniture, but the room was so large that it seemed empty despite the furniture. Although fires burned in two white-marble fireplaces at either end of the room, the air was still laced with frosty chill.

Buck left, closing the doors behind him, and I stood hesitantly, peering through the gloom, feeling lost and absurd in my velvet gown. I had the feeling that this was a dream fast taking on the qualities of nightmare. I was lost, locked in a museum, abandoned, forgotten, left to wander through these ancient rooms, through cold halls. Panic was just beginning to set in when I heard footsteps and saw Edward coming toward me.

He was resplendent in black pumps, black suit, shirt-front gleaming, white silk tie matching white silk cummerbund. His burnished golden hair was heaped in heavy locks over his forehead, and his cornflower-blue eyes showed his pleasure. He smiled, took my hand, led me across an acre of parquet to the cluster of furniture before one of the fireplaces. Although at least fifty candles burned in silver sconces and candelabra, there wasn't enough light. The figures grouped around the hearth looked hazy, as though seen through a mist.

'Your dress is smashing,' Edward whispered in my ear. 'It gives me evil thoughts.'

'Does it?'

'Better be glad we're not alone. Safety in numbers, you know.'

'I'm nervous,' I told him. 'I wish—'

'Here she is,' he said aloud.

I saw Nicola sitting on a sofa of pale-lavender velvet. Her dark hair was worn in two tight braids fastened in a coronet on top of her head. She wore a white dress. Her cheeks looked ashen, her eyes shadowy. Could this pale wraith be the vivacious creature I had seen on the moors, I wondered. The two greyhounds lay in front of the fire, not stirring as I approached. Burton Rodd stood up. He wore an elegant black suit, a masterpiece of tailoring, and a sky-blue satin vest embroidered with black-silk oak leaves. He was spotless, immaculate, his black leather pumps shining, his white silk ascot flawless. The exquisite clothes only emphasized the ravaged face and grizzled hair, made him seem older, wearier. He nodded, and his dark eyes took in every detail of the dress.

He arched one brow slowly. That single gesture spoke volumes.

Dorothea Rodd was sitting in a dark wing-backed chair turned away from the fire, and I didn't see her at first. She rose to greet me, came toward me with the agile grace of a young girl. She was tall and slender, with the loose, bony frame of her son, wearing a long-sleeved black gown that swept the floor, the full skirt rustling over starched petticoats. Amethysts sparkled at her throat and ears, the stones gleaming with blood-red facets. Her hair was lustrous black, streaked with silver, piled on top of her head in rich waves, and her face at one time must have been magnificent. The bone structure was perfect, delicately formed, and the dark-brown eyes gleamed like jewels. The lovely face was pathetically pitted and marred with pockmarks, but after a moment one didn't notice that. One saw only the eyes that still had the glittering clarity of youth.

'Come, dear,' she said, 'let me see you.'

She took both my hands in hers and stood back to examine me, a lovely smile on her lips. She stood like that for at least a full minute, studying my face, her hands holding mine in a firm grip, and for some reason I was not at all embarrassed. I felt completely at ease with this woman. She was a lady, in every sense of the word, a grand lady, and it was evident in her every gesture.

183

'It's true,' she said, her voice serious. 'You're as beautiful as they said you were.' She shook her head slowly, her lips drooping down slightly in a sad smile. 'Twenty years ago I would have loathed you on sight. Now I can only marvel—' She released my hands, sighed. 'Is it true that you are also intelligent? That seems terribly unjust.'

I didn't know what to reply. Edward came to my rescue. 'I assure you she's quite intelligent, Dorothea. Formidably so, in fact.'

'Unbelievable,' Dorothea Rodd said wistfully.

She seemed suddenly to remember her role as hostess. 'You know Edward, of course, and I believe you've met my son.' She paused, a rather malicious twinkle in her eyes. 'You haven't met my ward, though. Nicola? Come meet Miss Hunt, dear.'

Nicola rose, gave me a genteel curtsy and looked into my eyes, pleading with me not to reveal our secret. I spoke to her, commenting on her dress. She lowered her eyes, muttering something I couldn't hear, and then sank back down on the sofa wearily.

'This is quite an occasion,' Dorothea exclaimed. 'As you may know, I *never* entertain. I haven't seen anyone for years—besides those people at church when Burton condescends to take me. Social life! How I used to love it! Now, alas...' She sighed again, made a futile gesture. 'There is so much to compensate for it. I don't miss it, really. My books, my studies, my music, my plants—we must show you the conservatory! I have some rare specimens! There's no time for people, no need for them...' Again she paused, and her trilling voice grew soft, gentle. 'But I couldn't resist meeting you. Edward has talked of nothing else for the past three days. Ordinarily he's quite indifferent to women—I had to see the exception! Let me take your wrap, dear.'

I handed it to her. My back was to Burton Rodd. I could feel his eyes burning on the naked skin. I stood uncomfortably as Dorothea complimented me on the dress, asked where I had bought it, said she wished she still had the ability to wear such a gown.

We all sat down, except Burton Rodd, who stood with his elbow leaning on the mantelpiece, his face inscrutable. Edward stretched out in a large blue chair, spreading his long legs out in front of him. Dorothea led me to a sofa opposite the one on which Nicola sat. The fire crackled noisily, devouring a cedar log and filling the air with a tangy aroma, but the heat had little effect on the icy chill air.

'And how do you like the castle, my dear?'

Dorothea inquired.

'It's—well—'

'Dreadful!' she cried. 'That's what it is! Falling down over our heads little by little. Have you ever heard of anything so preposterous— living in such a place! But it's home. I know that sounds ludicrous, but nevertheless it's true. We've closed up most of it, shut it off, boarded it up. Sold most of the furniture—had to, my dear, in order to live. Now that Burton has the pottery factory, we have no financial problems anymore, but people simply can't *live* in a place like this in this day and age. I wish sometimes I had a calm little cottage somewhere in the country, but this is my home—a great empty wreck of a place, impossible to heat, a relic. I lived with my husband here, though, bore my son here, spent the best days of my life prowling around these corridors. I can't leave it. I intend to die here, and after that—' She snapped her fingers. 'Kaput! It can sink into the moors, stone by stone!'

Burton Rodd cleared his throat, causing all eyes to turn to him. He grimaced, clearly unhappy with his mother's words. He stood at the hearth, the dogs at his feet, his jacket falling open to reveal the exquisite blue vest. Dorothea laughed, a beautiful, trilling sound that floated on the air in silvery peals.

'Burton thinks I'm mad, of course,' she continued. 'He'd dump the place in a minute, move to London. No sense of background whatsoever, no feeling of heritage! Can't say that I blame him, really. He stays. He runs the factory. He respects my feelings. But it can't be very pleasant for a red-blooded young man! He has the soul of an adventurer, a wanderer. What he really needs is a good wife—that'd settle him down.'

'I don't think Miss Hunt is interested in all this, Mother,' he said in a cool, bored voice.

'Quite a problem,' she continued. 'The women he meets in London would never consider coming to a gloomy place like this, which is perfectly understandable, and the few eligible girls around here— La!' She clicked her tongue. 'You should see the way he treats them! Like cattle, or geese. For several years enterprising mothers in Castlemoor County have been grooming their daughters for my son, and he calls them empty-headed ninnies, laughs at their coy manoeuvres. Why, just last year Sukey Johnson—her father owns one of the largest farms and is district judge to boot— poor Sukey was all up in the air because Burton noticed her at church and talked to her for a few minutes after the services. Poor thing, she was all ready to move in for the kill, when—'

'Enough!' her son said loudly, interrupting her. 'Don't you think we should go in to dinner, Mother?'

'I suppose so, though why all this rush—'

'Oh, dear!' Nicola cried, speaking up for the first time. Everyone was startled by her exclamation. She blushed prettily and lowered her eyes. The tight braids on top of her head were unflattering to a face that needed to be framed with lustrous waves. The stark white dress seemed to drain all the colour away from her. She looked like a child of thirteen, an anaemic child at that.

'What is it, dear?' Dorothea asked.

'I've forgotten my coral bracelet. I—I left it in my room. I planned to wear it tonight. Will I have time to fetch it?'

'Of course.'

Nicola stood up hesitantly. She smiled meekly, but I noticed a sly look in her eyes.

'I wonder if Miss Hunt would like to come with me?' she said. 'I would like to show her my doll collection.'

'There isn't time,' Burton Rodd said impatiently. 'The bracelet isn't important, Nicola. You can fetch it later.'

'The dolls come from all over the world,' Nicola said, as though she hadn't heard him. 'Some of them are very old, very fine. One

188

belonged to Marie Antoinette, they say, and—'

'I'd love to see them,' I said quickly, helping her.

'Run along, children,' Dorothea said, 'but don't dawdle, or Burton will be fit to be tied. Really, Burton, all this rush to get to the table! I simply don't see—'

Nicola smiled, took my hand, and led me across the room to a small door that led down a narrow hall. Once out of the room, her whole manner changed. She dropped my hand, dropped the meek, childish manner. Her face was hard, her mouth set. She walked quickly down the hall, turned, passed through a large room filled with dusty musical instruments, moved down another hall. I had to move fast to keep up with her. She seemed completely unaware of my presence, although I had sensed her eagerness for me to join her. In fact, I felt that the whole bit about the bracelet had been merely a ploy to get me alone, away from the others.

We moved down a small flight of stone steps, across a short hall, and up another flight of steps. The walls and floor of this part of the castle were thick brown concrete, damp and ugly. Torches burned in wall brackets spaced at intervals, foul-smelling, flickering, affording very little light to guide our way. I followed Nicola's flashing white skirts, perplexed. Near

189

the end of the hall she stopped, waiting for me to catch up with her. She stood in front of a great yawning doorway cut into the wall, a flight of rough stone steps leading down into the darkness below.

'The dungeons are down there,' she said, her voice expressionless.

I peered down. Cold, clammy air billowed up from the darkness, and I heard whispering, scurrying sounds as though rats infested the place. Nicola took my hand again, held it tightly, as though afraid. Together we looked down the steps, the top ones plainly visible, the ones that followed spread with shadows, the others completely shrouded in pitch-black darkness. I was trembling, although I could not have said why. Nicola seemed to be listening for something. A torch burned on the wall behind us, filling the air with smoke and the smell of tar, yellow reflections licking the ugly brown walls. There was something fascinating about that flight of stairs leading down to the dungeons, an evil that seemed to beckon even as it repelled. I wanted to move down them, see what was below, and at the same time I wanted to flee, get away from that clammy air and those rustling sounds that came floating up from the black nest of darkness.

'How—how frightening,' I said.

She nodded grimly. 'Two hundred years ago, men were taken down there to be tortured, to be left to die, and now—' She glanced around, her face drawn, looking to see if someone were eavesdropping on us. She gave my hand a tug. 'Come, we'll go to my room,' she whispered.

The door to her room was about ten yards down the hall. She opened it and pulled me inside, closing the door behind her. She took a deep breath and released it slowly, as though we had been pursued down the hall, escaping some evil just in the nick of time. I frowned, disconcerted. Nicola stepped over to her dresser and picked up the coral bracelet that lay there in plain sight. She couldn't possibly have forgotten it. She fastened it around her wrist, stooped to peer at her face in the mirror, smoothed the skin over her cheekbones, pushed a stray hair away from her temple. I examined the room.

It was small, cosy, with a very high ceiling of painted blue plaster. The lower half of the walls was covered with white-painted wainscoting, the upper half with a faded paper with blue and violet swirl designs. The bed and dresser were white, violet counterpane on bed, blue cushion on the dresser stool. A towering white cabinet with glassed-in shelves contained the doll collection, lovely dolls of all shapes and sizes, all covered with a thin coat of dust. She pointed to the collection, clearly bored with it, and sank down on the bed.

'What lovely dolls,' I remarked.

'They're all right,' she replied. 'Dorothea went to a lot of expense, a lot of trouble, to acquire them for me when I was a child. I *had* to like them, to please her. I never played with them—too pretty, too expensive—but I always showed them off to anyone who came, to please her.'

She toyed with the bracelet, not looking at me. I had the impression she wasn't even speaking to me, but, rather, addressing her reflection in the mirror across the room.

'She wanted this room to be bright and cheerful,' Nicola continued in the flat, expressionless tone. 'So she got the fancy wallpaper and painted everything white. A perfect young room for a perfect young girl. Dorothea is sweet. I adore her. Her intentions are the best, always were. I'm just not capable of appreciating them. I often wish I could be the daughter she wanted so badly. It's a shame she didn't adopt some chubby little English girl—' Her voice trailed off, and I saw the sadness in her eyes, the tragic droop at the corner of her mouth.

I changed the subject quickly. 'You stay here

all alone? So far from everyone else?'

'Edward's quarters are just around the corner, in the tower, and Buck has his room down the hall, just a few steps away. Practical. He can keep an eye on me at all times.'

I remembered what Edward had told me about the girl, how she had gone to a 'school' that was really a private hospital, how she had come back to Castlemoor, to fall in love with Jamie and imagine a conspiracy when the boy was dismissed, how she needed to be away from here. She was mentally ill, he said, yet I couldn't completely accept that. I knew very little about such things, but the young girl who sat before me now seemed to be in complete control of herself. Disturbed, bewildered—yes, no doubt of that, but insane? I wondered.

'Why did you bring me here, Nicola? Certainly not to see the dolls?'

She shook her head, frowning. 'I have something to tell you,' she said. 'I have to tell someone. I must—' She gnawed her lower lip and pulled herself up straight, examining the hem of her white dress.

'I saw Jamie,' she said bluntly.

'You did?'

She nodded, avoiding my eyes.

'Where?'

'Here,' she whispered.

Her dark eyes were enormous, shadowy, and her face seemed even paler than before. She looked frightened, and when she spoke again her voice wavered. There was an urgency about her words, as though she were pleading with me to believe them.

'Two nights ago,' she began. 'I—I couldn't sleep. I heard noises. Shuffling footsteps, low voices. I told myself I was imagining them, but they wouldn't go away. It was late—two, three in the morning. I put the pillow over my head, told myself to sleep, told myself I didn't hear anything. I—it was useless. I sat up. I lit my lamp. Then I heard the cry—a scream, really, something terrible, terrible. I ran out of my room and down the hall, and when I reached the stairs that led down to the dungeons, I saw him—just for a moment.'

'You—you saw Jamie there?'

'Yes. I saw his golden hair, his pale face, his dark eyes. Just for a second. Coming up from below. Then he vanished, as though someone had jerked him back down. I heard shuffling in the darkness, heard a sound like a blow. Then—then I just stood there. I don't know how long. Buck came. *He came from down there.* He told me I'd had another nightmare. He told me not to say anything to anyone. It'd just upset them, he said, and I'd be punished.

I—I had to tell someone. I decided to tell you.'

'You're certain it was Jamie?'

'The pale face, the golden hair—it, it must have been Jamie.'

'Think.'

'Yes—yes, I'm sure.'

'It wasn't just a nightmare, as Buck said?'

'It wasn't a nightmare,' she replied, her voice level.

'But—Nicola—'

'You don't believe me,' she said.

'It isn't that—'

'Of course you don't. Why should you?'

'Be fair, Nicola. I—'

'I have a vivid imagination. I read too much. I'm mad.'

She composed herself. She looked me straight in the eyes. For a moment her eyes seemed to beg, to implore; then they went flat. I could feel her withdrawing. She stood up. She brushed her skirts. She was very thin, very pale in the white dress, but there was something hard about her now, something impenetrable.

'Maybe it *was* a nightmare,' she said. 'It's easier to be mad, much easier. Poor Ophelia—flowers and sadness and water. I should have known. I shouldn't have told you. Forgive me.'

'Nicola,' I protested. 'I—I want to believe you. I want to be your friend.'

She shook her head, firm. 'No, no, I don't need friends. Not now. They're going to send me away, you know. Dorothea has a friend on the Continent, France I believe it is, who has a house in the country and takes in paying guests. Burton has already persuaded Dorothea to write to the woman. I'll be leaving soon, no doubt. Perhaps it's best that way.'

'But—'

'Sunshine and green leaves and sky and young people laughing. I'll be a new person. I can be sane there—after a while.'

I felt helpless. There was so much I wanted to say. I couldn't find the words. The girl stood in front of the mirror, cold, lost to me, patting the sides of her hair. I felt as though I had betrayed her in some way, and I wanted to make amends, but the girl at the mirror was as hard as steel, her mouth set, her eyes cold. She ran a fingertip over her brow and turned her head this way and that, studying the reflection.

'Please,' I said, 'give me a chance.'

'Forget it,' she replied. 'I don't need anyone.'

'Won't you let me—'

'Shall we join the others?' she asked. 'We mustn't linger too long. They'll think I've stabbed you or locked you in a closet or something. I'm supposed to be capable of things like that, from all I've heard.'

She opened the door and held it for me. I stepped out of the room. She smiled a smile of bitter wisdom, closed the door, and took my hand as though nothing had passed between us. We walked down the hall, and as we passed the staircase leading up from the dungeons, I saw Buck Crabbe coming up. When he saw us, he stopped, his fists clenched. His eyes shot me a look of pure venom, and he moved up a few more steps, menacing. Nicola saw him, laughed softly, and waved to him. We hurried on down the hall, hand in hand. I felt Buck Crabbe's eyes watching every move we made.

CHAPTER ELEVEN

I had lost all appetite, and although the meal was lavish, I could only make a pretence of eating the succulent food Dorothea had had prepared for this occasion. I merely pushed the silver fork across the exquisite china plate. I sipped the wine in the crystal goblet and found it light, heady, and I drank more. The servant came to refill my glass. I smiled, nodded, and lifted the glass to my lips. Burton Rodd was watching me, amused. A cynical smile flickered on his mouth, and his dark eyes sparkled maliciously. I drank half the wine, glaring at him defiantly. He nodded slightly, as though to acknowledge my accomplishment. I set the glass down, a little too abruptly. When it clattered on the table, the others looked at me. I pretended not to notice.

'Ah, Egypt!' exclaimed Dorothea, who had been recounting her experiences as a young bride. With sunshade overhead and husband in tow, she had been an intrepid explorer, travelling from country to country with incredible zest. 'The hot sun, the burning sands, the Nile! Crocodiles, my dear, swarming around the boat like vile green logs! My husband was petrified and kept asking the boatman if there was any *danger!* I stood at that helm and tossed chunks of bread to the creatures, thrilled, simply thrilled when they snapped open their jaws to gulp the food.'

I only half listened. My head seemed to be spinning. I took another sip of the wine, hoping it would help steady the spinning sensation. I was suddenly intrigued with the candles in their heavy silver holders. The pear-shaped flames seemed to dip and dance, flinging golden light all over the huge, baronial table. We all sat at one end of the table, but even so we were far apart. Dorothea sat at the head, Edward on her left, her son at her right. I sat beside Edward, several feet away from him, in fact, and Nicola sat across from me, her eyes lowered, her face alarmingly pale in the shifting light.

'The pyramids! You've never see anything like them. They were excavating, and we actually went inside one of the grand ruins. Long passages all covered with hieroglyphics. I had the weirdest feeling! And when we saw the mummy, all wrapped up in dusty linen.'

I had failed with Nicola. I had wanted so badly to help her, to assure her of my friendship, yet it had been impossible to communicate with her. She had not spoken to me since we left her room. Once we joined the others, she had turned back into the demure, self-effacing creature I had seen when I first came. She showed Dorothea the bracelet, smiled meekly, withdrew into her shell. What demons haunted the girl? What living nightmare caused her to have such delusions? Her sickness must be deeply ingrained, as Edward had indicated. I felt a great compassion for the girl. I wished there had been some way I could have communicated it to her. Now, in her eyes, I was an enemy, incredulous, unbelieving.

'And Thebes! The stone cliffs at Deir el-Bahri, the temple of Queen Hatshepsut—more filet of sole, Miss Hunt? It's delicious, isn't it? I'll have the servant bring you another serving.'

'No,' I protested. 'A—a little more wine, perhaps.'

'But of course!'

She rang the tiny silver bell beside her plate. The servant came. She gave him instructions, and he refilled my glass with the sparkling, light-red wine. Edward indicated that he would have more, too. Burton Rodd smiled to himself. Across the great table, his face was like a mask, shadowy, all planes and angles, only the mocking eyes alive. I lifted the glass, and I spilled a few drops on the tablecloth. I dabbed at the stains with my napkin.

I was unable to concentrate on Dorothea's words. She had moved on to Arabia now, talking of palm trees and dates and coloured tents and camels. I looked up at the shadowy ceiling, where garlands of plaster flowers entwined with tarnished gold leaf against a dark-green background. Plaster cherubs held the immense chandelier which hung suspended over the table, thousands of multifaceted crystals glittering in the candlelight. I wondered what would happen if the cherubs dropped the chandelier. I envisioned a tremendous crash, a great explosion of sound, as crystal pendants scattered over the room. I almost laughed. I knew the wine was going to my head, but it was the only thing that made all this endurable.

I wondered what I was doing here, sitting in this great chair with its high, carved back. These were all strangers, even Edward, whom I didn't really know. This wasn't real. No, it was all a dream, going on and on, and I was asleep, watching it all through a haze. The huge, cold room, the shadowy ceiling with the ponderous chandelier, the sputtering candles, the people sitting so far apart, each lost in shadows—all imagined, not real at all. In a few minutes I would awaken, shake myself, see sunlight, and hear Bella making racket in the kitchen. I reached for the wineglass. It was empty. Why? When had I drunk the last of it? I couldn't remember.

'Would you believe it? He wanted to *buy* me! He actually made an offer. My husband was horrified, but I must say I was rather flattered, actually. He was a dashing fellow, the sheikh—tan face, great brown eyes, a wicked black moustache, the most dazzling white teeth! All wrapped in silk robes and turban, determined to have me for his harem. He looked mean when the guide explained I wasn't for sale. I was afraid he would pull out his dagger and slit the poor fellow's throat.'

'More wine, Miss Hunt?' Burton Rodd asked, speaking across the table and ignoring his mother's voice.

'No, thank you,' I replied.

'You're sure?' His voice was sarcastic.

'Quite sure.'

'It was dangerous. I know that, but I had to see the harem. He could have kept me there, locked the doors and never let me out, but I had to see how those women lived. Wretched sight! Fat, bloated creatures, most of them, lounging about on silk cushions and eating candied fruits, like a herd of cows! Jewels everywhere—rubies, emeralds, pearls galore. Gold bars over the windows, fantastic carpets on the floors. Sheikh Ahmed was a perfect gentleman, took me through there where no white woman had ever been before, and never once did he—'

Nicola rose, asked to be excused. When Dorothea protested, the girl said she had a headache and would like to go to her room. Dorothea looked concerned. Nicola said she was just tired, would be all right after she had rested for a little while.

'I wanted you to play for us,' Dorothea said. 'I know Miss Hunt would have enjoyed hearing you at the piano.'

'I think we're all finished, Mother,' Burton Rodd said, interrupting her. 'Shall we have coffee in the other room?'

'Why, of course,' Dorothea Rodd replied. 'I've been rambling on and on—no consideration at all. I so seldom have an opportunity to talk about my travels....'

Nicola left the table and moved out of the room like a wraith. Edward rose and helped Dorothea up. Burton Rodd came around the table and stood beside me. I wondered if I had the strength to get up from the table. My body felt limp, while my head seemed to be spinning dizzily. Pushing back the enormous carved chair and getting to my feet seemed like an insurmountable task. Burton Rodd laid his hand on my arm. I looked up at him and saw the irritated expression on his face. Dorothea and Edward were leaving the room.

'I don't need any help,' I snapped.

'I beg to differ with you,' he said smoothly. 'You're drunk. Another glass of that wine, and you'd have passed out. It's a wonder you're not unconscious now.'

'How dare you imply—'

'I'm implying nothing,' he retorted, the irritation showing now in his voice. 'Women are like children. They shouldn't be allowed to touch anything stronger than milk. Here—'

He pulled the heavy chair away from the table, helping me to my feet. I staggered a little. He held my arm tightly, supporting me, and wrapped his other arm around my shoulders.

'Do you think you can walk?' he asked tersely. 'I'd hate for you to fall on your face. It would be embarrassing to Mother. Here, one foot at a time. Easy, now.'

'I am *not* drunk,' I whispered angrily. 'You don't need to—'

'Shut up!' he said. 'I hope to hell the others didn't notice! Maybe the coffee will help. When we get to the other room, sit still and drink it black, and, for God's sake, don't say anything. Perhaps they won't see anything out of the ordinary. I'll cover for you.'

'This is *infuri*ating!'

'Come along, now. They'll wonder what's happened to us.'

He led me out of the room and down a long narrow hall. There were tapestries on the walls, green and blue and brown, all faded. The details stood out clearly, and I thought it extremely unjust of him to say I was drunk when everything was so sharp, so very clear. I was even aware of my feet moving, and I thought it splendid that one should be able to place one foot in front of the other and propel oneself in such a remarkable way. Why should he think me drunk, when I was so acutely aware of everything now? His arm was still about my shoulders, holding me tightly, and by tilting my head back and turning it sideways I could see his jaw, thrust out angrily, and his mouth, turned down fiercely at one corner. Such a grumpy man. Such a spoilsport! I wanted to run down the hall as fast as I could and see if I could slide on the highly waxed surface.

I tripped and almost fell.

He snorted. 'You're stoned!' he whispered hatefully. 'My God! Three glasses of dinner wine—just three glasses!'

'You counted,' I admonished.

'What would your gallant Edward say if he knew you were in this condition? If it weren't for Mother, I'd let you go to blazes, but she'd be upset and blame herself. You little lush! What other secret vices do you indulge in?'

'I think you're detestable,' I said primly.

'I know that. We're going into the room now. I'll take your arm. Try to walk straight. Don't trip. Sit down. Keep still.'

He led me across the wide parquet floor toward the fireplace. Edward and Dorothea were already seated, talking in low voices. They looked up as we came toward them. I smiled. Burton Rodd gripped my arm. He led me to one of the sofas and set me down, very graciously, very casually, as though he were merely performing his gentlemanly duties. The servant came in with a tray of coffee. When Burton insisted on pouring himself, Dorothea looked bewildered.

'Why all this sudden attentiveness?' she inquired. 'You've been solemn as the grave all evening, and now—'

'Now I'm trying to make up for it,' he replied, handing her a cup. 'Are you complaining?'

'Heavens, no! I merely wondered—'

'Cream or sugar?' he asked me, holding a cup of coffee toward me. His back was to the others, and he gave me a savage expression. 'Black? Fine. Need a cushion?'

'I'm perfectly all right,' I said, taking the coffee. The cup rattled in the saucer, and I almost dropped it in my lap. Rodd shot me another fierce look. I managed to take the cup out of the saucer without spilling any of the beverage.

'Why don't you play for us, Mother?' he said, sitting down across from me.

'Me play? What *is* this, Burton? You *hate* to hear me play. It drives you right up the wall.'

'Miss Hunt would love it,' Rodd informed her. 'Wouldn't you, Miss Hunt?'

'I—well, I suppose—' I stammered.

'Delighted,' he said. 'Do play, Mother.'

'I'm all out of practise,' Dorothea said, plainly flattered. 'I suppose I *could*. Fancy your asking me, Burton. What would you like to hear? Mozart, Chopin, Bach—'

'Chopin,' he said firmly.

Dorothea set her coffee cup down and moved over to the piano nearby. I watched as she brushed her rustling skirts, flexed her fingers and sat down at the instrument. As she ran her fingers over the keys, Burton Rodd grimaced. He settled back with a look of resignation as she began to play. She played horribly. The piano was old and out of tune, but the finest of instruments would have been to no avail. Dorothea banged and pounded, executing something that must have caused Chopin to turn briskly in his grave. Dorothea, plainly enjoying herself, was plainly unaware of her own ineptness. She finished the piece, turned, smiled, her eyes radiant.

'More?' she said.

Edward groaned. Burton asked her to play some Mozart. Edward looked at Burton as though Burton had taken leave of his senses. Burton poured another cup of coffee for me, sat down, and watched as I drank, gritting his teeth. Dorothea played three more pieces on the piano, and I drank three more cups of coffee. The giddiness was gone now, and so was the sharp magnification of my senses. There was a dull throbbing at the back of my head, and I had a suspicion that the pain would grow worse before the night was over. Rodd watched me closely. I prayed that he wouldn't ask her to play more.

'Well,' she said, rejoining us by the fireplace. 'That was stimulating. Quite! I do so love to play. Ordinarily, Miss Hunt, I haven't the opportunity. Burton loathes it, and even Edward, gallant though he is, shows very little enthusiasm. Do you play, dear?'

'A little. Not well.'

'Marvellous! You must play for us.'

'Mother,' Burton Rodd said warningly.

'Yes, dear?'

'We've had quite enough music for one night, don't you think?'

'I suppose so,' she said, sighing. She settled back in the chair. The amethysts at her throat and ears gleamed radiantly in the candlelight, purple with red fires. Edward poured another cup of coffee and handed it to her. Burton Rodd took out a slender black cigar and lighted it.

'Edward?' he said, indicating the box of cigars.

'No, thank you,' Edward replied.

'I forgot,' Rodd said maliciously. 'Bad for you, what? Must keep up the standards. No cigars, no whiskey, cold baths first thing in the morning, and plenty of exercise. Hale and hearty, and lots of red blood. That's the ticket.'

'You could use a little more exercise yourself, Burt,' Edward informed him. 'A few push-ups in the morning—'

'God forbid,' Burton Rodd said nastily.

'Tell us about your new song, Edward,' Dorothea said quickly, sensing the tension in the air. 'Did you finally locate it? You said the butcher's grandmother might remember all the words....'

'Saw her yesterday,' Edward replied. 'Magnificent old woman. Not only did she know the song I was telling you about, but she gave me three others I hadn't even heard of. One's really remarkable, all about May Day and the tragic accident that befalls a young man who...'

Edward talked about his work. I found it fascinating. He recited the song for us, and Dorothea asked him to recite others. One of them was terribly explicit. I asked if his publishers would permit him to include it in his collection. This caused us to swing into an animated discussion of censorship. All three of us had definite views on the subject, and I almost forgot my headache in the heat of discussion.

Burton Rodd leaned back on the sofa, his legs spread out in front of him, his arms folded over his chest. He held the cigar clenched in one corner of his mouth, and spirals of pale-blue smoke curled up to the ceiling. He flicked the ashes occasionally, the butt glowing bright orange. He made no contribution whatsoever to the conversation. He watched us with a rather mocking expression, indifferent now that my intoxication had passed. I was humiliated that he had seen me in such a condition and thankful that Edward and Dorothea had not noticed it.

We had been talking for perhaps half an hour when Rodd interrupted the conversation rudely. He took the cigar out of his mouth and pointed it at his mother. 'Haven't you forgotten something, Mother?' he said abruptly, breaking in on Edward, who was making a comment about a recent novel.

Dorothea looked up, startled, then puzzled. She plainly didn't understand what her son meant.

'The study,' he said.

'Oh! Oh, yes. I'd forgotten.' She turned to me, smiling. 'I want to show you my study,' she said. 'I have so many interesting things

210

there—books, souvenirs, art objects. Won't you let me show them to you?'

'I'd be delighted,' I replied, wondering why on earth her son should be so eager for her to take me there.

The men rose. Edward looked a bit disgruntled. Rodd stood with his arms folded, the cigar clamped in his mouth, his heavy lids hooding the dark eyes. Dorothea took my hand and led me out of the room. We went down a short hall, our heels tapping loudly on the hardwood floor. I moved with normal poise, with no desire to slide on the floor, no wish to stop and examine the portraits on the wall. My head throbbed violently, and I resolved never to touch wine again, under any circumstances. Dorothea led me into a small, crowded room brilliantly lighted with half a dozen oil lamps.

It looked more like a storage room or attic than anything else. Charts and pictures and maps were tacked on every available wall space. One corner was piled high with books and magazines that tumbled from their stacks, a Ouija board leaning across them, a huge, dusty harp with broken strings standing beside them. There was a shelf that held pots of plants, and from the acrid, bitter odour I guessed that they were herbs. There was a round table with fringed red cloth, astrology charts and crystal ball on it, and a bench, canvas-draped, with chisel and hammer and half-finished bust. Many exquisite art objects stood in a glassed-in cabinet—Egyptian vases, golden idols, an Arabian mosaic. The roll-top desk was incredibly cluttered with stacks of paper.

'This is where I really live,' Dorothea said, sweeping magazines off a chair and indicating for me to sit there. 'All the things I'm interested in—plants, astrology, sculpture, books! This is my retreat. I allow none of the others to come here, not even the servants. That's why things are in such a mess! Are you interested in astrology?'

'I know nothing about it.'

'Fascinating! I couldn't make a move without consulting my charts. You should investigate....'

Dorothea sat down at the desk and talked about astrology. She seemed a little nervous, her hands moving restlessly over the surface of the desk, straightening papers, fondling paperweights, jamming pins in and out of a red velvet pincushion. I knew she had brought me here for some specific reason, and the chatter about astrology was just a stall. I wondered what she wanted—rather, what her son wanted. I had no doubt that he had prearranged all this.

'My son tells me you write,' she said abruptly.

'Not exactly. I helped my brother with his first book. I plan to write another, one he had started.'

'I see. You must have great talent.'

'Not talent. Just determination and a knack of organizing material.'

'Excellent!' she exclaimed. 'That's precisely what I need—organization!'

'I don't quite follow you,' I said.

Dorothea turned to the piles of paper on the desk. She lifted a batch and laid them in my lap. I examined them. They were covered with neat, tiny handwriting. I read a few lines describing a ruined temple in the middle of the Arabian desert. The sentences were awkward, ungrammatical, rambling, yet they conveyed vivid impressions of sight and sound. I realized Dorothea had been writing her memoirs.

'Memoirs?' she said when I inquired about them. 'Hardly. Just a few recollections of my travel experiences. I've read so many travel books recently, all written by prim, prissy individuals who have no idea what it's all about, really. I said to myself—why, I could do it better! So *much* better. The things I saw! The things I did! How much more exciting than the solemn, tedious accounts I've read. I've spent the past year putting it all down on paper—quite abominably, as you can see.'

I handed the papers back to her. She examined them fondly.

'How many delicious hours I've spent with pen in hand, recalling all those splendid days! It would really be a shame if the book weren't published, don't you think? And no publisher in his right mind would accept it in its present condition.' She paused, looked at me with a frank expression. 'I need someone to organize this mess for me, someone to put it in orderly, coherent prose.'

'And—and you think I'm that someone?'

'Exactly!'

'But—'

'My dear, let me explain! I could hire some impoverished college student, of course, some legal clerk, some hack journalist, but this book is a woman's book—written by a woman, with a woman's reaction to everything around her. If I let a man handle it for me, it would lose that particular *feminine* flavour that makes it unique.'

'I wish I could help you, but—'

'Let me finish! I would pay you *handsomely*'—she named a price that was more than handsome; it was incredible—'and you could go anywhere you wanted to work on the manuscript: the south of France, Brighton, rent a cottage by the sea—'

'Why couldn't I work here?' I inquired.

'Well, you see—'

'I don't mean to be rude, Mrs Rodd, but I see all too clearly. Your son put you up to this, didn't he? For some reason—some reason I can't comprehend—he wants me to leave Castlemoor. This—this manuscript, and the exorbitant salary you would pay me to rewrite it for you is just—just a kind of bribe. Isn't that correct?'

Dorothea sighed and dropped her hands in her lap. 'Well, I tried,' she said. 'I told him it wouldn't work—not if you were half the woman Edward described to me. I told Burton you wouldn't rise to the bait, but he insisted I offer it. I've done my bit. It's rather a shame about the book, though. I really would like to have it prepared for publication.'

'I'm sure you'll be able to find someone to do it for you,' I said.

'I imagine so. My dear'—she looked into my eyes—'would you mind telling me what this is all *about?* I'm completely at sea.'

'What are you referring to?'

'You—and Burton. I've never seen him in such a state. From the moment he heard that you were coming to Castlemoor, he was in a tizzy. Said you had no business being here. Said he didn't intend to stand for it. For days he grumbled and cursed, and the day your trunks arrived and he saw you were really and truly going to come—' She made an expansive gesture. 'What is it all about?'

'I have no idea, Mrs Rodd.'

'But—surely? You don't—well, I assumed Burton had met you before, in London, that there had been something—between you.'

'I never laid eyes on your son until yesterday morning at the ruins.'

'Incredible,' she said. 'Then why is he in such a state? Why does he want you to leave? I've seldom seen him like this. I don't understand it. Not at all.'

'Neither do I,' I said, 'but I can assure you I have no intention of leaving Castlemoor.'

Dorothea smiled wryly. Her beautiful eyes sparkled. 'Bravo!' she exclaimed. 'You're a remarkable woman! Burton has met his match at last. He's so spoiled, you know, where women are concerned. It'll do him good to find one he can't push around. You bother him— that's a good sign, a very good sign. I suspect you could have him if you wanted him.'

I felt a blush staining my cheeks. 'Really, Mrs Rodd, I have no—'

'I saw the way he looked when he saw your dress. He thinks he's impervious to women. You proved him wrong when you removed your wrap. La! He's ready to tumble!'

'I'm not at all interested in your son,' I said firmly.

'Maybe not,' she said, smiling. 'But it does my heart good to see him reacting this way. I haven't given up hopes of becoming a grandmother!' She rose, extending her hand. 'Shall we join the men, my dear? This has been most interesting—most interesting. Burton may be disappointed, but I must say I'm intrigued. You must come back to the castle often, dear. I insist. This is all very stimulating.'

When we came back to the main room, Burton Rodd looked up at his mother expectantly. She shook her head slowly, indicating failure. He scowled, glancing at me irritably. He tossed his cigar into the fireplace and thrust his hands in his pockets. I said I must be going, and Edward said he would walk with me back to the house. Rodd snorted at that, jamming his hands deeper into his pockets and turning his back on us. Dorothea became the gracious hostess, taking my hand, saying she was sorry Nicola had had to leave us so early, expressing her pleasure at my visit, and bidding me return soon. There was a conspiratorial twinkle in her eyes as she said this last. Edward and I left. At the door I glanced back, to see Dorothea standing beside her son. She was tall and impressive in her black silk dress, her lovely hair streaked with silver, her amethysts gleaming in the glow of the fire. Rodd still stood with his back turned, his legs spread wide apart, and his shoulders hunched. Edward led me down the hall.

The torches were still burning in the courtyard—black shadows, yellow glow, an atmosphere of ruin, a smell of smoke and damp stone. Edward held my arm as we passed through the tunnel and out of the castle. We stood for a moment with the leaves of the oak trees rustling overhead, moonlight spilling silver through the branches. It was cold. My wrap was of no use whatsoever. We walked away from the castle, over the moors, my arm in his. Edward seemed rather moody, strangely silent. I asked him what was wrong. He stopped and looked at me. We were surrounded by vast empty land, clouds rolling heavily in the dark-grey sky, wind whistling over the ground.

'Burton,' he said.

'Burton?'

'He's undermining me. He never misses a chance to dig, to taunt. I don't mind ordinarily, but when he works through you—'

'Through me?'

'Tonight. The attention he gave you—helping you from the table and serving you coffee. He did it merely to irritate me. He knows—he senses how I feel about you—how I feel already.'

'Why, that's absurd, Edward. He dislikes me intensely, and I can assure you that I find him thoroughly unpleasant.'

'Do you?' He frowned. 'That'll change soon enough. Women find it impossible to resist him. I've never been able to understand it.'

'He has a certain appeal,' I said. 'I won't try to deny that. But I'm immune. Believe me. Right now I don't want to think of anything but—but the book.'

'That's—discouraging to me,' he said.

'Please, Edward, not now. Don't be gallant and—and attentive. I'm tired. I have a dreadful headache. I—can't we just be friends?'

'You wear a seductive dress, you look like every man's ideal, and you want me to be your—friend?' He spoke the words lightly.

'Yes,' I said. 'For now.'

'And later?'

'Later—we'll see.'

He looked into my eyes. He laid his hands on my shoulders, standing very close. He was so large, so male, so elegant in the fine clothes.

I was exhausted and strangely disturbed, and if he had wrapped those large arms around me and pulled me against him, I wouldn't have protested. His brow was creased, and his face looked grave in the moonlight. I wanted to reach up and smooth that brow, brush those golden locks away from his forehead. I was extremely vulnerable at that moment, but he didn't know it. He touched my cheek lightly and smiled and stood back, sighing. I was relieved and disappointed at the same time.

'I'll settle for friendship,' he said. 'I guess I'll have to. But I make no promises as to how long I'll settle for that. A day, a week, perhaps a month, and then'—he grinned—'then beware.'

He flung his arm casually around my shoulders, and we continued to walk over the moors. His arm was heavy, and it was uncomfortable to walk with it around me, but I wouldn't have wanted him to take it away. It gave me a feeling of warmth and security. I would always feel warm and secure with Edward, I thought, musing over his words. He was the kind of man any woman would want—gentle, protective, strong, amiable, capable of arousing the deepest emotions. I wondered why I had put him off, when I had felt so attracted to him. It would have been so easy to succumb to those hearty male charms, to welcome the advances he had been so clearly eager to make a few moments ago. He would settle for friendship for a while, he said, but I wondered why that was all I wanted right now. It bewildered me.

'You made quite an impression on Dorothea,' he said. 'I've never seen her so vivacious. It was almost worth hearing that hideous racket she made on the piano—just to see her so pleased.'

'I found her quite charming,' I said.

'She's a remarkable woman. Incidentally, what did Nicola want?'

'Why—what makes you ask that?'

'She seemed so eager to get you alone, so insistent that you go with her to get the bracelet.'

'She—she wanted to show me her dolls,' I replied cautiously.

'Dorothea's famous dolls! Nicola doesn't give a damn about them, but if you two have some dark secret—'

'She's disturbed, Edward. Really disturbed.'

'Of course she is. That's why they're sending her away.'

'Oh?' I said, very convincingly, I thought.

'At least that seems to be the plan,' he continued. 'I heard Burton discussing it with Dorothea yesterday. One of Dorothea's old school chums has opened a spa in the south of

France. Takes in paying guests, gives them health foods—I think there's supposed to be a mineral spring nearby. He wants Dorothea to send Nicola there. Personally, I think it's a grand idea. The girl needs to get away from here, as I've told you before.'

'Edward—' I began hesitantly. 'Your rooms are near Nicola's. Do you ever hear things—in the night?'

'What sort of things?'

'Well—noises,' I said inadequately.

He chuckled, plainly amused by the question. 'I hear creaking boards,' he said, 'and I hear the wind whistling through cracks in the walls, and I hear all the natural, normal noises of the place—rats in the wainscoting, and creaking of the joints. Rattling chains, stealthy footsteps, anguished moans—I don't hear those. I don't doubt that Nicola hears such things—at least in her mind. Why do you ask?'

'I just wondered....'

'If Nicola's been telling you tales, forget them. Forget anything she might have said. She's told me a few whoppers, believe me. I humour her. That's the only thing one can do—under the circumstances.'

'She seemed so—so sincere, so convinced—'

'She always does,' he said firmly.

We walked on silently. I thought about

Nicola and the tale she had related. I thought about the expression on her face, the urgent tone of her voice. In my mind I could see her standing at the top of the staircase. I could see the man coming up—pale face; dark, haunted eyes; golden hair. I could see the shadows swallow him up, hear the shuffling, the blow. It was vivid, and frightening. She had gone down into the dungeons once, she told me that day on the moors, and she had heard something then. She was subject to nightmares, vivid nightmares, and she was under a doctor's care. The dungeons were horrible, damp and fetid and evil, and no doubt she was obsessed with them. I could easily see why. She would be going away soon. It would be best to forget what she had told me, forget that pale face, those pleading dark eyes that begged me to believe her.

I couldn't help Nicola. I could only feel sorry for her.

We reached the top of the slope. Far away I could see my small house, lights burning in the windows, and all around distant slopes curved black and grey in the moonlight, an occasional boulder projecting up against the horizon. I looked around, finding a strange sort of beauty. I saw a lone tree, a rocky hill, a grassy slope. A faint mist shrouded the land, swirling and parting, and only half-obscuring the scene. Suddenly I stopped. I gave a little gasp of alarm. Edward jumped, startled.

'What is it!' he cried.

'There—' I whispered, pointing.

A figure moved through the mist, running toward the castle. I could not determine whether it was male or female, for it was completely covered with a hooded white sheet. The mist rolled, swirled, the figure disappeared and reappeared, and then clouds passed over the moon, and the moor was black and impenetrable. I saw a spot of white, or thought I did, and then there was nothing but the dark, walls of black surrounding us.

'What is it?' Edward repeated, calmer now.

'You saw—didn't you see—'

'I saw nothing,' he said, perplexed.

'But—you must have! It was—'

'Kathy, what is it? You're trembling—'

'You must have seen—' I whispered.

'There was nothing,' Edward said quietly. 'What did you think you saw, Kathy?'

'I—I don't know.'

'You *are* tired,' he said. 'Nervous, too.'

'Yes—I suppose that explains it.'

He laughed quietly. The sound was rich and reassuring. I wondered if I had actually seen the ghostly figure. It had been so real, and yet—so unreal. I closed my eyes. I was extremely tired. My nerves were frayed. I had a throbbing headache. Perhaps Edward was right. Perhaps it had been a figment of my imagination. I had been thinking about Nicola, worrying, and when I looked up I saw the figure. Bella had seen a ghostly figure, too, and she had frankly admitted that she had imagined it after listening to some of Alan's spooky tales.

'Describe it to me,' Edward said, grinning.

'I'm ashamed to,' I replied, still just a bit shaken.

'A figure in white?' he asked. 'One of the famous druid ghosts? The villagers see them all the time. Those ghosts are as common around here as mirages in the desert, and just about as substantial. I'm surprised at you, Kathy. You've been listening to too much local talk.'

'I—I guess I have.'

'Fear not,' he said teasingly. 'I'll protect you.'

'It seemed so real, Edward.'

'So do mirages,' he told me.

'I feel like a fool—crying out like that.'

'Nonsense. You just need a good night's sleep.'

He was in a good humour as we walked on down the slope to the house. I longed for my soft bed, the solitude of my room, a damp cloth over my eyes. As we strolled across the yard, I peered through the kitchen window. I could see Bella and Alan sitting at the table. Bella would have many questions. I would have to put her off until morning. Edward stood with me at the door. He clearly wanted to say something, but he couldn't seem to find the words. He finally heaved his shoulders and laughed softly. He doubled up his fist and tapped me gently on the chin, an exclusively masculine gesture that I found endearing. After I told him good night and opened the door, I stood there for a moment, watching him walk away. I doubted that I would have a very restful night. I felt sure my sleep would be filled with many dreams—and nightmares.

CHAPTER TWELVE

The wagon joggled over the moors toward Darkmead. Maud clicked the reins. Two days had passed since my visit to the castle, and I was going to Darkmead to do some shopping. Maud had come for a visit and agreed to drive me to town. I would walk back. The exercise would be stimulating, and it would give me an opportunity to think about my book. Although I had already outlined the first chapter and put my notes in order, I had been unable to begin the actual writing. Every time I took pen in hand I found myself thinking about other things—a face, a gesture, the hang of a jacket, a certain tone of voice. I scolded myself for this lack of concentration and blamed Burton Rodd for haunting me so.

Maud talked about Bella and Alan, who were currently quarrelling. Alan was supposed to have brought a wagonload of firewood yesterday morning, had failed to show up until the late afternoon, had received a frosty reception from Bella, engaged in a lively argument, and left resolved never to return. Bella had ranted and raved, but I was so engrossed in my own thoughts that I couldn't show the proper concern. Their arguments were like the bickerings of two small children, and I had no doubt that Alan would come back, sheepish and shy, ready to resume the romance. Maud thought so too, although Bella had told both of us this morning that she had no intention of ever speaking to *that one* again. Nevertheless, she was busily sewing on the dress she would wear to the bonfire festival tomorrow night, for which Alan was to be her escort.

'They're a couple of puppies!' Maud snorted. 'Prancin', yappin', waggin' their tails! That big dolt of a nephew—you shoulda seen 'im when 'e came in last night! Big mournful eyes, lip stuck out, 'ead 'angin' down. A cocker spaniel —to a T! Now, in *my* day....'

I listened as she related some of her youthful romantic escapades, but my mind wandered. I looked out over the moors—grey-brown, flooded with sunlight that poured silver-white from a pearl-grey sky. Rocks glittered as though encrusted with chips of mica. It had rained during the night, and I was amazed to see a fuzz of green on the horizon. Maud said there would be wildflowers, purple and white, after a few more rains, when, for a brief span, the moors would be a wonderland, doomed to vanish with the advent of summer. It was hard to visualize these barren acres covered with flowers. I stared out moodily as the wagon jolted along, half-hypnotized by the glittering rocks and Maud's drawling voice.

'An' no one knows where they come from....'

'What?...' I had been lost in thought and had no idea what she was talking about.

'Seven of 'em, there are. Big bruisers—all seven of 'em! Come here two days ago an' took rooms at the inn, *very* mysterious. No one knows why, although they say they're surveyors or somethin', sent 'ere to study boundaries or some such nonsense. Ain't logical—seven men! Don't mean nothin' good, I'll tell you that much. Everyone in Darkmead's wonderin' just why they're here. Some say they've come to cause contention at the factory. I know for a fact a couple of 'em've been hangin' about there.'

'What *are* you talking about, Maud?'

'The men. Wearin' suits an' ties, all clean an' neat, but disreputable-lookin' just the same. Saw one of 'em myself as I was leavin' the farm. 'E was walkin' along the road, brown suit, yellow tie, a funny instrument in 'is hand. Gave me a start, 'e did, his broad ugly face an' brown eyes an' coarse red 'air tumblin' about 'is 'ead. 'E carried a suitcase, too, 'e did, and from the way 'e looked, there mighta been a *body* in it.'

'Nonsense, Maud. The men are probably surveyors, just as they say.'

'*Seven* of 'em—all come to town at once? Not bleedin' likely! I don't believe a word of it. Strangers don't come to Darkmead unless they're just passin' through. These men've taken rooms at the inn, permanent-like, an' they seem to be *waitin' around* for somethin'. Oh, they go out, look over the land with their

229

instruments—four of 'em are out 'ere on the moors today, surveyin' supposedly. The townsfolk're nervous, you can bet on it! Somethin's up. Ain't no one 'appy about it 'cept the innkeeper's wife—the hussy in red who ain't no better than she 'as any business bein'. She's delighted at 'avin' all the rooms upstairs filled with great hulkin' males. I can just imagine the traffic on that staircase.'

We were passing under the oak trees now, the moors behind us. The wagon rattled over the bridge where I had first seen Edward and Bertie Rawlins. Maud continued to talk about the mysterious strangers. I found her tirade amusing. Every now and then she would turn to me, her lively blue eyes snapping, her lumpy face registering concern. She wore the same sad, drooping black felt hat she had worn the first time I saw her, the same old grey sweater and shapeless blue dress. She smelled of herbs and soil. Her feet were encased in the absurd high-buttoned black boots. I found her thoroughly enchanting, her frankness refreshing, her salty tongue delightful. She was like a character created by Chaucer in his bawdiest humour, brought here to enliven the staid Victorian era.

She stopped the wagon in front of the milliner's shop. I climbed down. Maud said, 'Ta-

ta, luv!' and drove on to carry a packet of herbs to the blacksmith, who hoped to be her next husband. I stood in front of the shop, examining the beribboned bonnets on display in the window. I had had no specific purchases in mind when I decided to come shopping today. I merely felt a need to get away from the house for a while, away from the books and notes and the stack of empty paper that taunted me to get down to work. One of the bonnets looked attractive, and I went inside to try it on. The pink ribbons did not go well with my golden hair. I tried on another one, green satin ribbons festooning a wide black brim, then another and another, and finally decided it was ridiculous to contemplate buying a new bonnet when I would have few occasions to wear it. I examined some material at the piece-goods store, fingering silk and velvet and glazed cotton, buying a bolt of golden-brown linen and asking that it be delivered. I bought a dress pattern, a few yards of ribbon, some hairpins. I left the store, passing the bakery, where delicious smells filled the air, and stepped into the stationer's shop.

It was small and quiet, an anaemic-looking clerk in shabby brown suit stroking his moustache at the back of the shop. I found some exercise books of cream paper ruled in grey with red margins and decided I must have them. They would be perfect for journals of my progress with the book. I bought some thin orange pencils in an olivewood pencil box and a mahogany ruler with edges bound with brass. I loved the shop—the smell of ink and paper and glue, the boxes of stationery, the multi-coloured bottles of ink, the table of novels newly arrived from London publishers, their dust jackets sleek and shiny, their pages uncut. I browsed over the table but found nothing of particular interest. The clerk solemnly wrapped my purchases in brown paper, and I left the shop, pausing before the plate-glass window in front to examine my reflection.

I looked rather drawn and pale, faint shadows under my eyes, skin too tightly stretched over cheekbones, but my hair, pushed back and fastened with pins behind each ear, fell in a luxuriant golden mass to my shoulders. I wore a beige dress printed with tiny brown and yellow flowers, bodice and waist snug-fitting, full skirt turned up slightly at the hem to reveal bits of starched yellow petticoat. Sunlight spilled on the sidewalk as I turned to examine my profile in the dim, smoky glass. I had never considered myself particularly vain, but recently I had been taking extra pains with my appearance. I wondered why. Who did I expect to see me in town today? Had I dressed so carefully for the grim, taciturn men of Dark-mead? The thought caused me to smile, and the clerk, behind the window, must have imagined I was flirting with him, for he dropped a whole armload of books, blushing furiously.

I laughed, turning away from the window. My good humour was restored. It was a lovely day, and I was delighted with my purchases. Why had I felt such lassitude earlier? I must get back and get to work. The long walk back to the house would be invigorating. I looked forward to it.

I had been so intent on studying my reflection in the glass that I had not seen the two men. They stood a few yards away, watching me. They wore city suits, tight at the shoulders, narrow at waist and thigh, trousers pipestem in cut. Their ties were garish, and both had the broad, coarse faces I associated with the underworld. They looked as out of place here in Darkmead as I myself must look. One man had dark-blond hair and cold grey eyes, a jagged pink scar running across his cheek, and the other had brown hair parted severely to one side, his face pitted with pockmarks. No wonder Maud had been disturbed, I thought. These men had a tough, ruthless look that would have disturbed anyone. I wondered if the others were as brutal in appearance. I had never, to my knowledge, seen a surveyor, but I felt certain a surveyor wouldn't look anything like this.

'Hey, now, there's the first interesting-looking sight I've seen since we got here,' the blond man remarked to his companion. His grey eyes were studying me with rude intensity.

'Not bad,' replied the pockmarked man, 'if your taste happens to run that way. Take the innkeeper's wife, now—there's a woman.'

'Too common. Too available. I didn't know Darkmead produced such tasty morsels as this one here. I wonder if she—'

'Forget it, Vic. You know our instructions.'

'Hell, nothing's going to happen around here for a while yet. I don't see as it'd hurt anything if I was to just *ask* her.'

'Yeah, if I thought *askin'* was all you'd do. Remember the last time? That little girl in Liverpool and the trouble you got into....'

I looked up and down the street, alarmed. Two or three bearded local men stood in front of the inn, smoking pipes and studiedly ignoring the two strangers. A farmer was loading sacks of seed into the back of his wagon in front of the feed store. Three or four young men were examining harness on the porch of the hardware store. Nothing could happen in broad daylight, I told myself, not with all these people around, yet I didn't like the tone of voice the blond man used. I would have to pass in front of them if I intended to walk toward the square, and that prospect wasn't pleasing. As I stood there, my heart beginning to pound, the blond man started toward me, his eyes narrowed. The other man gripped his arm, but the blond shook his companion's hand away. I backed against the stationer's window. It was only then that I heard the wheels grind to a stop.

The carriage was a small black victoria with a padded tan leather seat and great gleaming black wheels. A lovely black horse stood in the shafts. I recognized the horse at once. Burton Rodd looked down at me, his fingers curling about the handle of a silky black whip. He glanced at the blond man and shook his head, ever so slightly. It was a simple movement but unmistakably menacing. As the blond backed away, Rodd jerked his head at me. 'Get in!' he said sharply, and I hurried around the carriage and climbed up beside him, not daring to refuse. I set my packages on the floor at my feet as Rodd cracked the whip in the air. The victoria lurched forward so quickly I was thrown back against the seat. The harness jangled and a cloud of dust rose behind us as

235

the wheels skimmed over the unpaved road.

We turned off the main street and drove down a small, tree-shaded road that ran beside the river. I had been busy trying to keep my hair from flying in the wind, but now Rodd allowed the horse to slow to an easy trot. I smoothed the disorderly curls and turned to examine the profile of the man beside me. I saw the tousled black hair streaked with grey dipping forward over the lined forehead, a dark, arched brow, the twisted nose, the pink corners of the mobile mouth, the strong jaw thrust forward a little as he studied the road ahead and carefully ignored me. His fingers still curled about the whip handle. The other hand held the reins loosely yet firmly. He wore tight brown trousers tucked into the tops of his high black boots, and a heavy brown-and-black-checked jacket padded at the shoulders, tight along chest and waist, and flaring at the thighs. His tan silk shirt was rumpled, and his black tie was inexpertly knotted. He was sprinkled with dust all over.

He quite obviously had no intention of speaking to me, and I stubbornly refused to speak first. I watched the oak boughs arching above us, some of the branches hanging so low that their leaves almost brushed our heads, and observed the river winding at our side, green-brown, golden threads of sunlight swimming in the water and reflecting radiantly. The river wound in front of us. We crossed a stone bridge and followed the road up a winding, grassy slope with shabby grey and brown houses set far back. I could maintain my silence no longer.

'Where are you taking me?' I said peevishly.

'I'm going to the factory,' he said. 'As you're sitting beside me, it would be safe to assume you're going there too.'

'I don't *want* to go to the factory,' I snapped. 'I want to go home.'

He ignored this completely, clicking the reins and urging the horse to move at a brisker pace. The victoria passed over a bump in the road, and I was thrown against his hard body. I pulled away quickly, moving back to my side of the seat. Rodd seemed not to have noticed the contact. My skirts were flapping up, yellow petticoats billowing, and I had to clamp my hands on my knees in order to maintain modesty.

'I suppose you think I should thank you,' I said hatefully. 'I suppose you think if you hadn't come along when you did—'

'If I hadn't come along when I did,' he interrupted me, 'you would have been in a pretty mess.'

'I can handle myself, thank you.'

'You brought it all on yourself,' he continued. 'Parading around like that! Why can't you wear black and grey? Why can't you braid your hair and keep it modestly fastened? You strut around like a peacock in your outlandish clothes and expect to go unmolested. This isn't London, my girl! Around here women know how to conduct themselves. That dress you wore night before last—I'm surprised you haven't already been raped!'

'I—I've never been so insulted in my life!'

I was seething with fury, my cheeks bright pink, but, nevertheless, I was perversely flattered by his outrageous remarks. He *had* noticed, and he had been moved. The cold Burton Rodd was not as immune as he fancied himself to be.

'If you think for one minute I'm going to dress like the drab mournful women I've seen around here—' I began.

'I think you should be locked up in a convent and kept there until you are old and wrinkled and incapable of causing any more fuss!' he raged.

'Really, Mr Rodd, you're—'

The carriage jolted over a large rut in the road, throwing me forward. I braced myself against the board to keep from tumbling out. Rodd smiled to himself, and I knew he had deliberately raced the horse over the rut. I sat back, fuming, my arms folded about my waist, skirts billowing up disgracefully. I no longer cared. If he caught glimpses of well-turned ankle and silk-clad calf, so much the better! I stared straight ahead, lips held tightly together, cheeks still burning. Rodd seemed pleased with himself, his shoulders held at a jaunty angle, the smile not yet gone from his lips. I silently wished him all sorts of misfortune, and I knew that if he were able to read my thoughts he would have been delighted with my malice.

The road wound across a short stretch of open countryside—neat white farmhouse sitting far back against a line of trees, red barn and silo beside it, two fat brown cows grazing in the pasture nearby. A herd of sheep moved up a grassy green slope like a living cloud, the herder trailing behind in leather jacket and wide-brimmed hat. We turned, veering back toward Darkmead, and I could see the factory ahead—great gashes in the red earth, huddles of grey huts along the edge of the pits, large white buildings with black smokestacks rising against a darkening grey sky. Men pushed wheelbarrows up and down the sides of the pits, while others, barechested, moved energetically about the great, smoky kilns.

Burton Rodd stopped the carriage in front

of the huts. He turned to me for the first time since I had climbed up beside him. The ravaged face was lined with irritation, the dark eyes savage.

'I'm making a tour of inspection,' he said crisply. 'I should leave you here in the carriage, but I don't think that would be wise with all my men around.' He made it sound as though I secretly planned to seduce each and every one of them. 'Stay close beside me, do as you're told, and for God's sake don't ask any stupid questions. In fact, it might be a good idea for you to keep your mouth shut altogether!'

'You hold on!' I cried. 'I've taken just about enough—'

He swung lightly out of the carriage, came around to my side, and gave me his hand. I hesitated just an instant, and he almost pulled me down by sheer force. I felt like kicking him sharply across the shin, but men were milling around, openly curious, and I forced myself to maintain a cool, poised reserve. I walked at Rodd's side as though it were the most natural thing in the world, as though I belonged there. The man brought out all my worst instincts, making me feel like a spiteful, scratching schoolgirl, but I was secretly pleased to be here and found the tour quite fascinating, even though it had been forced upon me against my will.

We stood at the edge of the pits, watching the brawny men pushing the wheelbarrows laden with reddish-brown clay. Rodd inspected the soil, rubbing his fingers over a clod, watching it flake off. He asked several questions, his manner cool and authoritative. The men were plainly intimidated by him, great, muscular chaps with sweat on their brows looking as tongue-tied and awkward as schoolboys under his piercing gaze. One man accidentally dumped a load of clay, and he actually trembled when Rodd glanced at him. Rodd said nothing, but one of the foremen spluttered apologies. We went to the kilns—great blasts of heat, blazing red bellies of flame, brick black with soot. There was an odour of sulphur and acid and scorched flesh. The roar of the huge ovens was so deafening that I couldn't hear a word of the conversation Rodd had with the foreman there.

We walked into a long, narrow building with cracked concrete floor and tin roof. Machines clanged loudly, metal pounding on metal, wheels spinning, belts whirring. I had no idea what any of the machines did and was too stubborn to ask. Men stood in front of the machines, grim-faced, intent. They looked strangely dwarfed and inhuman, overshadowed as they were by the steel monsters of industry, and I was reminded of slaves in some curious hell. The place reeked of oil and sweat and unwashed bodies. We moved along the row of machines, Rodd tight-lipped and solemn, his eyes scrutinizing each and every machine. The men ignored him, or tried to, as their job was to concentrate on their machines. Rodd stopped abruptly. He looked up at a belt that was loose and frayed, spinning furiously on its metal wheel. I could see that it was about to break, causing no telling what kind of accident. The poor man who was in charge of that particular machine looked terrified as Rodd pointed to the belt.

Rodd led me over to a stack of boxes and told me to stand there. Then he called the foreman and went back to the machine. The man who was in charge of it looked on the verge of tears, his seamed, leathery face screwed up in agony. Rodd spoke to the foreman, ignoring the other. He did not shout, nor did he use any violent gestures, but he was a cold, hard instrument of fury. His eyes blazed. The corners of his mouth were white. He looked capable of murder at that moment. The workman turned pale. The foreman turned red. Rodd spoke for five minutes, and then the foreman called another man to run the machine, and the poor fellow whose neglect had caused this tirade took his lunch pail and cap and left the building, his shoulders trembling visibly.

The man was hanging around the door as we stepped out of the building. With cap in hand, he shambled over to Rodd, his eyes full of entreaty. He must have been forty-five years old, his hair peppered with grey, his tan face lined with a lifetime of defeat.

'Please, saar,' he stammered. 'I've a wuvf and three kiddies....' He laid his hand on Rodd's arm.

Rodd stiffened, looking at the man as though he were some kind of vermin. He flung the man's hand away and moved on sharply, not speaking. I was embarrassed. When we were several yards away, the man shouted a coarse insult. Rodd gave no indication that he even heard the remark. We walked across a stretch of pavement and around a group of huts.

'I found that—terribly cruel,' I said, unable to restrain myself.

'Did you?'

'You were brutal to that poor man.'

'Brutal?'

'Did you have to discharge him just because a belt—'

'If that belt had broken, the man could have been killed. Several men could have

243

been killed. Each man is supposed to inspect his machine in the morning, see that the parts are in working order, see that no dust or lint or rust has gotten in it. There was no excuse for such carelessness.'

'Still—'

'I suggested earlier, Miss Hunt, that you keep your mouth shut. The suggestion is still quite valid.'

'You can't push me around like you do those men, Mr Rodd.'

'Indeed? Can't I?'

'You certainly can't. I think—'

'Your opinions are not of the least interest to me, Miss Hunt. Come, I have much more to inspect.'

We entered a warehouse that smelled of glue and cardboard and excelsior. Rodd talked with a man about shipments to various parts of England, a difficult process because of Dark-mead's relative isolation. I looked at an enormous stack of boxes, watched men moving them on wheeled trolleys. After we left the warehouse we went to the packing room. It sounded like an aviary, as dozens of women chattered at their tables. They wore bright skirts and low-cut blouses, their arms bare, tendrils of damp hair surrounding their flushed faces. The merry babbling stopped as soon as they were aware of Rodd's presence. One plump middle-aged woman dropped a cup, almost went into hysterics, cut her hand on one of the jagged pieces she tried to scoop up. Rodd spoke to her in a gentle voice, told her to go to the first-aid station for bandages. He seemed far more tolerant with these women than he had been with the men.

The women ranged in age from late teens to early middle age. I noticed a few of the younger attractive ones casting sly glances at Rodd as he passed among them. One coy creature pushed her tangled brunette curls away from her face and moistened her lips with the tip of her tongue. Rodd gave no indication that he had noticed, but I saw his eyes narrow just a little as he passed the girl's table. She nimbly filled a box with excelsior, took up a stack of plates, and began to lay them carefully among the shavings. He paused just an instant, turned his head as though making a mental note. The girl leaned over a bit too artfully, revealed a bit too much cleavage. I wondered just how many of these simpleminded young things found their way to the castle. The man strutted like a pasha moving through a harem! I was disgusted, or at least I tried to tell myself I was. All the women, young and old alike, acted as though it were perfectly natural for me to be there at his side, but I could see they were eager to discuss my presence. What glorious gossip would fill the air when we left!

The packing room was well lighted, with long windows thrown open to admit sunshine and fresh air. I knew that before Rodd had taken over the factory, the conditions had been wretched, the women working in dim, crowded sheds that reeked of sweat and urine and had no ventilation whatsoever. He had introduced many improvements, such as the first-aid station, had done much to make working conditions more pleasant. He was hard and domineering in his demands and frequently brutal in his dealings, as I had witnessed, but I imagined his factory was as modern and well run as any in England. I had to admire him for that, however grudgingly the admiration might be given.

As we were leaving the packing room and walking toward the offices, I saw a man approaching us. Without question, he was a colleague of the two men I had seen in town. He had a hard, coarse face and black hair cut very close to the skull. He wore a tight brown suit and garish red tie and carried a small brown bag. Rodd seemed to be a little upset at seeing the man here. He told me to wait where I was and moved forward to intercept the man before he could reach us. They talked in low voices, out of my hearing range. The man seemed impatient. He doubled up his fist and frowned. Rodd, looking extremely irritated, spoke through tight lips that barely moved as he spoke. The man finally walked off, and Rodd came back to escort me up to the offices.

'Who are those men?' I asked as we went up the steps.

'Surveyors, I believe.'

'There's an awful lot of talk about them in town. People say they're up to no good. They —they don't *look* like surveyors. They look like hired thugs! And why should so many of them come all at once?'

'You needn't worry about them,' he replied crisply, holding the door open for me.

'You have dealings with them?'

'Perhaps. It's no concern of yours.'

'I find it peculiar that—'

'*I* find it infuriating that you ask so many questions, Miss Hunt! Can you keep that mouth shut while I go over the books, or must I put a gag in it? Believe me, I'm tempted to do just that!'

We passed through a large, airy room where several clerks worked meekly at cluttered desks and went into a smaller room with faded green carpet, huge mahogany desk, and

247

shelves crammed with dusty, yellowing ledgers. I stood at the window, holding back the green-and-white-striped curtains and looking out over the yard while Rodd discussed finances with one of the men who had followed us into the room. He examined ledgers, scribbled figures on a yellow pad, asked to see invoices, gave instructions. After thirty minutes, the man left, closing the door behind him. Burton Rodd and I were alone in the small, crowded room that smelled of ink and old leather. I was suddenly nervous as he looked at me with hooded eyes, his fingers drumming on the desk top. He left his chair and moved to the ugly black safe standing against one wall. He opened it, took out a dusty green box, and set the box on the desk.

'All right, Miss Hunt,' he said. 'Shall we get down to business? I had an ulterior motive in bringing you here, I'll admit. I wanted to talk to you, settle things.'

'Settle things?'

He nodded, opening the green box. He took out neat stacks of money, each stack fastened with a brown-paper band.

'Right,' he said tersely. 'How much do you want for Dower House? I want immediate possession, and I'm willing to pay dearly. Name your price, and let's get this over with.'

He began to pile the stacks of money on the desk. There was something absurdly melodramatic about the way he slapped one stack on top of another. He was brisk and determined. I stood by the curtains, silent. He finished piling the money up and turned around slowly in the swivel chair, looking up at me. He slumped a little in the chair, the material of his brown-and-black-checked jacket bunching at the shoulders. I had an insane impulse to straighten that crooked tie and brush that unruly lock of grizzled hair off his forehead. He was fidgeting, his hands on his knees. He seemed to be waiting for me to say something. A long minute passed.

'Well?' he said.

'Why are you so eager to get rid of me, Mr Rodd? Why do you want me to leave Castlemoor? I don't understand it.'

'I don't expect you to *understand*,' he snapped impatiently. 'I merely expect you to take the money and *go!*'

'First you get your mother to try to bribe me—'

'That was a mistake. I admit it.'

'—and now you offer me an enormous sum of money, all for a house no one would buy until my brother came along.'

'It's getting late, Miss Hunt. Ordinarily, I'm

a patient man, but—'

'Why? That's what I want to know. It—it has something to do with those men, doesn't it? The seven men who arrived in Darkmead two days ago? I don't know why I should think that, but I'm sure there's some...kind of connection....'

Burton Rodd stood up. His cheekbones were ashen, and the corner of his mouth twitched. He looked surprised, then alarmed, and finally he mastered whatever emotions he was feeling and looked at me with a cold, impassive expression. He was standing perhaps five feet away. As he came closer, I stepped back and found myself against the wall. Rodd moved slowly toward me, until his face was but inches away from my own.

'What do you know about that?' he asked quietly.

'It was a guess. I—I was right, wasn't I? There *is* a connection.'

'There could be.'

'What is it all about?'

'You must leave the house, leave Castlemoor.'

'I'm not leaving.'

'I told you before—I always get my way.'

I shook my head slowly from side to side, unable to speak, hypnotized by those dark, burning eyes. I noticed the little pouches under them, the skin light brown, stained with mauve, as though bruised. I noticed the way his nose twisted to one side beneath the slight hump. I saw the tiny lines at the corners of his wide mouth. I was unable to look away. I could feel his breath on my cheek and smell the odour of tobacco and harsh soap. He put his palms flat against the wall on either side of me, making me a prisoner. I wanted to cry, and it seemed all my will had gone. I felt weak, at his mercy.

'You're causing me an awful lot of trouble,' he said gently. The muscles in his throat moved when he spoke. The heavy lids drooped sleepily over his eyes. 'Take the money,' he said, the silky, rasping voice almost crooning. One hand moved to my chin, the long fingers cupping around it.

'Why—why do you want me to go?' I whispered.

'You little fool.' The words were tender. 'I don't *want* you to go. Can't you tell that?'

'Then—'

His mouth stopped me. It moved against mine, firm, gentle, the lips pressing and probing. He pulled me into his arms, swinging me around until I was leaning over backward, supported only by the steel-like grip at waist and

251

shoulder. I struggled only a moment. The arms grew tighter, the mouth more urgent on mine, seeking to destroy me. I felt black velvet shrouding me, a pleasant death, and against my closed eyelids I saw blue circles that revolved dizzily. Seconds passed, an eternity. Time ceased to be. Burton Rodd released me.

He went back to the desk, ignoring me completely. I leaned against the wall, trying to catch my breath. He tossed the money back into the dusty green box, shoved the box back into the safe, slammed the huge black iron door, whirled the dial of the combination lock. He straightened up and ran a finger along his temple. He seemed to be trying to remember something. He snapped his fingers, took a paper out of the top desk drawer, folded it, and put it in his pocket, and then he glanced at me as though I were a piece of the furniture.

'We'll go now,' he said, his voice harsh.

We went out to the victoria and rode away from the factory, passing through Darkmead at a brisk gallop. Burton Rodd clicked the reins, urging the horse to go faster and faster. I was tossed and jolted on the seat beside him and had to brace myself to keep from flying out. He was like a man possessed by demons, his hair whipping about his head, his face expressing no emotion whatsoever. It was only after we passed the oak trees and were on the moors that he allowed the horse to slow. He heaved his shoulders, seeming to relax a bit. He hadn't said a word to me, hadn't once glanced in my direction. He might have been alone in the carriage.

The moors were brown, dark now at twilight. The sky was dark grey, with apricot stains fading on the horizon. I thought the place had never looked so lonely and desolate. There was no sound but the noise of hooves pounding and wheels spinning. I was stunned, almost numb. The victoria passed over a slope, and I could see my house ahead, warm-yellow lights burning at the windows. Bella would be frantic with worry, I thought. Whatever would I tell her? The thoughts seemed to be formulating under water. I seemed to be swimming in rippling, invisible waves. Burton Rodd stopped the victoria in front of the house and sat impassively as I climbed out and gathered up my packages. When he finally looked at me, his face was weary. He seemed exhausted, battered, fighting to stay in an upright position.

'I haven't lost,' he said. 'There'll be another round. I'll win it. Don't think for a moment—'

He didn't complete the sentence. He snapped the reins and drove away. Bella came running outside, a look of alarm on her face, a dozen questions ready to pour forth. When she saw my expression, she stopped, looking at me as though she were seeing me for the first time, and then she looked at the carriage disappearing, over the slope. Bella shook her head and smiled to herself, took my hand, and led me into the house.

CHAPTER THIRTEEN

Market day was over. The animals were all gone, sold to the highest bidder, although their smell was still quite present. The produce had been sold as well, just a few rotten cabbages remaining in the bottoms of the empty bins. The stalls where local women had sold preserves and handmade lace and assorted items were all closed up now, and even the fortune-teller had left her gaudy tent to mingle with the crowd milling about the great clearing on the edge of town, where the towering stack of wood awaited the touch of fire that would start it blazing. A fringe of heavy woods surrounded the clearing, and the river was nearby. The sky was deep purple stained with black, and darkness was rapidly falling.

A deafening babble of voices filled the air, loud, shrill, husky. At least three hundred people crowded the clearing, pushing, shoving, trying to find a good spot near the woodpile where they could best see the dances. There was a concession stand where glasses of lemonade were being sold, and another, far more popular, where the innkeeper's wife was selling huge mugs of beer. Several of the men were staggering, and there had already been two fights, quickly broken up. An atmosphere of tension and excitement in the air threatened to explode if the fire wasn't lighted soon. Townsmen, ordinarily repressed, felt this was their night to break loose and roar. Decorum and sobriety were tossed aside for these few hours, and the coarse, rowdy mood of the crowd made me slightly uneasy as I stood near the gigantic pile of wood.

'When are they going to light it?' Bella said impatiently.

'Soon as it's good and dark,' Alan told her. 'Just hold on. It'll be worth the wait, I promise.'

'Your promises aren't worth much, Alan Dunne,' she said peevishly. Nevertheless, she allowed him to fling his arm about her shoulder. They were still edgy with each other after their argument, but I suspected that this night would find them firmly reunited. Bella wore a dress of buttercup yellow with tiny black stripes, Alan a blue silk shirt open at the throat and a shiny black suit that smelled of moth crystals and threatened to burst at all the seams. His hair was neatly combed, and his broad, amiable face was glowing with pleasure as he stood with his arm about Bella. I thought them the most attractive couple in the whole gathering.

'I've never seen so many people,' Bella said. 'The whole town must be here.'

'Looks that way,' Alan agreed, 'but a lot of folks stay away, thinkin' this celebration a bit too pagan for Christian tastes. You won't find many of the sober church members hangin' about. They're all at a big meetin' with the minister, tryin' to figure out a way to ban this celebration next year. These're factory folks, most of 'em, and farmers and townsmen who ain't too concerned about stayin' in the good graces of the deacons.'

'What're we going to see, for cripe's sake?' she retorted. 'A bunch of young people dancin' around a fire. That's so shocking?'

Edward, standing beside me, smiled. 'Wait till you see the dance,' he said. 'It stems from the ancient traditional rites that go back all the way to the Middle Ages. It's been toned down through the years, of course, but it's still a mite too flamboyant to please our Queen. She's suggested that all such celebrations be banned, but no one can ban the traditions in these country towns far from London, not local deacons, not even Victoria.'

'Bah!' Bella snapped. 'I'd rather be home cleanin' my pantry or makin' a batch of muffins. I don't even know why I let you bring me here, Alan Dunne. Back in London many a fellow took me to the music halls, and after I've seen those hussies dance the can-can, I'm not likely to be very excited about watchin' a pack of country yokels traipsin' about a bonfire.'

'If you want to go home—' Alan began warningly.

'I'll let you know when!' she replied testily, pulling away from him and brushing her skirts briskly. 'Right now I want something to drink, and I'd thank you to go buy me a glass of lemonade if it isn't askin' too much. A *gentleman* would've already considered a girl's thirst.'

Alan stalked away with a sullen expression on his face. Bella smiled pertly, delighted with her hoydenish treatment of him and smug in the knowledge that he would come back for more of the same. Edward chuckled, amused by this display of basic amorous tactics. He was plainly excited about the celebration, hoping to gather a lot of material for his book. He carried his leatherbound notebook and a quantity of pencils, and his attention was constantly being diverted every time he heard a snatch of song from someone in the crowd. He looked handsome in a rust-coloured corduroy jacket and dark-brown jodhpurs tucked snugly into the tops of his high brown leather boots. Bronze-blond hair unruly, tanned face aglow with anticipation, vivid blue eyes alight, he was finding it difficult to remain dutifully at my side. He gave my hand a squeeze, grinning.

'Seems like Bella should be giving me lessons in deportment,' he said in a teasing voice. 'I'm supposed to be a gentleman, and I haven't yet inquired about *your* thirst. Would you like a glass of lemonade?'

I nodded, and Edward followed after Alan through the dense crowd, frequently giving a gentle shove to someone who blocked his way. Bella turned to me, all concern. She knew I wasn't enjoying myself, knew I was nervous and on edge, however much I might pretend otherwise for Edward's sake. She knew I had been moody ever since Burton Rodd left me at the house the night before, and she suspected the reason, although she had asked no questions about that episode.

'Maybe we should've stayed home,' she said quietly. 'You look awful, Miss Kathy. I mean —well, you're dazzlin' in that green dress, and your hair looks stunnin' all loose about your shoulders, but your face is pale, even if you *did* use a little rouge, and you look ready to jump out of your skin!'

'Does it show that much?' I asked.

'Those men haven't noticed, if that's what you mean. Men are so concerned with the impression *they're* makin', they don't ever notice anything. A woman can tell, though. Mind you, I'm not makin' any accusations, but when you're with a man as big and good-lookin' as Mister Edward is and can't keep your mind on what he's sayin' and keep lookin' around the crowd like you're expectin' to see someone *else*—'

'Nonsense,' I snapped, irritated.

'Maybe so, but the person you *might* be expectin' to see is over there beside the empty bins, and he hasn't taken his eyes off you for the past half-hour.'

I looked up quickly. Burton Rodd was standing beside the brown wooden bins, his legs spread wide apart, his arms folded over his chest. He wore the same rumpled black suit he had worn that day in the ruins and the same white shirt with ruffled front. His head was lowered, his eyes raised and staring rudely at me across the street. He might have been completely alone, so immune was he to the jostling humanity that swarmed about him. His lips were turned down at one corner as though in scorn, and he paid no attention to the women who found it convenient to pass by him again and again. He was aloof, his eyes pinioning me to the spot. I looked away, trying to control the blush that threatened to stain my cheeks.

'He just keeps starin',' Bella said in a low voice, 'and he isn't the only one. See that man over there—the one in the tight suit with the pockmarked face and the cropped black hair? He's been watchin' you too. What an ugly lout he is.'

I glanced in the direction Bella had indicated. The man was the same one I had seen in town yesterday, the companion who had tried to restrain the blond who had approached me. When he saw that I was looking at him, the man averted his eyes, suddenly absorbed by a group of factory girls who were moving through the crowd arm in arm, flowers in their hair, bright skirts swaying. I stared at the man, and in a moment he looked back at me, shuffled uneasily on his feet, and turned his back. Bella had been talking, and I just now caught her words.

'...and I don't want to alarm you, Miss Kathy, but it's scary, downright scary. When I saw him, he stooped down with his instrument and tried to pretend he was busy payin' no mind, but I know for a fact he'd been hanging around for two hours, almost as if he was *keepin' watch*....'

'What are you talking about?'

'That man. He's the same one I saw this morning.'

'You—you saw him this morning?'

'First thing when I came downstairs. I looked out the kitchen window, and there he was—far off, granted, but watchin' the house. He had his instruments with him, and I didn't pay much mind at first. To tell you the truth, I hardly noticed. I was so busy gettin' the stove lighted and all, and I knew you wasn't feelin' well and was kinda worried about that—but when two *hours* passed and he was still there—' She shook her head, lips pursed. 'I can tell you, it bothered me. I went outside and put my hands on my hips and just stared at him, and he looked kinda shaken up, like I'd caught him doin' somethin' *sinister*.'

'Why didn't you tell me when I came down?'

'I didn't want to worry you, and he went off as soon as I stepped outside. Still, I had the feelin' he'd been there a long time, maybe even before *sun*up.'

'He's a—a surveyor,' I said. 'He was probably just doing his job—you say he had his instruments. Maud told me yesterday they were out surveying the moors.'

'Humph!' Bella snorted. 'You might believe that, but I don't! When I see a man with a face like his, I know he isn't up to any good. I don't mind tellin' you, Miss Kathy, if the men weren't with us, I'd be scared plum to death!'

Edward returned with a glass of lemonade. He raised an eyebrow when he saw that Alan hadn't come back yet. I drank the beverage quickly. It was extremely cold, a chunk of ice clinking in the glass, and I felt a sharp pain in my forehead from drinking too fast. I handed the glass to Edward, pressing my fingertips against my forehead. He smiled, said I drank it like a greedy child, and asked if I wanted another glassful. I shook my head.

'I'll just take the glass back,' he said, 'and—you'll pardon me for a few minutes, won't you? I ran into old Jed Bosley over there at the stall, and he said he'd just remembered a song his grandfather used to sing. Will you be all right?'

'Of course,' I replied.

'I'll just be gone a little while. They're going to light the fire in a minute or so. I'll try to be back before the dances start.'

262

He hurried back through the crowd. Darkness was almost completely upon us now, everything shrouded with shadows, the sky black and frosty with starlight. Torches burned, casting weird orange lights over the crowd and filling the air with the odour of smoke and tar. The crowd was restless and growing noisier. I cast a surreptitious glance in Burton Rodd's direction. He was still watching me, his face all shadowy, his body silhouetted dark against the yellow-orange glow of a torch that burned somewhere behind him. Now that twilight was gone and night was falling in earnest, it seemed to grow darker by the second. I could barely see Alan's face as he staggered toward us, his hands empty and a lopsided grin on his face. His neatly combed hair had slipped into one heavy lock that covered his forehead, making him look like a naughty schoolboy. He shoved a man out of his way, too forcefully, and he looked sullen when the man rebuked him.

'Where's my lemonade?' Bella inquired in haughty tones.

'Couldn't find any,' he replied.

'I see you found the beer all right,' she retorted icily.

'That I did, sure did,' he said, grinning. 'Want to make somethin' of it?'

Bella looked properly affronted, but she

couldn't prevent the corners of her lips from turning up in a slight smile. Alan looked so big and comical with his lopsided smile and fallen hair and tight, shiny suit. Bella permitted him to put an arm about her waist, sighing in resignation. Alan leaned his heavy body against her, and Bella brushed the hair off his forehead, only to have it fall down again. He shook his head impatiently like a puppy who despised petting. He must have consumed a large amount of beer in a remarkably short time to have become so inebriated so quickly, I told myself, remembering my own experiences with alcohol a few nights before. I frowned at the memory, certain it would haunt me for years.

Maud passed us, looking outrageous in high-buttoned boots, shapeless black dress, and an ancient black straw hat with tattered red velvet roses dripping over the wide brim. She was arm in arm with the brawny blacksmith, who looked even brawnier in his Sunday best. She raised a hand in greeting, clucked when she saw her nephew's condition, and patted the blacksmith's arm possessively, disappearing into the crowd. Alan staggered a little, leaning against Bella. She raised her eyes heavenward, as though seeking solace, although the smile still lingered on her lips.

I wondered why Edward hadn't returned. I

searched the crowd, thinking I might see him. I saw Buck Crabbe, his arm crooked around the neck of a plump brunette in blue who leaned against his chest. The girl was smiling, but Crabbe looked as surly as ever. People moved between us, pushing closer now that the fire was about to be lighted. I saw two or three men, who must have been surveyors, scattered among the crowd at various points. I did not see Edward, nor did I see Burton Rodd, who had left his station beside the wooden bins. I could feel someone watching me, an acute sensation, but no one was openly staring now. I felt nervous and apprehensive, as though something were wrong, as though something were about to happen. I felt alone, isolated in the crowd, and I wished Edward would return.

Ten men bearing torches moved out of the crowd and circled the pile of wood. They moved forward in unison, pushing the crowd back, widening the area about the wood, until there was twenty yards all around the pile. The crowd backed away, cursing, shoving, fighting to maintain their positions. There were loud cries, laughter, and finally silence as the men moved toward the towering pile, still in unison, and touched their torches to the wood. Small yellow-blue flames licked the wood like gentle tongues. Smoke filled the air. People coughed.

The flames darkened, turning orange, and began to devour the wood at the bottom of the pile. A hush fell over the crowd. We could hear the wood crackling, popping, and suddenly the flames shot up, exploding in fury, sheathing the whole pile in wildly dancing fire that illuminated the night. Sparks shot up, to touch the sky like glittering Roman candles, sprinkling down over the area the men had cleared. The heat was intense, even where I stood, and everyone backed away even more. The furious flames spit at the night for ten minutes. Charred bits of wood fell to the ground. Finally the blaze controlled itself, burning steadily now, the fury gone.

A constantly flickering yellow glow illuminated the whole large clearing. I could see the trunks of the trees that ringed the area. Wild shadows flitted over the crowd like intangible demons, black and orange, moving, shifting, creating a strange atmosphere. Faces were upturned to watch the blaze. I saw Buck Crabbe, alone now, the brunette in blue swallowed by the crowd. He was looking around, searching for someone, paying no attention to the fire. I thought I saw Burton Rodd, but I couldn't be certain. People moved about, standing on tiptoe, blocking my line of vision. Where was Edward? I wondered. I couldn't rid myself of the feeling of apprehension. I could still feel the eyes on me. The sensation was so strong that it was almost like a physical contact. I turned around quickly, hoping to catch whoever was staring at me, but I saw only upturned faces with shadows flitting over them, mouths open in awe, eyes reflecting the orange blaze. I stood close beside Bella and Alan. He seemed to be sober now. Both of them were absorbed by the spectacle.

More than ever, I felt alone. I told myself I was being ridiculous, but I couldn't shake the feeling of danger. It mounted steadily. I folded my arms about my waist. I could hardly stand still.

The crowd murmured with anticipation as the dancers appeared, stepping into the cleared area about the fire as though by magic. All were in costume, the boys in tight black trousers and white shirts with full, gathered sleeves, the girls in white dresses with low-cut bodices and flaring skirts with hems several inches above the ankles. Boys and girls alike wore garlands of flowers over their brows. The boys carried flutes, the girls tambourines. They began to play a strange, soft tune that reminded me of woodlands and glades, and they danced to the music, moving slowly, gracefully around the fire, doing something that looked like a minuet.

Bella expressed her disappointment to Alan and said she'd just as soon go home. He told her to just wait and she'd see something the can-can couldn't compare with. She stifled a yawn. He ignored her, leaning forward to peer at the dancers.

I could hardly see why Queen Victoria should have concerned herself about such festivals. The dance was innocuous, quite tame. Or was it? The flutes began to play shriller, faster. The tambourines jangled and thumped. The dancers moved faster around the flames, making little jump steps, the boys leaping in front of the girls. As the music grew louder, the dance became more frantic. Boys leaped high into the air like frenzied acrobats. Girls swayed wildly, skirts flying above knees. The flames crackled, a part of the music, burning bright orange and blue. Shadows of the dancers writhed on the ground beyond them, weird, obscene. The crowd was spellbound, fascinated. Bella stood with her lips parted, her eyes filled with amazement. Alan looked tense.

I closed my eyes. The shrill, discordant music split the air and shattered like broken glass. The crackling fire roared, popped, a great live thing mocking all decency. My eardrums began to ring. My head ached. The feeling of danger mounted, mounted, until I wanted to

268

scream. Where was Edward? Why hadn't he returned? Who was watching me? What was this evil that drew closer and closer? My hands were clenched, nails digging into palms. Against my closed lids I saw the obscene shadows, black on purple, and they seemed to taunt me.

Someone tugged on my arm from behind. I froze. The fingers closed on my elbow and tugged again. I turned.

Bertie Rawlins moved his lips without speaking. His face was even more thin and pale than I had remembered. The smudges under his blue eyes were darker, the hollows under his cheekbones deeper. The eyes were full of fear, and the thin white lips moved jerkily. He drew me away from Bella and Alan. We were completely surrounded by people who were absorbed in the spectacle that grew wilder and wilder, and we might have been alone in a dark forest of tall, immobile bodies that only smelled human. I could barely see Bertie's face. He was trembling.

'They got Jamie,' he whispered. 'It was *him* they found.'

'What do you mean, Bertie?'

'I seen you yesterday at the fact'ry. You didn't see me. I knew I had to tell you—they call me loony, loony-bird, but I gotta tell you....' He looked around frantically at the bodies pressing close to us. 'Not here,' he whispered hoarsely. 'They're watchin'. They know I know....'

'Bertie, try to make sense.'

'The other 'un. Yeah, him they're savin' for the moon dance.'

'Moon dance? Bertie—'

'It was *him* they found. The other 'un they're—'

His lips continued to move, but no sound came from them. The eyes implored me to believe him. His hands fluttered, jerked. He was like someone addicted to opium who had been deprived of it for a week. I thought he was going to faint. He staggered a little, leaning forward, and kept looking over his shoulder.

'Meet me by the river,' he stammered. 'In the woods, over there. I gotta tell you—you gotta believe—they're watchin' now. Please come. The woods, by the river. They won't see us there.'

He disappeared into the crowd. I was alone, surrounded by the bodies like tree trunks. The music was screeching. The flames cast a yellow glow that only intensified the darkness, shadowing faces, making black patterns in the air. I smelled sulphur and beer and perspiring bodies. My head was spinning. I no longer even knew where Alan and Bella stood. He was mad, mad, of course he was mad, and I couldn't follow him. It was insane even to contemplate it, but his face, his eyes, his voice, had all pleaded with me. I had to go. I had to listen to him. He was mad, but I had to let him talk. I couldn't let him huddle alone in the woods, babbling to himself, crazed with fear.

I would go tell Bella and Alan where I was going, and then I would go down to the river, through the woods. No, no, if I tried to explain it to them, I would waste too much time. They were both engrossed in the dances. The dances would last for at least another thirty minutes. I would be back before then. They wouldn't miss me. I hesitated only an instant, then began to push my way through the crowd.

It was difficult. People were packed solid about the clearing, rooted to the spot, refusing to move an inch in the fear they might miss part of the dance. I shoved against husky men in bulky jackets, murmuring apologies as I went. The crowd seemed to close in on me. I pushed and pleaded, my hair tumbling over my face. All the time, I felt the eyes watching me, but I could see no one following. A great slab of wood broke in two, sending a shower of sparks blazing up. The crowd stirred, pressing forward to watch the sparks drift down about the dancers. I was pushed back, caught in the movement. I was knocked against one of the surveyors, a red-haired brute with dark eyes who caught my shoulders to keep me from falling. I was on the verge of hysteria now. I pushed through the crowd, apologies forgotten, and when I finally reached the edge of the clearing. I was panting, my heart beating rapidly.

It was curiously calm here, the crowd behind me, the woods in front. I saw a wall of backs, and beyond, over the heads, far away, the flames that licked up against the black sky. The yellow glow hung over the crowd, but here there were only shadows. I could smell the rich, mossy smell of the woods, rotten leaves, damp soil, sappy bark. The music was distant, dim, drowned out by the crisp rustle of leaves and the hoot of an owl somewhere in the woods. I could hear a faint gurgling that I knew must be the river. I caught my breath. I pushed the golden waves away from my face and adjusted the bodice of my dress.

I hesitated again before going into the woods. Bertie was harmless. Everyone said that. He would do me no harm, but I suddenly wished I had never left Bella's side. If only Edward were here. He would understand. He would see why I had to indulge that poor frightened man with the living nightmares. He would go with me, and I would feel much better with him beside me; but he had vanished into the crowd. No doubt he was filling his notebooks with songs, collecting gems that would sparkle in the pages of his book, but I still wished he were here. I wished my throat weren't dry, my forehead hot, my pulse leaping. I felt dangerously exposed here on this strip of clearing, out of the crowd, not yet in the shelter of the woods. I felt the eyes on me, still, and I turned and moved quickly between the trunks of the trees.

It was very dark, and surprisingly cold. A chilly wind blew over the water, rippling through the brush, rustling the leaves. I walked very carefully, my heels sinking into the damp soil. The trees grew close together, tangled brush between them, leaving little room for passing through. I shuddered as silky strands of a cobweb brushed against my face. I walked into the trunk of a tree. I uttered a word I seldom heard and had never before used myself. My skirt caught on a thorn, the material ripping. I stood very still, knowing it was useless to try to go any farther until my eyes grew accustomed to the dark. There was rustling black darkness all around me, and little by little it lightened. Trees and brush began to take on shape and form, grew solid and visible.

The blackness melted into a misty grey, and I could see the few beams of moonlight that managed to penetrate the heavy canopy of leaf and bough. I saw that I was standing in the middle of a thicket, my skirt firmly fastened to a thorny branch. I began to separate the material from the thorns, trying to tear as little as possible. Birds called out to one another, shrill in the silence, and invisible animals scurried through the brush.

I could hear the river, and far away, through the trees, I could see the wavering veils of mist that hung suspended over its surface, the breeze causing them to swirl and stir like ghosts. I caught myself just in time. No nonsense, I warned firmly, no flights of fancy. Mist is mist. Bertie is waiting. There are no ghosts. I backed out of the thicket, holding my skirts up to keep them free from the thorns. I saw a kind of footpath that wound through the trees toward the river. I followed it, moving as slowly as before, stepping over roots, avoiding overhanging branches. A beam of moonlight slanted down through the trees ahead, gilding a cobweb with silver. Drops of moisture hung from the silken strands like glistening gems. The darkness was blue-black and grey, with shades of dark green. I kept my eyes on the mist that floated over the river. The heel of one of my shoes sank down in the soil. My foot slipped free, and I was almost thrown off balance. I retrieved the shoe and bent down to put it back on.

I froze.

It was here, all around me, that evil I had felt before. The wind had died down. The leaves no longer rustled. The birds had stopped calling. The air was still, filled with a heavy silence that caused the hair on the back of my neck to bristle. A few seconds ago I had been calm, confident, yet now I felt myself on the verge of panic. That feeling had returned: the eyes that watched, the evil that lurked. It was as though the woods had become a living thing that held its breath, waiting. I slipped the shoe on my foot. I backed against the trunk of a tree. I could feel the bark rough against my skin. The air was permeated with evil. There was a muffled thud, a snapping sound.

Something moved through the mists at the river's edge.

I wanted to scream, but I could only stare in horror as the figure in white stepped through a small clearing, paused, and looked back. It wore a hood with a peaked top and two holes for the eyes, all the rest of the body covered with a flowing robe, the brilliant white of the material gleaming, standing out against the foggy grey-white mist. I shook my head. I closed my eyes, saw whirling black circles, opened them, to see the figure standing as before. It was no ghost. It was something real, very real. I was not imaginging it, not this time. The figure seemed to hesitate for a moment, still looking back toward the river, and then it moved on, to be swallowed up by the mist.

Time stopped altogether. There was nothing but the woods, the evil, my fear. I was a little girl again, alone in the dark, wanting to cry but afraid to make a sound, afraid the things that lurked in the corners of my room would hear me and pounce. Those childhood phantoms had vanished by the time I was six or seven, but they had come back again, and I knew if I made a sound they would swarm around me. I felt something cold and damp sliding down my cheek. I realized my lashes were brimming with tears. The air was cold. The leaves were rustling again. I heard a low, moaning noise. I knew it was Bertie. I knew I must go to him. I moved quickly, following the pathetic sound.

He was by the edge of the river. He seemed to be stretched out, resting, his arms flung out, one leg folded under him. Then I saw that his head was held at a curious angle. It seemed to hang limply from his neck. His blue eyes stared up at me. His lips moved. The moaning ceased, followed by a gurgle, a rattle in the chest. I knelt down beside him, afraid to touch him. I whispered soft words. My tears splattered down on his face. He tried to lift himself up, and his head lolled crazily on his neck.

'Don't—don't move,' I whispered. 'I'll get help. Please—please don't—'

The blue eyes looked up at me. They were beginning to glaze over. The lips moved, but no sound came. The fingers of one hand lifted, imploring me to lean down closer. I did, my hair brushing his face. The lips moved again, and I could barely discern the words.

'The moon dance—they're waitin' for—the moon.'

I stood up. He was dead. His neck had been broken. I remembered the muffled thud I had heard earlier, followed by the snapping sound. I knew what that sound had been. So loud, I thought. I must go back now. I must tell someone what had happened. I started to move away, and then I saw something white on the branch of a bush. I pulled it free. It was a piece of white cloth with ragged edges, as large as a man's handkerchief. I stared at it, knowing where it had come from. I was strangely calm, all the fear gone now. I heard footsteps approaching and stuffed the piece of white cloth into the pocket of my skirt.

Burton Rodd came toward me. He looked livid with rage.

'What the hell!' he cried. 'I saw you leaving the crowd and slipping into the woods, and I couldn't believe it. I simply couldn't believe it! Have you lost your mind? What in God's name—'

I stepped aside so he could see the body. He stared down at it, then looked up at me, his cheekbones chalky. I watched as though in a dream as he knelt down, touched the rubbery neck, frowned, examined the curious position of the leg folded under the body. He tugged at a large root, and I saw that Bertie's foot was hooked under it. Burton Rodd stood up. He came over to me and stood very close, looking down into my face. Neither of us spoke. The mist moved around us. The water splashed pleasantly over the rocks. It was all dreamlike, and I was very far away, watching.

'It's Bertie Rawlins,' I said in a voice that didn't belong to me. 'He worked for you at the factory. Everyone said he was crazy. Children used to throw rocks at his house. That was wicked, don't you think? Children are sometimes quite wicked, even the best of them.'

'Shut up, Katherine. You're hysterical.'

'No. I'm quite calm. I've never been so calm in my life. He was Jamie's brother. Do

278

you remember Jamie? They killed him. They killed Bertie too. I know. I heard—'

'He caught his foot under that root and tripped. He broke his neck. It was an accident.'

I shook my head vigorously. 'No, you see, that's how it's supposed to look. I saw—one of them. All in white. Really. Not my imagination. He wore a white hood and a white robe, and he killed Bertie. You must believe me. I saw, with my own eyes....' I spoke in a curious singsong, and from somewhere far off another Katherine Hunt wondered why that voice was so peculiar.

Burton Rodd laid his hands heavily on my shoulders. He peered into my eyes. His face was very close. I could see every line, every crease. He spoke gently, but his voice was firm. 'You saw nothing,' he said. 'You saw nothing. Do you understand me? You did not see anything. Is that clear? I'm taking you home. I will tell Edward you were with me and grew faint and asked to leave. Katherine, do you hear me? No one is to know. No one!'

I nodded. The tears spilled down my cheeks. My shoulders trembled. I tried to make them stop. His arms wrapped around me, and I buried my face against his chest. He held me tightly, stroking my back. I did not care who he was. I did not care what he had done. He was here, and he would drive the phantoms away. They could not seize me as long as he was holding me in his arms.

CHAPTER FOURTEEN

It had been raining all morning, but now the sky was grey and leaden, hanging low over the moors. The sun was a small white blur behind a ponderous bank of clouds. The moors were wet, desolate, grey. I stood at the window in the study, holding the curtain back and peering out at the bleak land. I wished Bella were here. Her merry chatter would have helped to relieve the melancholy that held me in thrall, but Alan had come for her a short while ago. They were going to spend the afternoon at Maud's farm, inspecting the batch of new baby chicks and roaming over the fields. They would not return until later this afternoon. It was just now eleven. The whole day waited, empty, depressing. I didn't know how I would get through it.

Letting the curtain fall back in place, I went

over to the desk and sat down. I stared at the neat stack of clean white paper set to one side, the bottle of blue ink, the new pen. I took out my notes for the first chapter and examined the outline I had made. The clock ticked loudly. Outside, the wind whistled over the moors with the sound of whispers. A window rattled. I put the notes away and folded up the outline. I tried not to think of what had happened night before last, but everything came back, each detail sharp and clear, tormenting me.

Burton Rodd had not brought me home after all. The dances ended just as we returned to the clearing, the crowd dispersing. People swarmed around us, pushing, staggering, laughing, shouting at one another. Rodd held an arm about my waist, supporting me. We stood still as people moved in every direction, waves of humanity that crashed around us. The fire was almost gone, a heap of crackling orange coals that men were already covering with sand. Edward came tearing toward us, his hair dishevelled, a frantic expression on his face.

'Where have you been?' he cried. 'I've been looking everywhere.'

'She was with me,' Burton Rodd said calmly. 'We were watching the dances. She grew faint. I'm taking her home.'

'I believe I can manage that, Burt,' Edward

said coldly. 'I brought her. I'll take her home.'

'Bella—' I began.

'She and the boy have already left. I told them to go ahead, that I'd find you. She looked worried. I told her everything was all right.'

'Did you get your song?' I asked brightly.

'Yes, fantastic luck! And I got a great lead.'

Rodd was reluctant to turn me over to Edward. He did not want to make an issue of it, but neither did he want to run the risk of my telling anyone what had happened. I broke away from him, telling him I would be perfectly all right, and thanked him for his attentiveness. Silently, with my eyes, I told him I would say nothing about the body in the woods. Edward drove me home, concerned about my headache, but bursting with excitement at his discovery. A family in the next county had a whole folder of songs one of their ancestors had written out in longhand. Edward had met the head of the house, a poor farmer, and he had agreed to let Edward come to the farm and make copies of all the material.

'It'll take at least two days,' he told me as we drove over the moors. 'I'm leaving first thing in the morning. Of course, many of the songs will be duplicates of ones I've already found, but I expect to discover....' I only half listened, my mind whirling. Edward was so enthusiastic about his good fortune that he hardly noticed my silence. Bella and Alan were already at the house when we arrived. Edward kissed me casually on the cheek, said he hoped I got a good night's rest, and promised to come see me as soon as he returned to Castlemoor.

That would be tomorrow. Today I faced long, solitary hours that would sap all my energy and drain my emotions. I wished I had asked Bella not to go. She would gladly have stayed, but I would have had to make some kind of explanation for the request. Never before had I felt the isolation of this house so strongly. It was as though the moors were a vast, empty sea, the house a solitary vessel anchored in the middle of it. The land undulated like grey waves, and the whistling of the wind only intensified this feeling. I had the feverish sensation that the house might sink, exactly like a boat, and be swallowed up by the land, the sea.

I felt I was losing my mind. I knew I couldn't go on like this. I had to find something to hold on to.

The portrait Damon Stuart had painted of my brother stood on the desk, beside the carved-ivory elephant. That so-familiar face stared up at me, ruggedly handsome, alarmingly lifelike. The tousled golden hair looked as though it had just fallen across his forehead, and the wide pink mouth, curled with humour, seemed about to speak. The blazing brown eyes held mine, and they were very stern. What's all this nonsense? they seemed to inquire. Hardly your style, old girl, this. Sitting around, brooding, feeling sorry for yourself—that's not my Kathy. Better do something, right? Where's the old Hunt spirit?

My mood lifted, almost as though Donald had actually been speaking to me. I could feel his presence here in this small room filled with his books and papers, and it comforted me. I would go make a pot of coffee. I would cook something for lunch, and this afternoon, as soon as I'd finished eating, I would start to work on the book, despite the headache, despite the desolation. I would also draft the letter I knew I must send to the police. I didn't want to send it, but I knew I had to, even if it meant the arrest of Burton Rodd.

I went into the kitchen and dropped coffee beans in the grinder. I put water on to boil, ground the beans, and made the coffee. I sliced bread, and took the ham out, carving off two thin pink slices. All the while my mind worked coldly, methodically, all emotion repressed. I had been hysterical after I found the body, and yesterday I had been prostrate, still too

284

stunned and shaken to see things clearly. I had to inform the police of what I had seen in the woods. It had been insanity to wait this long.

Burton Rodd had appeared suddenly at the scene of the 'accident', much too suddenly. He had examined the body and declared the death an accidental one. How could he be so sure? Why had he insisted so firmly? He ordered me to keep quiet about what I had seen, and, numb, bewildered, I had agreed. If he had not been responsible for Bertie's death, then why had he been so determined that it be kept quiet? I remembered those few minutes in his arms, and I shuddered now to think I had been in the arms of a murderer.

There were so many things still unanswered, but it was safe to assume Burton Rodd had murdered Bertie Rawlins. There could be no other explanation for his strange conduct. I had to face the truth, however unpleasant it might be.

I had just finished drinking my first cup of coffee when I heard someone pounding on the front door. The noise echoed through the house, loudly, persistently. An unreasonable panic seized me. I almost dropped the empty cup I still held. I stared about the room frantically, looking for a place to hide. My pulse leaped, and I could feel the skin drawing tightly over my cheekbones. The pounding continued, shattering the silence that had prevailed a moment before. I stood up shakily, scolding myself for this absurd reaction.

I opened the front door. Nicola stood there, her fist raised ready to knock again. She stepped inside quickly without saying a word. I closed the door, puzzled. I noticed that she carried a large flat brown box. She went into the study and set the box on the desk. She stood in the middle of the room, looking around at the books. When she saw the portrait of Donald, she started. She moved closer, examining it, and then she looked up at me.

'For a moment I thought it was Jamie,' she said.

'Did you—want something?' I asked. The words were ludicrous under the circumstances, but I could think of nothing else to say.

Nicola didn't reply. She seemed not to have heard me. She wore a cloak of heavy dark-sapphire velvet, the hood fallen back to reveal her jet-black hair falling in loose, lustrous waves as it had been the first time I saw her. There were spots of colour on her cheeks, and her lovely face was serene. She took off the cloak and draped it over a chair. Beneath it she was wearing a dress of sky-blue silk that emphasized her mature bosom and slender waist. The nervous child had disappeared. She was a woman, beautifully poised, completely self-possessed.

Nicola looked at me with a frank expression in her black eyes.

'I'm really not mad, you know,' she said quietly.

'Nicola—'

'Don't say anything,' she interrupted me. 'Don't apologize, don't try to reason with me. I'm not mad. They—they would like to have believed I was, but I'm not, and after today I'll no longer have to pretend. I will be free.' She smiled, a pensive look on her face. 'Dorothea is going to be amazed at the change in me. I'm glad. I think she and I can be friends now, away from Castlemoor.'

'You're leaving?'

'In thirty-five minutes,' she replied calmly.

'Dorothea is going with you?'

She nodded. 'Burton is driving us to the station this afternoon. He's quite eager to get rid of both of us—for reasons of his own. There was a spectacular scene with Dorothea. She had no intention of leaving. Burton insisted. He called her a coward, said she was afraid to face the world. She threw a vase at him—quite priceless, a Ming. She said there wasn't anything in the world she was afraid of, and he

287

said she was afraid of herself, and she called him an unnatural son, throwing his mother out into the cold, and he said cold, my ass, you're going to one of the most exclusive resorts on the Continent—they went on like that for two hours.'

'Wasn't this all—rather sudden?' I asked.

'The decision to leave now? Yes, but when Burton makes up his mind to do something, he wants it done immediately. Yesterday morning he came into the breakfast room and announced his decision. That's when he and Dorothea had their fight. He wanted us to leave then and there; I mean, he actually wanted to put us in the carriage as soon as we'd finished breakfast. After she'd made up her mind to go, Dorothea said it would take at least a week to get ready. He said now or never. She said he was insane. They compromised—he would pay for complete new wardrobes if we would leave today. We are going to spend a week in Paris, buying clothes.'

'He seems anxious to get you both away from Castlemoor,' I said.

'I know. It's not—natural. Something is wrong, but—I don't care about that. I'm leaving. That's the important thing. And Dorothea is radiant. I've never seen her so excited, so happy.'

'And you?' I said hesitantly. 'You don't look—unhappy.'

'This is the happiest day in my life. After today, no more Castlemoor, no more dark halls, no more noises, no more Buck. Sunshine, green leaves, fresh air, and people—lots of people. The place will be swarming with men, handsome men, young men, rich, rich men. I plan to pick one out and elope with him.'

'Indeed?'

'I don't think I'll have too much trouble,' Nicola said firmly. 'When we get to Paris, I'm going to select a stunning wardrobe—red satin, gold lamé, black velvet, and I'm going to have my hair done in a new way, very chic. I've just been reading about Lola Montez—I look like her, did you know that? She captivated the world. I think I can managed to captive at least one suitable man. I can hardly wait to get started.'

'If you're leaving in'—I glanced at the clock—'in twenty-five minutes, why did you come here? Surely they don't know you've come?'

She shook her head. 'I slipped off. Typical behaviour, to be expected of me. I went to my room to say goodbye to my dolls.' She laughed softly. 'Dorothea was pleased. They won't miss me. They're busy loading the trunks and making last-minute lists. I'll join them in the courtyard just in time to leave.'

'How did you get away without them seeing you?'

'There's a little side door in the south wall. Everyone else has forgotten about it—the wood's warped, the latch rusted. The boughs of the oak trees bend down and hide it from outside. I discovered it years ago. I've found it very convenient.'

'Why did you come? Not just to say goodbye?'

'Not just to say goodbye,' she replied. 'I wanted to show you something.'

She stepped over to the desk and opened the flat brown box. I was nervous and apprehensive, suddenly afraid. Nicola took out the white hood and flowing white robe. A piece of material had been torn out of the robe, a piece the size of the square now hidden in my bureau drawer. She spread the robe over a chair, dropped the hood on top of it. She was calm, but I could see that she was being deliberately dramatic.

'My ghost,' she said simply. 'That day on the moors, I told you I saw a ghost slipping down the hall. I—I still didn't understand everything then. I thought it really might have been a ghost, that I really was losing my mind.

290

I know better now.'

I managed to look at the robe without revealing any of the horror that seemed to freeze my blood.

'Where did you get that?' I asked. My voice was quite steady.

'Night before last I saw my famous ghost again, going down the stairs that lead to the dungeons. I didn't panic—for once. I told myself I had to *see*. I waited a few minutes and then started down myself. I was about halfway down when I saw a white blur in a niche in the wall. I reached up and found these.' She indicated the robe and hood. 'He'd left them.'

'He?'

'Buck, of course.'

'Why—why would he have done that?'

'Following instructions, I suppose.'

'Whose instructions?' I asked carefully.

'Burton's.'

'I see.'

'No,' she said calmly, 'I don't believe you do. I don't know why it should be so important to me that you understand, but it is. Perhaps it's because you tried to be kind to me and because I was rude to you. I know I wasn't making sense for a while. No wonder you thought me mad. They almost succeeded.'

'Succeeded in what?'

'In driving me mad.'

I didn't say anything. Nicola perched on the arm of the sofa, spreading the light-blue silk skirts out. She was beautifully composed, her face registering no emotion. Her voice was cool and controlled.

'I know what that sounds like,' she said. 'I know a doctor would say I was suffering from delusions, that I had a feeling of persecution, but there's no other explanation for it. I *did* see those things. I *did* hear those noises.'

There was another explanation, but Nicola could not know about it. By accident, she had been exposed to a tiny part of a great intrigue, and she could only relate it to herself.

'Burton was trying to drive me mad,' she said. 'Buck was helping him do it.'

'Why—why should Burton want to do that?'

'I don't know. I suppose he thought Dorothea was going to leave me her jewels—what few there are. Perhaps there's some other reason I don't know about. Anyway, there's my ghost—a white robe and a hood with holes cut out for the eyes. Quite real. Everything else was real, too.'

'What about Jamie?' I asked. 'You said you saw him.'

She shook her head slowly, and her eyes were sad. 'I don't know what happened to Jamie,' she said quietly, 'but I—I didn't see him.'

'You imagined it?'

'I saw someone who looked like Jamie,' she replied.

She glanced at the portrait of Donald. I remembered Bertie's words. I understood them now.

Nicola talked on, not aware of what she had just told me.

'I don't understand it,' she said. 'I won't even pretend I do. Burton is a strange man. He always has motives for everything he does. If he wanted to—to send me away, he had his reasons. Well, I'm going now. I will be out of his way. He can have Dorothea's jewels. He can have everything. I only want to get away.'

She stood up, pensive, her fragile face suddenly very young. She began to put on the dark-sapphire cloak, adjusting the heavy folds about her shoulders, pulling the hood over her head. I watched as though in a trance. The room seemed to spin around, slowly at first, then faster and faster, and I was amazed that I could stand quite still and watch her so calmly and not fall over. Pushing a jet-black curl away from her temple, she took my hand and peered into my eyes.

'I must go now,' she said.

'Yes,' I whispered.

'Is something wrong? You're pale. Your cheeks....'

'No,' I said, my voice steady now.

Nicola looked relieved. She smiled.

'I'm going to be happy, Kathy,' she said. 'I wanted you to know. I haven't been happy before—not really. I'm going to forget Castlemoor and start a new life. I was quite serious about eloping with a millionaire. Of course, I'd like a title, too. Maybe I'll find a duke or marquess, or even a Russian prince. I know I've read too many novels, and happy endings are supposed to be bunk, but you just wait and see. I'll write.'

I walked to the front door with her, still in a trance. I opened the door for her, and Nicola stood on her tiptoes and kissed my cheek, then hurried toward the slope, her dark-blue cloak billowing behind her. I did not know if I could make it back into the study. I braced myself against the wall and closed my eyes. After a moment the dizzy sensation passed, and I was able to reach the sofa. I sat there for a long time, my eyes closed, my cheeks burning, my whole body limp and empty. Only the monotonous clicking of the clock broke the silence that settled over the house.

The giant jigsaw puzzle that had been haunting me for so long was fitting together. Each piece, mysterious in itself, fit neatly with another to form the complete picture. It was horrifying, but as I sat there in the silent house, shaken, stunned, I realized that the picture was real. As I worked on the puzzle, a curious calm came over me. I wanted to cry, to swoon, to resort to every known feminine trick in order to avoid the truths that presented themselves, but I couldn't. My mind was cool, sharp, pushing me toward the inevitable conclusion, and I knew I must act. I sat, and I thought, and all weakness dropped away.

Donald had come to Castlemoor to do a book on the Celtic religions. He had intended to send for Bella and me, but something had changed his mind. His last letters were mysterious. Maud had told me that he had worked himself into a state of nervous exhaustion, and Edward had verified that, adding that my brother had given way to delusions about cults and ghosts. The 'accident' had happened on the moors, and my brother's body was sent to London in a sealed coffin. The coffin had never been opened.

I came to Castlemoor, and on my first day I encountered the overwhelming superstition of the local folk. Was it just superstition? Alan thought so. He had recounted the story of Ted Roberts, the local drunk, who saw figures in white chanting and dancing among the ruins where a girl was tied to one of the phallic columns. Milly Brown's body was found shortly thereafter, and although Alan was convinced she had been murdered by her lover, others were not willing to accept this explanation. Neither was I. Not now. I did not believe in ghosts. I did not think Milly had been butchered by a band of phantoms who walked the ruins at night. I believed Ted Roberts had seen his figures in white, and I believed them to be as tangible as flesh, as tangible as the figure I had seen down at the river's edge.

The first time I saw Nicola, she had told me of her 'nightmares'. She told me of seeing a figure in white moving down the halls of the castle and going down the steps to the dungeons. She told me about Jamie, the golden-haired young stable boy who had been discharged and, subsequently, disappeared, leaving Castlemoor without a word to anyone. Later, at the bridge, Bertie Rawlins made a curious sign, frightening me, and, convinced that I was not 'one of them,' told me about his brother. 'They got Jamie,' he told me. He mumbled about 'the secret of the stones,' and I had passed him off as a harmless eccentric. He had been eccentric, and harmless, but he had possessed knowledge that no one would listen to. It had led to his death. I cringed, remembering the smell of moss and mud, the cry in the night, the figure that moved through the mist. I remembered the twisted body, one leg folded beneath it, the head hanging loosely on the rubbery neck. The image would not go away. I could not avoid the truth, no matter how ugly it might be. That murder was part of the truth, as was the other, earlier murder.

I found an amulet among my brother's things. It was valuable. It belonged in a museum. I had wondered how Donald could have obtained it. On my first day at the ruins, I had stumbled across an identical amulet, old, priceless, the leather thong quite new. How many such amulets were there? Ted Roberts had seen several figures in white. Had each of them worn one? I believed now that Donald had found the amulet at the ruins, dropped there accidentally by one of the men, just as the one I had stumbled over had been. Burton Rodd had been looking for the amulet that day.... Burton Rodd had been in the woods immediately after Bertie's death, and he seemed to be in league with the strange men who had come to Darkmead, the men with coarse, brutal faces. I wondered who they were. I wondered if they frequently wore white hoods and flowing white robes, if they had secret signals known only to each other, if they chanted and danced by moonlight and performed ritual ceremonies.... It seemed very likely.

I was calm, analytical. Such cults had existed over the centuries. I had read of several of them. There had been one centred around Stonehenge, and human sacrifices had been performed, people butchered on the stones. A similar cult had existed in Monmouthshire, and there had even been one in Scotland. All had been disbanded, the cultists imprisoned, and supposedly such bizarre religious cults ceased to exist. In the course of his research here in Darkmead, my brother had discovered just such a cult actively surviving in our civlized age. It seemed incredible.

It was like something out of one of Mrs Radcliffe's novels of mystery and romance. I could hardly believe it. This was the age of Victoria and Disraeli, the age of steel and steam and industry, and yet I had proof that the cult actually existed. I glanced at the hood and robe still draped over the chair. In this day and age.... And yet, I thought, the vast moors offered perfect cover, far from the eyes of the civilized world. The superstition of the local people was an asset. They were ready to believe in the 'ghosts' that danced among the ruins at night, and sophisticated outsiders would only smile and pass the whole thing off as a rather charming example of native nonsense. Yes, I could see how the cult could exist, and I no longer doubted its existence.

Nicola had seen a man coming up from the dungeons. He had dark-golden hair, brown eyes, a pale, tormented face. She had thought him Jamie, but just now she had said he was someone who looked like Jamie. She had glanced at the portrait of my brother. The last piece of the puzzle fit into place. The picture was complete.

'They got Jamie,' Bertie Rawlins had whispered when he spoke to me in the crowd around the bonfire. 'It was *him* they found.'

My brother had been abducted. Jamie had been murdered, his face and body disfigured. Buck Crabbe 'found' the body and identified it. Jamie's body was sent to London, buried beneath a tombstone bearing Donald's name. But why? Why had they gone to all that trouble? Why had they murdered someone else and indulged in the elaborate pretence? Donald had discovered 'the secret of the stones,' but why hadn't they just murdered him? Why had they abducted him and kept him alive? Why had they run that risk?

I remembered Bertie's last words: 'The moon dance—they're waitin' for—the moon.'

I stepped over to the bookcase and selected several heavy volumes. I was amazed at my own calm. Another Kathy, far off, watched with incredulity as her twin spread the books out on the desk and turned the pages. My brow was unfurrowed, my gaze level. My lips were pursed with determination as I ran my finger down the pages that mentioned the moon dance. For perhaps ten minutes I read, pushing one volume aside for another, and each book told me the same thing. I understood at last why they had not murdered Donald immediately.

The moon dance was an ancient ceremony especially reserved for enemies of the cult. It was held twice a year, under a full moon, and those who dared desecrate the sacred ground or blaspheme the religion were sacrificed in a particularly gruesome manner. Although the offence may have been committed months before, the offenders were held captive, reserved for this special ceremony.

Donald was alive. He was in the dungeons of Castlemoor.

Burton Rodd had left to drive Nicola and Dorothea to the station, and as it was in the next county, it would be hours before he could return. Edward was in the next county, collecting songs, and he would not be back until tomorrow. For several hours, Castlemoor would be empty, except for a few servants—and the man who was languishing in the dungeons, waiting for death, or salvation.

I had no idea why I should be so calm. Hysteria would have been the normal reaction. Why wasn't I hysterical? Why didn't I fall across the sofa in a swoon? I felt bloodless, numb, all emotion suppressed. Later, I would give way to them. Later, I would let them wash over me like a great tidal wave, and I would react, I would cry, I would experience every emotion at its fullest, but not now. Now there was only the thing I must do, and I knew I had to concentrate every fibre of my being on going through with it. There was no time to feel, no time to think, no time for caution. I saw a woman in the mirror across the room. Her face looked hard, cold, no longer young, no longer beautiful.

I found a pen and scrap of paper and quickly wrote a note to Bella and placed it on the hall table where she could not avoid seeing it. I picked up a small oil lamp not much larger than a cup and dropped a box of matches in the pocket of my dress. I took my forest-green velvet cloak from the closet and put it on, left the house, and hurried up the slope toward the castle.

The wind was savage. It caused the cloak to

whip about my shoulders like fluttering wings and tossed my voluminous skirts up above my legs. It tore at my hair and sent it whirling about my head in tangled auburn waves. The sky was heavy, wet, grey. The air was damp and laden with the smells of rain and mud and new grass. I could see the castle now, a ponderous grey monster, waiting, menacing. The topmost branches of the oak trees scratched against the battlements. I walked beneath the trees. The boughs bent down and almost touched the ground along the south wall.

I pushed aside the branches laden with thick green leaves, and I found the door Nicola had described. It was very small, and the wood was warped, the hinges crusted with rust. The latch hung loose, long since broken. I tugged at the knob, but the door wouldn't open. The wood had swollen, and the door was stuck in the frame. Nicola must have slammed it when she went back inside. I wrapped both hands around the brass knob and pulled. The hinges screeched loudly. The door flew open. I stepped into a long, narrow hall that smelled of mildew and decay. The floor was damp. I took a few steps, and a great gust of wind blew the door shut behind me. There was nothing but darkness and damp and the fierce howling of the wind outside.

CHAPTER FIFTEEN

I was paralysed with terror. Damp, darkness, wind, slick walls closing in on me, heart pounding rapidly—for a moment I was lost, and I knew I could never go on. I reached into my pocket and took out the matches. I struck one—the acrid smell of sulphur, a tiny yellow explosion, wet walls brought into relief. I lighted the small oil lamp, and a warm-orange glow blossomed inside the gloss. The glow spread, licked the walls, dispelling the menacing darkness around me. I started down the hall. It was very narrow, the rough walls pressing close on either side, the ceiling so low that I had to stoop a little to keep from brushing my head against it.

The hall twisted and turned and seemed to be slanting down toward the bowels of Castlemoor. The sound of wind was far behind me now, but there was a slight, scratching noise like tiny claws, a rustling, rushing along the floor. I dared not look down. If there were rats, I didn't want to see them. I brushed aside a tattered curtain of cobweb, dusty grey, and found the doorway that led into a much larger hall, with a smooth concrete floor. In the glow of my lamp I could see ornate wall brackets that held the burned, charred remains of torches long since extinguished. The air was fetid, and I had the feeling that it had been decades since this hall heard the sound of normal footsteps. The brick walls were dusty, espaliered with a growth of moss-green fungus.

I had no earthly idea where I was. I had lost all sense of direction. Castlemoor was like a great labyrinth, and these lower regions were even more complex. I could almost feel the groaning weight of the place hovering above me. I moved down the hall slowly, my heels tapping loudly on the concrete floor. The noise echoed loudly, bouncing from wall to wall, and it sounded as though I were being followed by a legion. I went up a flight of narrow stone steps, down another hall, down steps, across a broad, tiled space, up a short flight of steps, darkness all around me, broken only by the glow of my lamp. I heard the sound of running water, though I couldn't tell where it came from, and felt gusts of clammy cold air that swirled around like icy fingers stroking my cheeks and arms.

I stopped to gather my forces. I had been

moving up and down halls for at least twenty minutes, and I knew I couldn't possibly find the dungeons unless I was first able to locate the halls I had traversed the night of my visit. The tapestries, the portraits, the furniture, would guide me, and I was sure I could find the hall that led to Nicola's room, but here I was hopelessly lost.

I could feel the panic gathering force. It threatened, strong and alive, ready to take over and render me helpless. What if I couldn't find my way? What if I continued to travel these halls until the lamp went out—rats, darkness, damp, dust, ceilings that groaned, terror. No, I wouldn't allow myself these thoughts. I pushed them aside forcefully, determined to let nothing hinder me. I raised the lamp high, pools of orange light spilling about me.

At the end of the hall, the wall seemed to curve, and I saw a staircase of rough, stone steps that curled up around it, steep, without benefit of railing or banister. I realized that this must be the lower level of one of the towers, and the staircase must lead up to the floors above. I hurried down the hall and stood in the well of darkness, looking up at the spiral staircase that reared up so dangerously. The steps were damp, and I knew one slip could mean a fatal fall. I set the lamp down and pulled off my shoes. I moved up slowly, staying close to the wall, afraid to peer down at the yawning space around me. I climbed up, up, higher and higher, and realized I must have climbed what would have amounted to three stories in a regular house. I grew dizzy. The hand clutching the lamp trembled. There must be a door somewhere, I reasoned. The stairs had to end.... The stone was cold to my stockinged feet. The clammy air swirled, fiercely now, and it reverberated against the circular walls with the sound of whispers, loud and violent. It was as though an army of phantoms was protesting my intrusion, warning me to come no farther.

The landing was flat and narrow, not two yards across. It dropped down sharply to the floor, hundreds of feet below. I was trembling. I had always had a great fear of high places, and now this fear was magnified. It seemed some evil force pulled at me, compelled me to peer over that edge and jump into the black void. I leaned against the wall, panting, gripping the lamp tightly, and trying to master the sensations that plagued me.

The door was small, and it was locked. I set the lamp down and tugged at the door, frantic, ever aware of the yawning space behind me that beckoned. I knew I would never have either the strength or the nerve to go back down that curling spiral staircase. I had to force the door open. I pulled with all my might, to no avail. After a moment of near-hysteria, common sense prevailed. I took a hairpin out of my hair and forced it through the lock, twisting, turning. The lock clicked. The door swung slowly open toward me, revealing the back of a tapestry that must cover it from the other side. I put my shoes back on, retrieved the lamp, and lifted the edge of the tapestry, slipping under it and stepping into a room that looked vaguely familiar.

It was small, semicircular, the walls concealed by blue and grey tapestries with faded gold-and-rose designs. Large white pots sitting around the floor contained dark-green rubber plants and ferns, layered with dust. Dorothea and I had passed through this room, hadn't we? I walked through it and proceeded down a long, narrow hall with torches burning in wall brackets, making my oil lamp unnecessary. The walls were adorned with old portraits in tarnished gold frames. Yes, that gorgeous woman in farthingale and neck ruff looked familiar, as did the raven-haired man in black velvet, his cruel face and glowering eyes so like Rodd's.

A door stood half-open. I stepped through

it, finding myself in the vast, cavernous room where we had gathered that night of my visit. It was very dark and icy cold. I started across the parquet floor, my heels tapping, the oil lamp making a moving orange glow that washed over me and only heightened the darkness all around. I was certain now that I could find my way to the dungeons. Nicola and I had left through a door across the room, gone down a hall...yes, I was on firm ground now, no longer lost. My spirits lifted. In a few minutes I would see my brother again. I knew he was in the dungeons. I knew he was still alive. Together we would expose this whole sordid mess to the world outside. I quickened my steps. The lamp spluttered. My footsteps echoed throughout the room.

Someone coughed.

I blew the lamp out quickly, instinctively, more a reflex than a conscious action. Layers and layers of cold black darkness surrounded me. The room, half as large as a soccer field, seemed to close in on me, growing smaller and smaller. I stood dead still, not daring to move, hardly daring to breathe. I had heard a cough. There could be no doubt about it. I felt a presence here in the room with me, a sense, a smell, a feeling that was unmistakable. Someone was watching me with eyes grown accustomed to the darkness, while my own were still blinded by the glow of the lamp. Blue and orange globes floated in front of me, glimmered, faded, disappeared, while the blackness thinned, grew misty. Shapes of furniture seemed to spring out of the dark, grow sharper, and I was gradually able to discern form and dimension.

My terror was so great that I hardly felt it. It was like a numbness, so intense that it allowed nothing to penetrate. As my eyes grew accustomed to the dark, I looked around the great room, nests of shadows floating from each corner like silent black waterfalls. The lighter pieces of furniture took on definite shape, faded colour, lavender velvet, ivory satin, veiled with black mist. I saw something solid at the edge of one of the floods of shadow—tall, dark, straight, still. The tangible force of presence seemed to emanate from there. It was a man. I could barely discern the glimmer of eyes that pinioned me to the spot. There was a movement, a blur, and the form disappeared, drowned by the shadows.

I waited. At any moment I expected to see a dark form rushing toward me, hear a blood-curdling cry, see the blade of a knife glittering wildly before plunging down at me, to end it all. Minutes passed. The evil was so strong that it filled the room, swirling around me, gathering force. I watched the cascade of blackness, waiting. I could hear the wind, far away, the noise penetrating the thickness of stone and concrete, and the ticking of a clock. There was a loud creak, as though someone shifted body weight from one foot to another, then a gush of air, held breath finally released. Silence prevailed. The shadows stirred. The clock ticked—a second, a minute, five, an eternity.

Nothing happened.

The terror subsided. The numbness began to wear off. I must have imagined the whole thing, I told myself. There was no one else in the room. It was my nerves, tension, an overactive imagination. The evil was still in the air, as real as a strong perfume, but I tried to convince myself that it came from within, from my mind. My skin seemed to sting with pricks, and I could feel the blood coursing through my veins. I must have been standing in the same position for ten minutes, maybe more. Nothing had happened, no bloodcurdling scream, no lunge, no knife. A nervous laugh rose up inside, but I was still too shaken to give vent to it.

I moved slowly toward the door Nicola and I had left by the night she took me to her room. I could see it clearly, at the outer edge of one of the rippling black waterfalls of shadow. I tried to make no sound, but my skirts rustled and my heels tapped gently on the bare wooden floor. I held the lamp tightly, although I dared not light it yet. The room seemed to watch my progress toward the door, and I could feel hostile eyes burning into my back, causing my flesh to creep. Twenty yards to go, fifteen, ten. I wanted to scream and make a mad dash for the door. I moved slowly, slowly, my shoulders trembling.

I was at the edge of the cascade of shadows. I peered into it—dense blackness, moving, stirring, and there, against the wall, a tall form, eyes, teeth, breathing. I paused, staring. Nothing was there. Something moved—a tapestry rippling. I reached the door, pulled it open, and darted into the hall.

I had to lean against the wall for a moment to regroup my forces. One torch burned in a bracket at the end of the hall, and it gave enough light for me to see that I was on the right track. Down that hall, around a corner... yes, I knew the way now, but I was too weak to move on just yet. My shoulders still trembled, and I felt my cheeks wet with tears I hadn't known I had shed.

Nerves, I told myself. Of course there had been no one in the room. I had imagined it.

Everyone had left Castlemoor except a few servants, and what could a servant possibly have been doing in the room, in the dark? I had come too far to let myself lose control now. I must go on. I must find Donald and get him away from this place. There was no time for nerves, no time to linger. I moved quickly down the hall.

I turned a corner and started down a small passage with wet brown concrete walls, torches burning at spaced intervals. I vaguely wondered why the torches should be burning if everyone were gone. Did they burn all the time? Perhaps. There must be some logical explanation. I turned another corner and started down the hall that would eventually lead me to the steps that went down to the dungeons. My footsteps echoed loudly.

Too loudly.

I stopped, glancing over my shoulder. The echoes lasted just a little too long, long enough for me to realize they weren't echoes at all. I listened. The sound stopped.

Someone was following me.

I stared at the end of the hall where I had turned the corner. A torch burned smokily there, washing the wall with flickering yellow light. There was a shadow on the wall, black, stamped clearly against the yellow, head and shoulders projected in profile. Someone was standing just out of sight around the corner, leaning forward. The shadow moved, magnified to gigantic proportions by the light as the figure moved closer. The torch spluttered, and the shadow disappeared. Others took its place, weird, gyrating wildly—a tree branch, a galloping horse, two dancers.

All right, I told myself. No more of that. I had given way before, summoning up vivid horrors, but I didn't intend to do it again. The shadow *had* been there, its shape resembling a man's head and torso, and the footsteps *had* echoed a little too long, but this was a long hall with walls of solid concrete, and no doubt the acoustics were peculiar. I moved on down the hall, paying no attention to the sound of footsteps that echoed around me. I glanced back once, quickly, and it seemed a figure darted into the obscurity of shadows, but I merely scolded myself and moved on.

I reached the great hole in the wall where the steps led down. I could smell mildew and decay, a horribly fetid odour that caused me to recoil. No torch burned nearby. The steps led down into a yawning pit of darkness. I hesitated, shuddering. I heard rustling, scurrying noises that rose up from the well. I stood stiffly at the top of the steps, trying to summon enough courage to start the descent. I urged myself to move, but something seemed to hold me back. I couldn't go down. I had lost control of my body and was unable to force myself to take that first step.

My skin prickled. Great gusts of clammy air swooshed up the steps and whistled against the walls and stroked my cheeks. There was an aura of forbidding evil, and voices unheard cried out, protested, warned me to stay back. I knew that if I once started that descent, I would never return. I would be swallowed up by that evil, destroyed. Nothing, nothing could induce me to go down. This was insanity. I should have taken my proof, gone for help, brought a whole fleet of men with me to investigate Castlemoor. I had come this far, but I couldn't go down into the dungeons alone, not for anything....

Then I thought of Donald. I squared my shoulders, lit the oil lamp, and started down the rough stone steps.

The steps were wide and narrow, gradually curving down at an angle. I moved carefully, the lamplight revealing damp brown walls streaked with a moss-green fungus. In this confined area, my footsteps echoed even louder than ever, ringing like a battalion pounding on the rough stone. Down and down, closed, confined, a damp mossy tunnel, fetid-smelling and alive with scurrying sound—the aura of evil was thick, alive, surging around me. I clenched the lamp. I thought of Donald. I sensed something behind me. It was a curious sensation, instinctive, a feeling of vulnerability rather than anything definite. I looked over my shoulder, but I saw only darkness, yet I could not shake the feeling. I felt exposed, watched, followed.

Something rustled near my feet. I saw a large grey rat scuttling down the steps, making a weird squeaking noise that sounded like a scream in the strange echo chamber. Down and down I went, and I suddenly realized that I must have been in the dungeons at first, or at least a part of them, before I climbed the spiral staircase. The hall leading away from the south wall had slanted down sharply, and it seemed now that I had come down almost as many steps as I had climbed earlier.

I saw flickering light ahead. Descending the remaining steps, I came out into a large, cavern-like room with passages leading off from it in every direction. The floor and walls were concrete. Torches burned in black iron brackets. There were chains on one wall, rusty manacles attached. I stood in the middle of the room, puzzled. Donald was here, somewhere, but there were half a dozen passages, each leading in a different direction. I frowned. I wondered why the torches should be burning here. It was.... It was almost as though someone had been expecting me.

I heard footsteps approaching from one of the passages. I stood very still. I seemed to have stopped breathing, and I had to restrain an urge to laugh, because this was not real. It wasn't happening. It wasn't happening to me. It was a nightmare, and as the footsteps grew louder I knew I would wake up and stretch and see the sun and no longer feel the dreadful evil that held me captive. I dropped the oil lamp. It shattered at my feet. I shook my head slowly.

Edward stepped into the room from one of the passages. He was smiling, and he wore a flowing white robe.

'Congratulations,' he said calmly. 'You've done remarkably well. We never dreamed you'd actually find your way here. I was sure you'd get lost, that we'd have to come find you, bring you here.'

'You knew I was coming?'

'I knew you would come eventually. You see, I didn't underestimate you. I knew you were too intelligent, too inquisitive to accept things as they were. I knew you'd begin to piece things together and come to Castlemoor. More specifically, we saw you coming across the moors this afternoon. Fancy your knowing about the door in the south wall.'

'Nicola told me about it.'

'Ah,' he exclaimed. He nodded soberly. 'She—knows.'

'Of course. Her "fragile nerves" made it relatively easy to convince the others she was having a breakdown. Convenient that Burton finally took her away. Convenient for her. Otherwise, I'd have had to kill her.'

'But—'

'Surely you suspected me, Katherine?'

'No.'

'You suspected Burton?'

I nodded.

He chuckled. 'No, my dear, he hasn't enough imagination for anything so grand. He's too sober, too sensible, too corrupt. This takes—purity, and purpose, a total dedication to ideals. Burton's too dense, too stupid to see what's been going on right under his nose. He'll be easy to deal with—when the time comes.'

'I—I can't believe this—'

'You're a fool,' he said. 'It's a shame things worked out this way. I rather fancied you for a while there. I was almost willing to risk contamination.'

'Contamination?'

'There are only a few of us left,' he said solemnly, 'a few with the pure, unsullied blood—direct descendants of Boadicea and all those Celtic ancestors who ruled this country before the invasions. Just a few of us, but we'll unite, we'll overcome, we'll overthrow—'

'You're insane,' I whispered.

'A typical reaction, that. The great visionaries were always laughed at, mocked, insulted. We'll overcome. We'll have our revenge. It'll take a long time, granted. I may not live to see it, but that day will come, and England will belong to its rightful owners.'

I was right. He was insane. I could see it clearly now. His handsome face looked pale and drawn, deep shadows under the radiant blue eyes that gleamed with a fanatic light. He seemed to be consumed with an inner flame that burned fiercely, and it had always been there. The heavy, masculine charm, the hearty manner, had concealed it before. I was afraid, and I was trembling, yet I was fascinated by the spectacle of the man who had a curious splendour in his flowing white robe. The ancient Celtic priests must have had that same golden-bronze hair, those same rough-hewn features illuminated by a fanatic glow as they wielded the sacrificial knife. I was horrified by the man, yet, at the same time, intrigued by the phenomenon. I backed away a step. He smiled, the wide pink lips stretching slowly, curling down at the corners. The vividly blue eyes sparkled with pleasure as he sensed my terror.

'Afraid?' he asked tenderly.

'You—you can't get away with this,' I stammered.

'Come, don't toss platitudes at me. Have some dignity. You're going to die, but your death will be an honour, a tribute to the only true gods. In ancient times, maidens vied for the privilege of such a death. You'll be a splendid gift.'

'You killed Jamie,' I said.

'Yes. The colour of his hair determined it. Had he been a brunette, he would be alive today.'

'And Bertie.'

'Sheer necessity. He knew too much.'

'And—Donald—'

'That will come, in time.'

'The moon dance,' I said.

'You *are* well informed, Katherine.'

'He's here. My brother is here.'

'He's quite comfortable, actually. Well taken care of. He gave us a hard time once or twice, tried to escape, almost made it once.'

'Nicola saw him.'

'Yes. That was unfortunate. Another of her "delusions," the one that finally convinced Burton he must send her away. Most fortunate for her.'

'Edward,' I whispered, 'you can't really believe in this. You can't really...believe you'll succeed.'

He ignored the remark. 'I liked Donald, truly. I tried to discourage him. I tried to persuade him to give the whole thing up, but he persisted. He made a grave error. He probed too deeply. He saw too much, suspected even more. He showed me the manuscript. I knew then that he would have to be punished.' He paused. 'As do you,' he added.

He moved slowly toward me, the white cambric robe billowing, softly rustling. His wide mouth was still stretched in a smile, but the face was hard, a mask, the eyes like blue agate. For a moment I was too stunned to move, and then I turned quickly, intending to flee back up the staircase. Buck Crabbe moved casually down the last few steps, blocking my way. He had been in the room. He had been behind me along the hall and down the staircase. I had imagined none of it.

'What have we got here,' he said.

'No,' I whispered.

'A regular prize,' Buck said. 'Nice, what?'

'Very nice,' Edward replied.

'Dandy,' Buck said. 'Just dandy.'

He loomed there like a giant in doeskin trousers and leather jerkin, a terrifying mass of male strength. I stared at him in horror—tight bronze-blond curls clinging to skull, broad, bony face with long nose, wide mouth, and flat, expressionless eyes. He raised his large hands and flexed the long fingers, cupping them around air, grinning.

'I've been looking forward to this,' he said.

'Come, Buck,' Edward said quietly, reasonably. 'We mustn't be selfish. She's a plum. Her death must be shared.'

'I'm gonna kill her now. I've been waitin' a long time—'

'I know what you want to do, Buck, and I'd like nothing better than to turn her over to you here and now and watch the—proceedings. It would be a satisfying experience, granted, but we must think of the others.'

'They needn't know about it.'

'Ah, but they'd find out. We're having a meeting tonight, as you very well know. She'll be our special guest. Her execution will be a formal one, on the stones, a treat for everyone. If I let you kill her now, the others would feel cheated.'

I stood very still, caught between the two of

321

them, looking from one to the other—a mad-
man in white cambric robe whose handsome
face was transformed, and a giant bully with
brutal face whose urge to kill had nothing to
do with religious zeal. Edward was insane, but
he really believed in his cult. It was real, sacred
to him. Buck Crabbe believed in nothing, but
the cult enabled him to indulge his innate
sadistic instincts. I did not know which of them
was worse. Both were warped, twisted by an
evil that had removed everything decent and
humane. They continued to talk as though I
were an inanimate object they were appraising.
Buck was sullen, eager to kill me now and be
done with it. Edward was calm, patient, ex-
plaining why that was unfeasible.

They were perhaps eight yards apart, Edward standing in the middle of the room, Buck
still in front of the staircase, and I was directly
between them. The torches burned fiercely,
flinging blue-orange shadows over the brown
walls and filling the air with the odour of smoke
and tar. The voices echoed, Edward's melodic,
Buck's harsh. The sound whirled around the
room and drifted away down the various dark
passages. My eyes were fixed on the passage
directly in front of me, some twenty feet from
where I stood. If I moved quickly, I could reach
it. I braced myself, my body taut as an arrow

ready to leave the bow. The men continued to argue, ignoring me. I took a deep breath and flew toward the passage.

I reached the entrance and stumbled. My heel broke. I fell to the floor with stunning impact. White cambric billowed about me. Iron fingers pulled me up. Edward held me against him, my face buried in folds of cloth. Buck was shouting. Edward silenced him with a word I couldn't understand. I was trembling violently. Edward held me away from him and looked down into my eyes. He was smiling. I tried to break free. He raised one arm, the great white sleeve fluttering like a rustling wing. He released me and clenched his fist. He looked at me almost tenderly before smashing the fist against my jaw. I cried out as the pain shot through my body and blankets of darkness smothered me, heavy, wet, pushing me down, down into a white-hot oblivion of pain and terror.

Sensation piled on sensation, dark, murky, vivid, obscure. I was drowning, enormous waves breaking over me, and I welcomed them. A light burned dimly far, far above me, and I tried to reach it, failed, fell back down into a pit full of shifting black shadows. Layer by layer they lifted, and reality returned, ever so slowly. My eyelids were heavy. It took great effort to lift them. I was in a small cell, not much larger than a broom closet, rotten straw on the floor, damp stains on the wall, a barred window looking out onto the hall, where a torch burned briskly and shed enough light for me to study my surroundings.

I was on a narrow cot littered with rags. I sat up. My head whirled, but my jaw no longer hurt. There was a dull ache, but the pain was gone. I must have been here for a long time, two or three hours at least. I went to the door and looked through the bars of the window. A heavy lock secured the door, and there was no way I could escape. I staggered back to the cot and sank down, my temples throbbing. Panic rose up, disappeared. Fear vanished. All feeling vanished. A numbness set in. Trancelike, I sat on the cot and waited. I was objective, curious, almost as though this were happening in a novel I read, not real at all, a fiction that did not really involve Kathy Hunt. I watched the shadows cast on the wall by the fire, and time passed without my being aware of it. Fifteen minutes, twenty, an hour, two: I don't know how long it was before I heard the footsteps in the hall outside the cell.

Buck unlocked the door and pulled it open. The hinges creaked loudly. He jerked his head, summoning me. I stood up on shaky legs. Buck wore a white robe too, now, of a coarse white linen not nearly so fine as the one Edward wore. Edward was behind Buck, waiting casually in the hall. I took a step and stumbled forward. Buck caught me, supported me, led me out of the cell, holding my elbow firmly. The three of us began to walk down the hall, one on either side of me, their robes swirling with the movement and rustling, Buck's stiffly, Edward's with a soft, silken sound. The hall was long and narrow and seemingly endless, and soon the brick walls gave way to walls of solid-packed earth braced with strong wooden beams. We were in a tunnel smelling of damp earth and root and the smoke of torches that burned in brackets every fifty yards or so. Alan had once mentioned a secret tunnel that was supposed to lead out onto the moors, although no one was certain it actually existed. This must be that tunnel, I thought. It really did exist, and it went on and on, endless.

We must have walked at least a mile. The tunnel grew more narrow, and there was a new smell, curious, like peat. Buck still held my elbow. His face was impassive. I glanced at Edward. He seemed to be meditating, his eyes far away, unseeing, his full lips moving silently, one heavy wave of dark-gold hair fallen across his brow. His hands were clasped in front of him, and he had the appearance of a priest going to some sacred ceremony. I moved like an automaton, awake yet asleep, aware of everything around me, yet curiously detached. It was as though I had been given some potent drug that allowed me to move but prevented me from feeling anything.

Far ahead, two torches burned, one at either side of a small door at the end of the tunnel. Buck released me and hurried to open the door. Edward fastened his hand around my wrist, pulling me along with him. I moved jerkily. Buck held the door open, and we stepped outside.

The door was completely hidden by a towering pile of broken stones. We stepped around them. The sky was dark black, starless. An enormous white moon spilled milky light over the ruined city, gilding temples and columns and ruins with murky silver and spreading bizarre purple-black shadows over walls and ground. Far away, among the ruins, I saw flickering orange flames that burned like an apparition from Hades, and I heard the distant chanting, a strange, murmuring sound, monotonous, rhythmic, music made by a coven of lost souls, satanic. Centuries disappeared, time vanished, and I was in a living nightmare of the past. Numb, trancelike, I walked beside

Edward, my body moving of its own volition, while inside a silent scream shattered all semblance of reality.

Buck glided ahead of us, passing through misty light and shadows, his robe floating about him, now silver, now a mere white blur in the darkness. The moonlight illuminated parts of the city, picking out each detail in sharp silver-blue and black, while other sections were in total darkness, masses of impenetrable black that seemed curiously alive with movement. Edward's fingers were like iron bands fastened about my wrist, pulling me along beside him. He was mumbling to himself, but I couldn't understand what he was saying. We stepped over stones, moved around columns, passed through stretches of darkness alive with darker forms moving quietly and whispering with the sound of wind, phantoms risen from the past to observe this revival of their long-dead rites.

Ahead, the flames seemed to burn more brightly as we drew nearer. The fire burned in the circles of stones where I had talked with Burton Rodd. I remembered the altar with its brown bloodstain. No, I cried, no, no; but no sound came. The cry was silent, inside, piercing nerve and fibre while I moved along beside the man in billowing white cambric, drawing nearer and nearer the circle. I could see the

columns now, glowing reddish orange with firelight, and through the stones I saw the figures
in white moving slowly around the altar, their
shadows following them like black spokes of
a revolving wheel. The muted, monotonous
chant was music heard in nightmare, an insane
sound droning on and on and sweeping away
all hope.

Buck stopped at the portals of the circle and
pulled on his hood, then moved inside. The
chanting stopped abruptly. The silence that
followed was even more terrifying than the
sound had been. It hung over the city like a
threat. The stillness was the stillness of death.
Edward and I moved toward the circle. Our
footsteps sounded incredibly loud. I could
hear now the crackle of the flames and smell
the odour of oak boughs burning. Edward
tightened his grip, and I felt sure my wrist-
bone would snap. It was useless to cry out,
useless to struggle. I moved through hazy
nightmare air shimmering with imagined horror, for it couldn't be real.

We moved into the circle of stone. At least
twelve figures stood in a semicircle behind the
altar, all in white robes with hoods that concealed their faces. I could pick out Buck only
because of his enormous size. All of them raised
their arms in unison and chanted some ritual

greeting in a language unlike any I had ever heard. Edward returned the greeting, pronouncing the unknown words in a harsh, guttural voice. He was the only one who did not wear a hood. He released me. Two of the others moved forward solemnly and took hold of my arms and led me to the altar, standing guard while Edward launched into a tirade long and loud and completely incomprehensible to me. The fire burned fiercely. The wood crackled. The circle was filled with orange glow and black shadows and figures in white who gave ritual replies to the sentences Edward unleashed with furor. I felt a cold terror as I listened to those mad voices.

I remembered the factual accounts I had read about these ceremonies. I remembered all the gruesome details. I shook my head, trying to push those lurid pictures out of my mind, but it was impossible. As the fire crackled, and the furious, incomprehensible tirade continued, I kept seeing graphic scenes I had read about with scholarly relish—a stone, a girl, a group of robed men removing their robes one by one, and one by one approaching the stone, the girl. It couldn't be happening, I told myself. Things like that happened only in the pages of musty old books. This couldn't be real. Please, I whispered to myself, please, don't let it be real...don't let it happen....

I closed my eyes, my lips moving in silent prayer.

I must have fainted, for when I opened my eyes I was leaning against the altar, and the only sound I heard was the sound of my own labour-ed breathing. All else was silent. I lifted my head. The figures were standing in a wide circle around the altar, spaced out several yards away from me. The fire had burned down to a heap of glowing orange coals. There was no move-ment, no sound. I felt curiously languorous and empty-headed, no longer afraid, no longer truly aware of my plight. There was an empty cup on the altar beside me, a few drops of liquid spilled on the stone. I smelled a strong, cloy-ing odour. They must have forced me to drink some kind of narcotic, I thought, and I tried to sit up. When I moved, it was as though I were moving under water.

Edward was approaching me. His face was severe, his mouth turned down, his eyes like agate.

'You have sinned,' he said. 'You must pay.'

I tried to answer him, but no words would come. Edward frowned, and then his face seemed to soften, grow human again. He took a deep breath, swelling his chest. His robes swirled softly, blue-white with shadow, the material rustling. He glanced over his shoulder at the cultists stationed around the circle, then turned back to me.

'I'm sorry, Kathy,' he said, his voice low-pitched, barely audible. 'I'm going to be merciful. I've persuaded the others to forgo the customary procedures. There will be pain, yes, but it will be over quickly. You'll be spared the other....'

I stared at him, and I saw that he held a great curved knife in his hand. The blade gleamed and glistened. He took another step and raised the knife. It was very long, very sharp. I studied it objectively, thinking how lovely it was, steel reflecting the glowing orange coals. I heard a shout, but I paid no attention to it. I was fascinated by the blade. I was aware of flurried movement, low voices, a maelstrom of activity, but it didn't concern me. There was the blade, only the blade. Edward paused a few feet away from me, a look of bewildered amazement on his face. Why? What was wrong? Then I saw his face contort with savage anger, and the drug stopped working, and I saw death and tried to scream, and he raised the knife for the final plunge. An orange flash streaked across the air; he let out an anguished cry, and strong familiar arms pulled me away from the altar as Edward fell hurtling to the ground.

CHAPTER SIXTEEN

Now, in June, it was over, and London was warm and green and full of noise and activity. From the hotel window I could see the park across the way, blue pond afloat with toy white boats, children playing under leafy boughs, nursemaids in starched uniforms keeping an eye on their charges or pushing black perambulators along the sun-flecked walks. Elegant carriages and humble carts clattered down the street. Beautifully dressed women studied the windows of expensive shops, and a tough-looking man in leather apron cried the virtues of the flowers in his white wooden cart. I had missed all this during the weeks at Castlemoor, but now I felt a certain sadness that made it all seem less inviting than before.

The door flew open, and Donald came charging into the room, tossing his top hat on the sofa, flinging his gloves on a chair. His handsome face was aglow with excitement, dark-brown eyes sparkling merrily, cheeks ruddy with health. Seeing him now in his gleaming brown boots, plum-coloured suit, and white silk shirt with ruffled front, I found it hard to believe that just a few weeks ago he had been thin and pale, cheeks sunken, dark smudges under his eyes. For a few days the doctors had been deeply concerned, but with proper nourishment and care, he had soon lost the haggard look and regained his energy, enough to fight with the reporters who clamoured around him as he left the hospital, enough to sit through hours of hearings at Old Bailey while the cultists were tried and convicted. They were behind bars now, and Edward was buried in a musty country cemetery. The policeman who had shot him had received a promotion.

'It's done!' Donald cried. 'I've signed a staggering contract. They agreed to everything—and handed over a whopping big advance. Seems everyone's eager to know about the man who returned from the dead. My publishers believe the book will be a fabulous success.'

'I'm so glad,' I said feebly.

'They want an exposé—a personal account of my adventures—but I told them I intended to include chapters of scholarly information as well. Readers will skip the academic sections, I know, but I intend to include 'em just the same.'

He pulled off his jacket, tossed it on a chair,

and loosened his brown silk tie. 'Where's Bella? She's going to have to get a move on! We're leaving for Castlemoor first thing in the morning.'

'Oh?'

'I've already made the reservations.'

'Well, you can cancel mine,' I said firmly.

'What? What is this? What do you mean?'

'I'm not going back to Castlemoor.'

'Nonsense! You know I have to be there to write the book, and you know I can't do it without you. What's the matter with you? You look like you've just made peace with God and taken the last sacraments.'

'Nothing's wrong with me. I just don't plan to go back to Castlemoor. Aunt Clarice came to call this afternoon while you were at your publishers. She wants me to spend the summer with her.'

'You've lost your bloomin' mind, that's what! I know for a fact you'd rather cut off both arms and part of one leg than to spend three days with that old hag! What is *wrong*, Kathy girl?'

'Nothing!' I snapped irritably.

'Ah, so—' he replied quietly, drawing the words out. 'I know. Yes, indeed. You've been moping around here for the past month, and it just now dawned on me *why*.'

'What do you mean by that?'

'I mean Mr Burton Rodd hasn't come to pay his respects. I saw the way you looked at him during the trial, and the other day Bella gave me a few details about what was taking place while I was in that cell. She said you and Rodd—'

'She knows absolutely nothing about it!' I cried. 'And furthermore, I don't intend to discuss it one minute more. Wild horses couldn't keep Bella away from Castlemoor, now that Alan's back in Darkmead, but as for me—'

'As for you?'

'I'm going for a walk,' I said abruptly. 'There are times, Donald, when I find you absolutely impossible to live with, and if you think—'

'I think you'd better go for your walk if you're going, because we've got a tremendous lot of packing to do.'

I marched out of the room, my blue eyes blazing, spots of colour on my cheeks. Donald burst into gales of loud laughter as I slammed the door behind me, and that made me all the more furious. I walked angrily down the hall with its pale-grey walls and thick maroon carpets, passing glittering mirrors that hung in gilt frames and large pots containing dark, waxen green plants. I swept down the curving staircase and passed through the crowded lobby, paying no attention to its heavy chandeliers or grey marble columns. I stepped outside, welcoming the sunshine and all the heady odours of London that filled the early summer air.

Donald had touched a sore spot. I knew it. I knew I had no reason to be angry with him. I *had* studied Burton Rodd all during the trial, admiring his cool, crisp manner and complete command of the situation. He had been extremely handsome in his elegant black suit and tailored white shirt, blue satin ascot about his neck, and I hadn't been the only woman to find him impressive. One of the female reporters covering the trial devoted a whole column to 'the dashing Mr Rodd' whose suspicions had first alerted the police about the cult. I thought the article in incredibly poor taste and had tossed it in the wastebasket immediately.

I owed my life to Burton Rodd.

I tried not to think of that terrible night when it had all come to a head. Much of it still remained hazy, due to the narcotic they had given to me, but I remembered Burton Rodd holding me in his arms while the policemen rounded up the last members of the cult and put them in handcuffs. He had been suspicious for weeks, ever since Jamie's mysterious disappearance and Donald's 'accident,' but he knew he had to have concrete proof of the existence of the cult before he could take action. He had finally sent for the police, those men in tight suits whose hard faces had aroused such distrust in Darkmead. He had tried his best to make me leave Castlemoor, sensing the danger I was in, and after the day in his office when I refused to take his money, I had been under constant surveillance.

One of the men had been assigned to watch me at all times, for my own protection, and he had been on duty night and day until that very afternoon I left the house to go to Castlemoor. Another of the men had learned that the cultists intended to meet that night in the ruined city, and they had concentrated all their force on the ruins, hiding among the rocks, hoping to catch all the cultists in one swoop. Burton Rodd had driven Nicola and his mother to the train station and returned immediately to join the men at the ruins. Night fell, and they waited among the shadows. Soon the figures in white began to appear, one by one. A fire was built, the chant began, and a little later Edward and I stepped from behind the rocks and started toward the circle of stone. Rodd had wanted to close in immediately, but the officer in charge of the police insisted they wait until they could actually prove a crime was intended. They surrounded the place, standing just outside the glow of firelight, and they waited until Edward took the knife out and started toward me. They closed in. Edward panicked. He refused to drop the knife. He lunged toward me. Burton had swept me off the altar just in time, even as the policeman fired the bullet that proved fatal to Edward.

It was over. The nightmare was ended. My brother was back, bursting with good health now, and the trial was over. Even the newspaper reporters had stopped hounding us. Everything was settled...but I wasn't. I had been utterly miserable during the past three or four weeks, and I knew the reason why. I could not forget that ravaged face. I could not forget those strong arms around me, those hard, firm lips pressing mine. I may have been unduly conscious of Burton Rodd during the trial, but I knew he hadn't been entirely oblivious of me. More than once I had caught him staring at me. I had not misread the look in his eyes; I was sure of that, yet he had made no attempt to see me since the trial. He knew where I was staying. He knew I wouldn't rebuff him if he came to call.... Well, I couldn't care less, I told myself. I didn't give a hang what he did. Life was rich and full of possibilities. I had done very well before I met Burton Rodd, and I could do very well without him.

I was furious with myself, furious with Donald, furious with the man who said love conquers all. I wanted no part of it if it made one feel so grouchy and sad. I would forget Mr Burton Rodd, but I certainly didn't intend to go back to Castlemoor, where I would be bound to think of him every minute of every day. I would brazen it out with Aunt Clarice first—tea and crumpets, good works, sensible young men with secure futures whom she would force upon me with monotonous regularity. Better that than being all wrought up and snarling every time someone stepped into a room. Donald could do his book very well without me. I definitely wouldn't go back.

I stopped in front of one of the expensive shops half a block from the hotel. There was a stunning bonnet in the window, light-blue straw adorned with yards and yards of pink velvet ribbon. It would go beautifully with the blue silk dress I was wearing at the moment. I peered at the price tag. It was fantastically expensive. Donald would have conniptions if I bought it. It would serve him right! I went into the shop and bought the bonnet, as well as a pink velvet bag, two pairs of gloves, a blue silk parasol, and a box of linen handkerchiefs. I told the clerk to charge them to my brother and left the shop laden with packages and feeling absolutely glorious. I wondered how in the world I could have been so despondent such a short time ago. I could hardly wait to see Donald's expression when I walked in with all these packages.

Burton Rodd was standing in front of the shop, almost as though it had been prearranged. I felt my pulse leap. I almost dropped my packages. I quickly gained control over myself and met his eyes with a cool, level gaze that showed complete lack of concern. He might have been a rather dull acquaintance, out of sight, out of mind, or someone met at a party and forgotten as soon as the music stopped playing. He wore an elegant black suit and a pearl-grey satin vest embroidered with darker-grey fleurs-de-lis, smoky-blue ascot, and dark-grey top hat, which he swept off his head as soon as he saw me coming out of the shop.

'I suppose you expect me to believe this is a coincidence,' I said in a cool voice.

'On the contrary,' he replied. 'I was on my way to your hotel when I saw you going into the shop. I've been waiting out here while you've been laying the foundation for your brother's bankruptcy.'

'He just signed a wonderful contract this morning,' I said icily. 'I seriously doubt that my purchases will send him to debtors' prison.'

He grinned. There was something different about him, something that had not been there before. It was more than the elegant new clothes, went much deeper than the surface. The face was still ravaged, still lined, but the tragic stamp was missing. The dark eyes sparkled, no longer brooding, and there was about him a new vigour that affected his whole personality. It was as though an oppressive weight had been lifted from his shoulders, giving a jaunty spring to his carriage and making him even more formidable. I summed up these changes in him while the grin played on his lips.

'How have you been?' he inquired.

'Smashing,' I said nastily. 'And you?'

'Busy.'

'Indeed?'

'I left for France immediately after the trial,' he informed me. 'My mother sent me a wildly incoherent letter about an eccentric Russian countess and a secret formula and a fantastic new business enterprise. I rushed across the channel post-haste. I finally located her in a musty laboratory in the slum district, wearing a soiled blue smock and surrounded by bottles and burners and glass tubes and baskets of violet petals. She handed me a bottle of perfume, introduced me to the countess, and said they had formed a partnership to manufacture the stuff. I was horrified, as you might imagine, yet surprisingly enough, the scheme is quite sound—so sound that several avaricious French businessmen were moving in, hoping to take over. I put an end to that. For the past three weeks I have been consulting lawyers, signing papers, making arrangements to sell the factory in Darkmead.'

'You're going into the perfume business?'

He nodded. 'Incredible, isn't it? The business is going to boom, and someone has to keep a firm hand on the reins while the women dash about in the laboratory. They already have a staggering number of orders from leading boutiques, and the countess is experimenting with a face cream that is supposed to remove wrinkles and restore a pearly glow to dry skin.'

'Amazing,' I said.

'I've even sold the castle,' he continued. 'Have you heard of Lord and Lady Cleland? They're vegetarians and antivi-visectionists who have an enormous following—a cult, you might say. They believe the world is going to end in a year or two, and they want an isolated place where they can await the dire event surrounded by their apostles. Castlemoor is ideal. My lawyer is drawing up the final papers this afternoon. They want occupancy no later than September. That'll give me just enough time to take care of all the final details at the factory and gather up the various items Mother wants shipped to France.'

'And then?' I inquired.

'I have my eye on a house on the outskirts of Paris,' he said. 'It's small and unpretentious —no dungeons—but surrounded by acres of parkland and countryside. I've almost decided to buy it.'

'Will you?'

'That depends,' he said quietly.

We were still standing in front of the shop. Burton took the packages from me, gripped my elbow, and started walking me down the street toward the hotel. I was confused and bewildered, unable to sort out my reactions to all he had been telling me. We walked slowly, and the silence between us was unnerving. I felt I had to break it.

'How is Nicola?' I asked.

'Making life hell for an Austrian diplomat, an English lord, and a miner from America who apparently owns half the state of Montana. I think the American has a slight lead on the others. The last time I saw her, she was babbling about the challenge of frontier living and the fascinating possibilities of copper and silver.'

'Nicola will do well for herself,' I said.

'I expect to have news of an elopement any day now.'

We were nearing the hotel. I stopped.

'You—you said you were on the way to the hotel when you saw me going into the shop. Do you have—business there?'

'Of sorts.'

'Really?'

'I planned to bring you one of the first bottles of perfume turned out by the new firm. It's in my pocket.'

'I rarely wear perfume,' I said peevishly.

'And to ask you how you'd like to live on the outskirts of Paris.'

The world shimmered with radiance, but I would have gone to the stake before letting him know what these last words had done to me. I tossed my head and became suddenly very interested in a shop window.

'Well?' he said.

I looked at him, my brow arched.

'How would you like to live on the outskirts of Paris?'

'What an outrageous question.'

'I fail to see anything outrageous about it!'

he said testily.

'I hardly know you, Mr Rodd.'

'I'll be in Darkmead for the rest of the summer. You'll have plenty of time to get to know me.'

'I'll be very busy—'

'You damn sure will.'

'Really, Mr Rodd, I see no reason—'

'At the end of summer we'll leave for Paris—'

'Nonsense,' I interrupted.

'As man and wife,' he concluded.

'You're dreaming.'

'You'll be on that boat with me,' he snarled.

'I wouldn't think of it,' I said blithely.

'You'll think of it,' he retorted. 'Twenty-four hours a day.'

'You're terribly sure of yourself, Mr Rodd.'

'Not at all. I'm just sure of you.'

'Are you?'

'Quite. Do you have anything else to say?'

I started to make a scathing retort. I held it back. Burton Rodd looked down at me with glowering eyes, ready to fight some more if necessary. I smiled. He was determined to have his way, and any further argument would have been futile. He saw the smile and knew that he had won. He took my arm possessively and led me toward the hotel. I wondered if he knew his victory was one I had been planning for a very long time.